When Night Awakens

Ken Paiva

Hi Tom,

Thanks so much for reading
"When Night Awakens." I hope
you find it a great read.

All the best,

Ken Paiva

First published by Endeavour Press Ltd in 2017.

For my dad, who taught me that amazing things can be accomplished through perseverance and hard work.

Table of Contents

1. Andre, Elise - O Rest Ye Merry...

December 24, 19:30 Hours – Eschdorf, Luxembourg

It was Christmas Eve. Across the Ardennes Forest, scenes of the season were imprinted like a Currier and Ives post card. New snow had fallen, painting a fresh coat on the heavily laden evergreen trees. The flakes unfiltered by the furs came to rest as a velvet-like blanket spread across an already whitened ground. Playing off the moon, the snowy surface reflected as a dim glow yielding the only light in an otherwise black forest.

The seasonal canvas painting a serene image of the Ardennes that Christmas Eve was a ruse. In revelation a pure deception, harboring dark secrets of the reality of war, whose true landscape beneath its snowy mask would expose a scarred and cratered earth, littered with frozen corpses.

At the edge of the Ardennes, where the dense snowy woods relented, laid the beleaguered town of Eschdorf, in the north-western part of Luxembourg. Nestled between Belgium to its west and north, Germany to its east and France due south, the tiny country of Luxembourg had a rich history, dating back to its founding as a Roman fortress in the Middle Ages. Its recent history however, had been written by Germany, which violated Luxembourg's neutrally and invaded in 1940, annexing the country as a province of the Third Reich. It remained under German control until the autumn of 1944, when Allied troops fought their way from the beaches of Normandy and the D-Day invasion to free it from occupation.

For the past few days the people of Eschdorf had watched in disbelief as their town, liberated by the Allies only three months prior, was again overrun by the powerful German juggernaut. The massive German Offensive had caught the Allies completely off guard and pushed a deep bulge into the lines. In so doing, the German war machine wrapped itself around the small town of Eschdorf and others like it, in an embrace much like a boa constrictor would its prey. Those who stayed in Eschdorf during the latest German occupation were suffocated by their guests, driven down to live in dank basements while soldiers billeted in their beds, forced to sacrifice much of their food and living in fear, subject to interrogation at any time.

The German Government, and in particular the Security Service arm of the SS – the Sicherheitsdienst – considered the town's inhabitants German citizens and felt many had refused to comply with an edict issued in September, when Ally liberation seemed imminent, to leave the town and relocate behind German lines. They suspected many who stayed behind were collaborating with the Americans or eluding conscription into the Wehrmacht. The latest German occupation saw SS visit the town daily, checking papers and questioning anyone they deemed suspicious.

One of the town's elders, Andre Verhoeven, paced in the basement of his cobbler shop that Christmas Eve, concerned about the pending American assault. Andre knew about the attack, not due to connections with outside groups like the resistance or underground, but because he could see the signs of the German army preparing for battle. His anxiety stemmed from the health and well-being of his niece Elise, who was nine months pregnant and due to deliver at any time.

He watched helplessly the day before as SS soldiers questioned men and woman in a schoolhouse basement that a number of them had congregated in, accusing a few of collaborating and subsequently carting them off for "interrogation." If not for Elise, Andre would have probably been shot on the spot for his intolerance of what he considered a witch hunt in a town that only wanted the war to leave. Sure, Andre knew of a number of townsfolk the SS would execute had they known of their distaste for Hitler's Government – he himself being one of those people. Elise had held his hand tightly and pulled him back when he started to rise.

For all his dislike of Nazi Germany and what it represented, Andre knew he was all Elise had left. An only child, her parents had perished in an artillery bombardment only three months before. Sadly enough, this occurred when Allied forces were liberating the town after the first German occupation of almost four years. Her husband avoided being conscripted in the German Army, but was found able-bodied and ushered away to help undertake railroad repairs. This, five months after she found herself with child. Elise endured the latter months of her pregnancy without the very people who had always been there for her. She had fought through the emotional strain of losing her parents and clung to the hope that her husband, René, would somehow survive and reunite with her. Until then Andre, her father's brother, did all he could to provide his niece Elise, comfort and support.

Andre himself lived a no more fortunate life. He lost his wife to sickness before the war. His only child, a son, was an artist at a Parisian school when the German occupation occurred. The young man was erroneously identified as an underground agent and shot on his bicycle at a roadblock by the Gestapo investigating an incident of sabotage. Such was the plight of many civilians during these unpredictable and volatile times of war. Few, if any families escaped intact without suffering loss. The war was a malevolent, unconscionable beast, feeding relentlessly upon homes, land, livestock, food and of course most regrettably people, be they man or woman, elder or child.

So, with Elise in his care, Andre did not fight as she tugged his sleeve that day, silently pleading for him not to engage the SS guards. Instead Andre sat quietly in that damp school basement and watched in horror as the SS *played* with the lives of the townspeople, picking the unfortunates and ushering them away.

Andre had witnessed one young girl getting special attention from one of the SS, his hands under her shirt before pointing her to the door with the other selected ones. He could only imagine what had happened to her since and had worried that Elise, given her pregnancy, might also make an interesting *suspect* for the SS on their next visit. Her strikingly deep blue eyes were accentuated by high cheek-bones and flowing dark hair, which shined like silk and always got her attention. Andre surely didn't want her noticed by the wrong people. It was partially why he had relocated them to the basement under his cobbler shop as soon as the SS had left that day. Additionally, he couldn't face his neighbors after his lack of action with the SS. They, of course, wouldn't judge him, they were all powerless, but Andre still felt shame for his lack of response. The final reason for moving to the basement of his shop was to make it easier to leave Eschdorf altogether. It was a plan he had thought about since the Germans arrived, and he sprung it on Elise as they ate their

Christmas Eve dinner of fruit preserves and stale bread in the chilled, musty cellar air.

"I don't understand!" Elise questioned. "You want to leave here? To go where?"

"Your father's farm. We will be safe there."

Elise laughed softly. "Dear uncle, in case you haven't noticed, I'm not exactly fit for travel."

It was Andre's turn to laugh, or perhaps it was a sigh.

"You are a strong girl, and the farmhouse is little more than a mile away. The town will soon be under attack. Artillery shells, tanks, and of course soldiers, shooting at anything that moves. How can you have your baby under these conditions?"

Elise's face lost all traces of her smile. "We will be safe here in our basement as we've been before. The soldier's know there are civilians in the basements and will leave us alone."

"Like the SS left us alone under the school?" Andre questioned cynically.

"But we are no longer under the school," Elise protested. "And when the Americans come, they will drive the Germans out, like before."

"Perhaps eventually they will. But tell me Elise, where do you think the German's will take shelter when the shelling starts?"

Elise paused for a moment. "What would they want with a large pregnant woman?" she pondered, hungrily shoveling a last spoonful of preserves in her mouth.

She and Andre exchanged glances, both knew he didn't have to answer her thoughtless question. She studied his face. "Do you really think we could make it to the farm?"

"I do," he said.

"But it is Christmas Eve. Do you actually believe the Americans will attack? Are we really in danger here on Christmas Eve?"

Andre looked away, contemplating her question. "I honestly don't know. But I do know that I would like to get away from here before the bombs start falling."

"But Uncle, it's Christmas Eve!"

"All the more reason to go, Elise. We have celebrated Christmas at the farm for as long as I can remember. Why should this year be any different?"

Elise grew quiet, tears clouding her bright blue eyes. She felt herself suddenly trembling, Andre's words bringing confusion, anger; a reality that jolted her like a hard slap in the face. Elise had only recently convinced herself that her uncle's cobbler shop could provide her a marginal measure of security. The past year had been a nightmare – a horrific dream from which there was no redemption. And now, as she began to settle, no, accept her dismal situation, Elise was realizing that in addition to her loss – both parent's dead and her husband taken to a labor camp – her baby's life was at risk as well. *Maybe I have been naïve*, the thought flashed by... *Maybe war simply results in death. Perhaps there is no salvation once caught in its storm. But no...* her mind screamed in obstinate protest. *Damn it – it's Christmas Eve and my baby deserves better!* Memories of past Christmases overwhelmed Elise in a hurricane of emotion. A tear ran down her cheek as she recalled the elation felt those months back, at the thought of a Christmas baby. Christmas was not supposed to be like this... but then again... there wasn't supposed to be a war. Elise's hands cupped her face, elbows thumping the table, a numb tingling reverberating to her fingers, now wet with tears that hung off her cheeks.

"Everything is different this year!" Elise cried in resignation. Drawing strength from a deep breath, she uttered in a sarcastic tone, "Perhaps even the German army is celebrating this Christmas at *our* home!"

Andre kept his demeanor calm, cautious not to further upset his niece. "It would be silly of me to think that no one could find the farmhouse, even though it is well concealed," he acknowledged.

Elise wiped away a tear that was hovering about her chin. Her eyes pooled to a steely blue, a resolute calmness suddenly about her. "Perhaps we should go and see," Elise spit out, defiance and desperation forcing a meek smile that pulled at the corners of her mouth.

Andre's face beamed, a hollow victory, but one he accepted gladly. "My sweet Elise," he bellowed out. "That's my girl!"

2. Conley - The Patrol

December 24, 19:34 Hours – Ardennes Forest, Luxembourg

The eleven man U.S Army patrol moved carefully, plodding through the thick, snow-plastered woods as unobtrusively as possible. Their mission was to check the flank, northeast of Eschdorf, in support of a large-scale attack on the German-held town later that night. They had left from Hierheck, about seven-tenths of a mile south of Eschdorf, with orders to find the enemy and note their position but not to engage if possible. The men were from Third Army, of the famed 26th Infantry Division, known as the "Yankee Division", a name derived from its New England roots.

Third Squad, Company G of the 328th Infantry Regiment had drawn the assignment.

They had hiked about two miles thus far and all had been quiet despite hearing gunfire from the distant woods. The men of Company G knew that other nearby towns were under American counter-attack this night, so the sounds of war were not a surprise to them. Each man hoped they would find the enemy soon. Every step forward was farther from their post and all just wanted the patrol to be over. The sooner they could locate the Germans forward lines, the faster they could head back to their camp, the promise of a meal, some warmth and perhaps an hour of rest.

Private William Conley was situated towards the back of the squad. Like his fellow soldiers, he was numb with cold, scared and wondering how they could possibly find the enemy without engaging them. Conley was a likeable kid from South Boston. He was 19 years old. Before being called up, Conley worked as part of his family's business. It provided Conley a good sense of responsibility, and having dealt with adults at a young age, a mature presence for a 19 year old.

The battlefield however, played no favorites with age. Young, old and everywhere in-between, death and dying sometimes broke the most mature of men while allowing others to rise in valor. None of this filtered through Conley's mind that night. He only considered this wasn't the night or place he wanted to die.

The thicket became heavy with foliage, the squad navigating through dense, wooded forest, nearly devoid of light. Conley wondered how his patrol could possibly remain unheard, given boots crunching snow and branches crackling as they passed. He uttered silently that, if God's will be done, he stay safe, and did his best to put his trust in that belief. It was difficult for a man to hold his faith in war because it was constantly being put to the test. It seemed to go one of two ways for most – they either held on to the religious beliefs they had as their only hope, or abandoned them altogether. Conley had grown up in a family of devote Catholics, and while he never prescribed to the entire doctrine, he did believe that having a personal relationship with God was key, and that strong belief in the face of diversity was pivotal to surviving in time of war. He never shared this sentiment with anyone, but used it as justification for making it through the past two months.

Over that time, he also learned to put his faith and trust in something else, the man who walked immediately in front of him, Sergeant Bo Morgan. Morgan was the best soldier Conley had ever met. He was cool under pressure, thought before making decisions, and always considered the welfare of the men first, never intentionally placing them in harm's way.

Morgan assigned Private Jenkins, as point man to lead the squad through the snowy thicket. Everyone liked Jenkins – he had good instincts when it came to sniffing out Krauts. Conley struggled to keep the man in front of him in sight as the thin moonlight left little visibility other than ghostly shadows on a whitish backdrop. Suddenly, Conley found himself almost walking into Morgan. Up front Jenkins stopped, dropped to a knee, and one by one each soldier did likewise.

They waited as the black, foreboding night consumed them. The seconds ticked off and Conley could hear his heart thumping through the many layers of clothes that still failed to keep him warm. As he knelt and shivered, Conley's mind raced, wondered what Jenkins had seen or more likely heard. Was something out there or was Jenkins just listening for sounds, anything that might indicate the enemy was watching... and waiting.

The seconds turned into a minute. Conley felt his legs cramping but was disciplined to stay down and quiet. He was beginning to believe Jenkins must had heard something, but found the lead man and those in front him slowly rising one at a time. Watching Morgan stand, Conley awkwardly regained his own footing, and on stiff, partially frozen limbs, resumed pacing behind his Sergeant. He wasn't sure whether to feel elated that nothing had been discovered or disappointed because the march into the black abyss would continue until the enemy was located. As the steps crunched beneath his boots, Conley noticed the woods now opening up a bit, thinning from dense trees to more patchy brush. He felt the terrain starting to rise and now realized why Jenkins had stopped. The riser and opening in the thicket seemed to be a good spot to stage an ambush. As the thought passed, suddenly there was a flash and explosion, followed by the loud buzzing sound of a German MG-42 machine gun. Conley heard screams and shouting as chaos ensued and the men dove for the solid dirty-white ground and any cover that could be found.

"Sarge," Conley called out, unceremoniously clutching the ground. "Up on the crest – see the muzzle flash?"

"I see it! Damn, I'm hit," Morgan groaned as he pulled himself to cover by a downed tree.

Conley was about to rush the few feet forward to his Sergeant's position but another explosion and more violent screams stopped him. Out in front, Conley heard one of the men screeching, "Stay down! Booby traps everywhere. Fucking potato mashers hung from branches!"

Another voice penetrated the frenzied darkness. He recognized it as Donato's. It was a gurgling sound – one of a man in his dying moments. "Help me! Please… Help!"

Shit, Conley thought, knowing there was likely no immediate aid to be had. Donato was a new man, a replacement who had just joined the outfit the day before yesterday. It was his first patrol.

The MG-42 rattled again, shots ringing out in the direction of the voice. Conley used the distraction to worm his way to Morgan.

"How bad, Sarge?" he said, rummaging for a bandage in his coat and straining to see where Morgan was wounded.

"Son of a bitch," Morgan grunted. "Upper leg! Not too bad, but don't think I can walk."

Conley rose slightly to wrap Morgan's leg, but Morgan pushed him away. "Stay down… and listen! You've got to flank that nest and hit it with a grenade or two. If you don't flank'em, those bastards are going to pick us apart!"

The MG-42 raked off another long eruption answered by a brief burst of an American BAR (Browning Automatic Rifle) and rifle fire.

It was encouraging to know some of his squad was alive and returning fire. "Belson's still out there," Conley said, referring to the BAR man's attempt to engage the enemy. As if responding to his words, the branches to his right splintered, the German machine gun searching for targets. Conley flattened on his stomach, brought his rifle to fire, but Morgan stopped him.

"Take my Thompson!" Morgan hissed, tossing Conley his machine gun. He also peeled off his ammo belt and pulled a grenade from his coat. Conley took the Thompson from Morgan and traded it for his M1. He also took Morgan's ammo belt in exchange for his own and tucked Morgan's grenade in his front pocket next to the one he had been given from supply for the patrol.

The MG-42 again swept the area, forcing Conley to again callously hug the ground. Stitches of frozen earth exploded in a line just to his right, bits of ice embedding into exposed skin as it pelted them. Morgan seemed to pay it no attention. "Go left and try to flush those bastards from behind. If you can't - find your way back to company and let them know the Krauts have positions east of Eschdorf."

The thought of leaving Morgan wounded and alone didn't sit well with Conley, but an order was an order. He hoped it wouldn't come to that. Conley saw a dark stain growing in the snow around the Sergeant's upper leg. "You sure you don't want me to patch you up?"

"Isn't time son! Just do your job!" With that Morgan pulled his uniform belt from beneath his field jacket, wrapping it around his thigh to use as a tourniquet.

Conley rose partially and turned to his left. He looked back at Morgan and nodded, his resignation now giving way to fear. He had relied so heavily on Morgan to keep him alive these past months – it seemed a strange twist of fate that Morgan's life now depended on him.

"Hey," Morgan called out, over the chaotic gunfire, pulling Conley from his thought paralysis, "watch out for those damn booby traps!"

Conley focused, nodded again and crawled off. He navigated around the base of the rise but found the going difficult as the foliage became denser again. Trying to be stealth while navigating the thicket and snow, watching for booby traps, yet staying alert for the enemy was not an easy task and harder still in the murky darkness. Conley had to force himself to move forward – fighting the sickening feeling expanding in his gut and the ominous awareness that each movement forward might be his last.

Just then, on the other side of the rise from Conley's position, a flare went off – a blessing and a curse. A booby trap, suddenly made visible, something he never would have seen without its canopy of overhead light. A German grenade he knew as a potato masher hung upside down by its cord, only a foot in front of him. Conley recoiled and stopped just short of the bush from which it hung. Had the flare not revealed the German grenade, he would have traveled into the device, triggering the fuse and in a quarter-second of recognition witnessed the flash that blew his head off.

But while the flare had illuminated this trap to Conley, it also rained light over the immediate area, causing the German machine gun crew to go to work on the targets it exposed. The MG-42 buzzed in bursts and total chaos ensued as men were exposed in their positions previously hidden by the night. When the German machine gun paused all that was heard was a single rifle returning fire.

Still at some distance from the main rise, Conley hoped he could get a grenade off without being detected. He knew time was critical and couldn't linger. Conley forced a long breath, was now ready to move. A grenade exploded near the enemy position, perhaps one of the men had taken out the German machine gun. His enthusiasm was short lived however, as a burst from the MG-42 spoke otherwise. Conley got into motion crawling around some brush to a location that revealed the nest through some thicket. Darkness was returning, the flare's light starting to dim. Conley had to move fast to keep the nest in sight. Staying low, he pulled a grenade from his pocket.

Rising to his knees, he reached for the pin. As he did Conley saw the snow move out in front of him and instinctively dropped behind a downed tree. Icy cold seeped into his uniform, but he didn't feel it, adrenaline and fear coursing through his veins. Willing himself to peek over the log Conley spied a German crawling in snow camouflage, only fifteen feet away. The German solider blended in perfectly with the whitened earth, and Conley would have traveled right into him if he had not seen the motion and taken cover.

Conley tucked the grenade back in his pocket, squirmed over to an adjacent tree and pulled himself up against its base, readying his Thompson. He didn't think the German had seen him. The man's focus had been to the right, away from him and toward the gunfire. Conley collected himself, slowing his breath and staring his shaking hands into control, things that Morgan had taught him. He counted off to three, then spun around the tree, expecting the German to be still on the ground out in front of him. The German had moved quickly, however, rising to carry out a flanking mission of his own. Conley was startled to find himself face-to-face with the enemy soldier. The barrel of the German's gun, a large bayonet fixed, greeted him at chest level, a quick plunge all that was needed to end it, there and now. Conley gasped, his heart nearly pulsating out of his body. Their eyes met for an instant, shock and fear consuming both men. The German lunged with the bayonet - Conley pulled the trigger. The Thompson ignited, exploding the man's chest through his white camouflage and driving the German back at point-blank range, collapsing him hard to the ground.

Conley instinctively dashed over the dead German and jumped into the brush that the enemy soldier had occupied moments before. He was shaking all over, the image of the German, the bayonet, all so close, his first face-to-face kill. The chattering machine gun pulled him back. Conley regained focus, thought of his job, Sergeant Morgan who needed him, his platoon – those who remained, they were depending on him to silence that machine gun. He again fought the shaking, regained control. Rising slightly, Conley stole a quick glance toward the nest. He hoped the blast from his weapon seconds before hadn't alerted the Germans. If they turned their machine gun toward him, the bush serving as cover would offer as much protection as a cardboard box during a tornado.

Satisfied that he hadn't been seen or heard, Conley laid the Thompson down and removed the grenade from his pocket. He pulled up to his knees and reached for the pin. Conley's numb, ridged fingers didn't respond as they should, and he momentarily lost his grip on the grenade after pulling the pin and releasing the handle. His heart stopped as he fought to wrap his throbbing fingers around the metal pineapple, its internal timer sequencing down to ignition. Conley reclaimed his grasp, glancing up at the nest just as a white sheeted German turned toward him. The soldier spun towards him, raised his rifle to fire. Conley heaved the grenade and dove to the ground. The throw was not perfect, but the resulting explosion did stop the firing. Conley quickly retrieved his Thompson and followed by emptying his clip, then dispatching his second grenade, this one more on target.

Conley reloaded the Thompson and waited, but as the smoke cleared, there was only silence. He slowly, cautiously made his way to the nest and checked that the enemy was dead. Then Conley began carefully retracing his way back to the Sergeant, vigilant to avoid any remaining booby traps among the clumps of dark, thick foliage he had to navigate.

It was unsettlingly quiet as he picked his way back toward Morgan and the remainder of the squad. Smoke wafted like a lazy fog mixing with the smell of gunpowder and cordite, stinging his lungs with each breath. Conley expected to find some activity from the remaining squad but to his surprise it was deathly still. As he reached the bottom of the rise only lifeless shadows lay before him. Conley spied Morgan crouched by the tree they had taken cover behind. He bent down next to his Sergeant and noticed a dark stain across his Sergeant's chest. One touch told him Morgan was dead. Conley pieced together a scenario whereby Morgan pulled himself up to the log to provide additional rifle fire. His Sergeant was likely caught by the MG-42 when the flare lit up the area.

The recognition that Morgan was dead turned Conley's stomach, and the urge to retch hit him as though he had been gut-punched. The man he relied on to guide him through all this madness was suddenly gone. Conley had thought the Sarge immortal. Morgan had been with the squad since the Omaha Beach landing in June. How could Bo be caught by a stray bullet? Conley slammed his fist against the tree-limb, his eyes red and watery. It was then a second realization struck him. Conley was the sole survivor of this firefight. He'd have to find his way back to his lines alone.

Conley felt a wave of panic rise within him and tasted bile. He spit it out as if doing so would change everything. Closing his eyes he tried to visualize reversing course back to his outfit. Conley half convinced himself he could make it back, but when he opened his eyes the world of obscure shapes and shadows of the gloomy night ran up his spine like a small animal being chased up a tree.

Suddenly, he heard voices and the storm in his gut intensified to the degree it bent him over. Conley strained to make out the dialog, hoping, praying it was English. He had to force himself to breathe as the pumping in his chest was so loud all that could be heard was muffled cadences. Finally he managed to straighten, his gut easing just a bit, and was able to discern the dialog realizing that it was clearer only because it was closer. It was guttural, definitely not English. Additionally it was coming from the direction he needed to travel in order to reach his division.

Conley looked behind him into the eerie blackness, knowing his only option was to travel further into the Ardennes and away from his lines. He was concerned he couldn't negotiate his way back from deeper in the forest but thoughts surfaced of a more pressing issue... would the Germans find him before he could find sanctuary in those woods?

3. Mueller - The Ride from Eschdorf

December 24, 19:49 Hours – Road outside of Eschdorf

For lingering moments, silence hung like dense fog over the dark Ardennes Forest. Then, from the empty quiet, a faint rattling sound emanated that with the passing seconds translated to an engine, somewhat laboring as it navigated the black, desolate road.

The vehicle, a German Sd. Kfz 7 half-track, left fresh tracks as it lunged through the darkness. Although the Sd. Kfz 7 design could be utilized in many armored variations, this vehicle was more a truck with tracks than a mechanism of war. It carried no weapons and was instead fitted with three rows of bench seats for the transport of personnel and small supplies. The canvas top usually in place on such a bitter night had been commandeered, likely for an officer's use.

Exposed in the open cab and protected only by a cracked windshield were two soldiers from the Fuehrer Grenadier Brigade, straining to see ahead of them in the unyielding darkness. The men shivered, helmets low, shielding them from the harsh and gripping wind that enveloped the open body vehicle. Their breath rose in plumes as they peered into the inky void of road ahead.

Additionally, there were two men in the back of the vehicle, also from the Fuehrer Grenadier Brigade, and they fared no better. The men, a sergeant, who led the trip and a young private were also subject to the biting air that seemed to find every opening in their clothing, creating a bone-chilling numbness that permeated their entire bodies.

In the front of the vehicle, Hans, riding shotgun, peered nervously ahead down the murky roadway as though he held control of the vehicle. Driving an eerie desolate road with minimal lights for navigation was difficult and with the snow and ice a dangerous proposition. He'd do all he could to help Wolfgang, the driver, get the half-track safely to its destination.

Wolfgang leaned over the wheel negotiating the vehicle through the empty black corridor that defined their passage. His back ached but he felt it necessary to pitch forward in his seat to provide the best view possible of the dim road, if only to afford him a few additional inches of visibility. Rather than focus on his throbbing back Wolfgang thought of the risky mission. Night patrols were the worst and somehow he had found his way to being selected for this dangerous duty far too many times. His stomach twisted whenever he headed out into the unknown without the remainder of his squad.

Wolfgang's coughing half-track announced its coming long before it arrived, making his vehicle the perfect target for an unseen enemy. His officers told him this time was different. They painted a picture of Americans in gross retreat, running in fear of the great German war machine that had struck quickly and ferociously.

Thus far, based on what he saw, the rumor was true. His unit met limited resistance and the enemy they did encounter were easily defeated. The Americans, as he had been told, seemed to be in full retreat. He hoped that "Watch on the Rein" as the German offensive was called, would divide the allied forces as planned and lead to a negotiated peace that would send him home, back to his wife and children. He wanted to believe the information the officers conveyed was factual and not some fabrication to help motivate the troops.

Because there were other stories circulating through the ranks as well, depicting a much different scenario. Some of the front line troops reported that the Americans were regrouping, counter-attacking and gaining back ground lost to the German army in the initial attack. There was some shelling in town only this afternoon and Wolfgang wondered what was really true. He certainly hoped the enemy was in retreat and not between him and the destination of his vehicle this night.

Wolfgang felt an elbow from Hans and quickly regained focus, sighting a fallen tree in front of him. He pulled the half-track partially off the road to his right and around the downed sapling. Wolfgang expected the vehicle to skid but the tracks held tight and together he and Hans breathed a sigh of relief.

"That was too close, stay alert!" Hans grunted loudly in German, never taking his eyes off the road from his passenger's seat, as if doing so would keep the half-track on course. "It's bad enough we are an easy target in this slow moving piece of shit. I don't want to die because you can't stay awake!"

"Ya," Wolfgang replied, barely acknowledging the reprimand as he peered ahead into the darkness. The little light provided by the dimmed bulbs on the half-track made the going very slow and hazardous. The partially covered lights were supposed to make his vehicle less visible, but they also limited what he could see in front of him. He negotiated yet another turn and with it another shiver of cold.

In the back of the half-track, one of Wolfgang's passengers, Unterfeldwebel (Sergeant) Eric Mueller was collecting his thoughts as well. He gazed in the faint light at Private Johann Vogel, seated adjacent to him, considering what the young soldier had been doing a year ago. *He was probably with his family and getting ready to celebrate the Christmas holiday*, he thought. *Now he is just a scared rabbit, far from home and like the rest of us, trying to stay alive another day.*

Mueller was an old man by the standards of war. At 28 he was a seasoned veteran, serving in North Africa as well as Sardinia, Italy and the infamous Russian front. He cut his teeth in North Africa as part of the 90th Light Infantry Division. Although a new recruit, Mueller knew his way around a gun, having grown up hunting with his dad. He quickly established himself as a weapons expert and marksman. As the 90th gained status as a strong fighting force in Rommel's Africa Corps, Mueller too built a reputation as a soldier's soldier and was promoted to Corporal (Unteroffizier). By the time his unit was assigned to Sardinia and Italy, he was a hardened soldier, knowing well the barbaric nature of war.

So he thought.

As a newly promoted Sergeant (Unterfeldwebel), Mueller and his squad were shipped to the Russian Front as a replacement unit. There, Mueller experienced a savagery and brutality he had never seen in his three years of war. The Russian Army was merciless, and seemed to take pleasure in the art of death, burning, pillaging, even raping without conscious. On an icy, starlit night, much like this night, while retreating from a burning village under siege, Mueller took hot shrapnel in his left leg and was left for dead. Only by a determined will to live was he able to limp back to his lines. After a three month rehabilitation, he was reassigned to the Fuehrer Grenadier Brigade.

Seeing so much of war and brutality hardened him, but living with this inhumanity also gave Mueller pause to question the extremity of it all.

As a result, Mueller's philosophy was that of a pragmatist. A dedicated soldier, he would kill the enemy without hesitation, realizing there would always be collateral damage resulting in death to civilians and destruction of property. But Mueller held the conviction he was fighting to defend German soil and not political ideologies supporting the wholesale slaughter of those not aligned with the Nazi regime.

Mueller shifted his six foot frame in the seat in an ineffective attempt to stretch his stiff and rigid legs. He felt the bitter air lapping at his face and brought a gloved hand up to wipe his tired, wet eyes. If visible his eyes would reveal a soft blue hue, like an early morning sky before fully awoken by the sun. Under Mueller's dinged and scraped helmet was a cluster of beach sand hair. In his younger days, Mueller certainly presented the image of the model German soldier, the prototype that Hitler boasted was the best fighting man in the world and one of the master race. He still presented well, although war had roughened his features and curbed his enthusiasm toward the great German war machine.

Despite his rugged good looks, Mueller was still a bachelor. He was sought after by a number of young ladies over the years, but women never seemed to take precedence over his schooling initially then the military, which now consumed his time and energy.

Mueller looked at his watch but could not make out the time. He felt as though they should have already arrived at their destination, an outpost just off the roadway between Eschdorf and Heiderscheidergrund. Mueller had new orders and food supplies for the squad of ten men guarding the post. The distance to the outpost was only three miles, but he realized with the iced over roads and limited visibility, it would be a slow trek.

Despite the cloudless, bright night, the road traversed the dense Ardennes Forest and its tall, snow laden trees blocked out much of the moonlight. Mueller knew they weren't even half way to the post. He wondered what he would find when they reached there. Given the fluidity of the front lines the past day, Mueller wasn't sure which army would be there to receive the supplies he had to distribute.

The half-track slowed down as it negotiated a number of hair-pin turns that snaked a path through the thick Ardennes Forest. Another downed tree limb caused Wolfgang to veer right and partially off the roadway. As he tried to negotiate the half-track back on the main artery, the front end of the vehicle suddenly erupted in a flash of fire and smoke. The right front tire had hit a mine and the vehicle jerked like a toy, careening off the road and spiraling on its left side before skidding into a tree.

As the four men on route to Heiderscheidergrund suddenly came to understand, Christmas would yield no mercy that year.

4. Conley – On the Run

December 24, 19:58 Hours – Ardennes Forest, Luxembourg

Conley had taken three steps when he heard the words clearly: *Americana! Halt!*

Part of him wanted to end it all right there, surrender and be done with the war. But he had heard stories about the Germans not taking prisoners during this December offensive. He wasn't ready to bet his life on being captured by a compassionate enemy, especially after they saw the carnage he had just left behind.

He jumped over a log and spun to a kneeling position, firing a long burst from the Thompson in a wide arc. As the Germans dove for cover, Conley used those seconds of opportunity to bolt into the dark woods in an effort to distance himself from the German patrol. Conley ran with abandon, believing fully that his life was contingent on escaping. He could hear his heart kicking at his chest, lungs burning with each breath, sucking in rapid swallows, tasting it, stale and grimy. Conley's feet kicked out from under him as he turned sharply and he skidded into thick, dense brush. Conley found himself momentarily held captive by a prickly shrub. He pulled free, feeling the sharp thorns tear through his uniform, drawing blood. Driven by fear, he continued deeper into what seemed a dark abyss, picking up speed and getting comfortable dodging the trees and shrubs. Conley knew it was dangerous to run without caution. The woods were full of booby traps, snipers and enemy patrols. What sent him reeling however, was a downed tree hidden by the overgrowth in a patch of shrubbery. He landed hard, his helmet rolling off, a stone digging in his left hip. The cold had numbed him so the impact was not fully felt, but it still hurt like hell.

Conley rose slowly and a bit dazed, drawing air in quick shallow gulps. He took a few drunken steps, nearly tripping over his helmet. After recovering it, he secured it on his head then awkwardly rubbed his side where the stone had made its mark. Conley looked back, gave a quick listen but did not wait to hear anything. Instead he lurched forward, resuming his dash away from any pursuing enemy. Conley held his stride until he was breathless again and panting almost a half mile later. Conley was confident that the German patrol couldn't have kept pace, but also knew he was farther from his lines and deeper in enemy-held territory.

Seeing a cluster of shrub with a natural opening, Conley jumped in to catch his breath and access his situation. He slammed a fresh clip of ammo in the Thompson, peered into the darkness and listened. The blackness surrounded him like a blindfold, but all his ears perceived was calm and quiet. Conley brought up a sleeve to clear sweat running down his face. He knew the perspiration that warmed him now would chill him to the bone if he didn't continue moving at a strong pace. Conley realized he'd have to circle back to find his unit. He'd wait in this brush for a few moments and see if he picked up any sounds of the German patrol still in pursuit. If nothing was heard he'd start making his way back via a circuitous route. Conley had little idea as to what his route would actually be but figured he could discern the general direction needed to find his lines.

As he stopped to catch his breath, Conley realized how dogged-tired he was. His side throbbed from the fall he had taken, legs felt numb and rubbery, and his temples pulsed – the tension beating along his brow like a drum. He closed his weary eyes for a moment and found himself thinking of home and oddly how his dad was running the family business without him. Conley had no illusions – he knew that his father, mother and younger brother could manage the business just fine. *Boston By-Products* was a current-day recycling company. They would secure various types of material scraps from local textile mills and sort, bail then sell them to material manufacturers to be used again in their production processes. The business would never make them rich but provided a steady income for his family. For young Bill Conley it meant a part-time job throughout his school years and a full-time one after graduation. That was, until his draft letter arrived.

Suddenly, some nearby hedges rustled as if stirred by a gusty breeze. Conley stiffened, as thoughts of home vanished, and he flattened himself low in the brush pulling the Thompson into position. For the moment all was quiet again. Conley lay prone in the bush, his gun focused on the hedge, its shadow, like a ghost, staring back.

Conley considered the possibilities as his gut swirled in storm again. He felt certain he would have heard anyone sneaking up. Had he stumbled next to another German machine-gun nest? No, they never would have let him get this close. Perhaps he came upon a sniper or even a wounded man? Seconds passed. Conley's mind spun in all directions. He began to question whether the bushes really moved at all. Abruptly, the hedge fluttered again. Instinctively, his finger closed on the trigger. Conley knew firing his weapon would advertise his location, but he'd rather do that and be alive than wait too long and end up on the wrong end of a bullet. At that moment, the hedges parted – Conley swallowed hard, the muzzle of the Thompson trained, his finger applying additional tension to the trigger. The hedge opened - a large badger exiting, foraging the ground in search of food. Conley jerked back, initially startled until he recognized the inquisitive scavenger. As he considered how close he came to unloading his Thompson on the harmless creature, Conley was suddenly overcome with laughter. The unmistakable sound of an MG-42 in the distance came as a sobering reminder that there was little to laugh about on this night given his current situation.

5. Mueller – Finding Refuge

December 24, 20:21 Hours – Road outside of Eschdorf

Hans died instantly, taking the brunt of the blast, the mine detonating almost immediately beneath him. Wolfgang was ejected violently from the half-track and also killed, his neck broken as his head struck the frozen unforgiving ground.

In the back, private Vogel had looked over the edge of the vehicle just as the mine exploded, taking shrapnel in the face and neck. He and Mueller were rolled out of the vehicle as it turned on its side, both men hitting the ground hard. Mueller felt his head spinning and the urge to both vomit and pass out. Oddly, he recalled the same feeling during a shelling incident somewhere on the eastern front. He spit out some bile and shook his head trying to clear it. Taking a deep breath, his lungs convulsed as they filled with acidic smoke from the burning engine.

"Ah…, Ah…!" Vogel moaned nearby. Mueller could see Vogel's shadow in the dim light cast by the burning engine compartment. He moved toward the wounded man and felt pain stabbing his side. *Damn*, he thought, knowing his ribs were bruised at best and possibly fractured.

He came up on Vogel who was semiconscious. The man's face and neck was a bloody mess. The smell of burning and gasoline filled his nostrils and set off an internal alarm. With difficulty, Mueller awkwardly dragged Vogel away from the vehicle, fearful of it exploding once the flames licking the engine compartment found the fuel line.

Mueller's ribs felt they had been blow-torched, but he never released his grip on Vogel until the wounded soldier was safely away from crackling half-track. Then he collapsed in a panting heap.

Breathing deeply and rubbing his throbbing side, Mueller forced himself to his knees searching out ahead of the half-track. He spied the two other men lying motionless. Hans was close to the vehicle, Wolfgang a dark clump a short distance away in the snow. Mueller was fairly certain that Hans was dead, being directly under the blast, but knew he needed to check him and distance him from the half-track if there was any sign of life. Slowly but with purpose, Mueller forced himself up and over to his stricken comrade. In the glow of fire, Hans looked peaceful in death, as though he had found release. Mueller caught himself getting lost in the moment and realized doing so could get him killed. He quickly distanced himself away from the vehicle, crawling ahead to check Wolfgang.

"Unterfeldwebel, Unterfeldwebel...," he heard Vogel crying out. "I cannot see! I'm blind! Unterfeldwebel...,"

After a quick verification, Mueller released Wolfgang gently and stumbled his way to Vogel who shook uncontrollably, consumed by panic. "Stay calm, stay calm," Mueller uttered, trying to convey a reassurance he didn't feel. "Your eyes are swollen from the blast, that's why you can't see. You will be fine," he added, unbelieving of his own words.

Mueller rummaged in his pockets and found his standard issue bandages. He wrapped Vogel's face as gently as he could to stem the bleeding and cover his wounds. The frightened man quieted down after being bandaged and given additional assurance.

With Vogel calm for the moment, Mueller sat and contemplated his options. He knew he was only a mile or so from the town, but was certain he couldn't carry Vogel that far given the stabbing pain in his ribs. He knew of a farmhouse nearby from a past patrol, and thought that to be his best option. Once he had Vogel settled, he could then trek to town and summon help. He looked around him and saw the trees break where a narrow pathway cut off the main road a short distance behind him.

Mueller forced himself up and hobbled back to the vehicle, the flames still burning, although seemingly contained in the engine compartment. His eyes darted up and down the back of the turned vehicle until he spied what he was looking for. His machine pistol was there, dangling by its strap on a turned bench. He reached into the vehicle, unhooked it, and slung it over his shoulder before returning to Vogel.

"Help me Unterfeldwebel, I don't want to die," Vogel grunted hoarsely as Mueller knelt by his side.

Mueller could hear the desperation in his partner's voice. He wanted to be honest with the young soldier but didn't want to further upset him. "I'm wounded too. I can't make it back to town, but there's a house up the road we can go to." Summoning all of his strength, he helped Vogel to his feet and the two men staggered toward the path, off the main road and in the direction of the farmhouse.

Once on the path, the woods surrounded them in a canopy of hearty fir trees that suffocated the moon's light and filled the narrow road in an eerie darkness. As they approached the farmhouse, Mueller could see that it had been demolished by fire. The dark silhouette of only a few timbers was visible against the backdrop of blackened trees. Mueller tried to recall the last time he had seen the farmhouse. It had been only a few days since the patrol, he thought. He remembered marveling that the house had survived the war untouched, perhaps due to its unique location, hidden in the thick woods. The fates of war he supposed.

He heard gunfire in the distance but couldn't place whether it was to his front or rear. The Americans are no longer retreating he rationalized but have regrouped and are counter-attacking. Slowly, he continued dragging Vogel along.

"How much farther?" Vogel moaned anxiously, needing more help with each step.

"Just a bit," Mueller replied, unable to tell the young man the farmhouse had been destroyed. He still hoped to find refuge in the basement, out of the bitter cold. He stopped in front of the house, searching the dark for anything that might act as a shelter. As he did, Mueller remembered a barn which he thought was attached to the main structure, common in that area of the country. Seeing no barn, he wondered if he had remembered correctly or if it was located elsewhere on the property. He noticed that the path continued beyond the house.

"Are we here?" Vogel persisted, in obvious pain.

"Almost," Mueller replied, "Just a little farther ahead."

Hoping he wasn't mistaken, he navigated Vogel past the burned timbers. The wounded man was now like a lead weight, and Mueller's ribs screamed in protest with each step he plodded through the snow.

After trudging along for another few minutes he saw the barn, silhouetted against a pasture where the woods and path opened to a large expanse. It stood, based on the profile he saw, seemingly untouched. It was an extensive structure employing an oversized central double door that provided access for livestock and farm equipment as well as an adjacent entry door. To Mueller's eyes and aching ribs it was a thing of beauty. He gave thanks, and with renewed effort, guided Vogel along until they were at the entrance.

"Is this it?" Vogel grunted through measured breaths as Mueller leaned him against the entry door frame.

"The farmhouse is gone," Mueller answered honestly, "but this barn will do."

Mueller knew the double doors were secured from the inside and was almost as certain the side door would be locked as well, but it opened with a push. He peered into the darkness, wondering if anyone or anything inhabited the place on this frigid, wintery night. He wanted to ready his weapon, but despite leaning against the door frame, Vogel was still pressed against him and the gun was not easily accessible. He breathed deeply and against his better judgment entered the barn on faith that an ambush didn't await him.

They hobbled into the darkness, the moonlight giving little away through the open door. Mueller looked around but could see nothing. It was deathly quiet. He staggered with Vogel to the far side of the barn to minimize the draft from the door. Mueller could feel Vogel shivering and thought that maybe the wounded man was going into shock. Mueller gently placed him down, then covered him as best he could with hay found covering the barn floor.

Mueller looked around him, hoping his eyes would adjust to the darkness of the barn and allow him to discern its interior. But around him all was black; he needed light. A thought came to him and he cursed himself for not having remembered it before.

He turned to Vogel, "There's a flashlight, blankets, and food supplies back at the half-track. I'll get them and return in twenty minutes."

Vogel moaned, "No, don't leave me. I don't want to die alone."

"Just twenty minutes, maybe even fifteen," Mueller reiterated.

"Please Unterfeldwebel Mueller!" Vogel pleaded, his voice weak, shaking with fear.

Mueller ran his options through his head. For all he knew, the half-track had burned completely and the supplies were cinders. But if he could retrieve them, they were the best option he had for survival, both Vogel's and his.

"Grenadier Vogel," Mueller continued almost in a whisper. "I want to help you. Please, let me help you. I'll only be gone a little while, and then you'll be warm and comfortable. There is also a medical kit in the half-track. I can recover that too and better bandage your wounds."

Vogel was silent for a number of seconds. "What if someone comes? I can't defend myself like this."

Mueller reached to his side and pulled out his Lugar. He found Vogel's hand in the darkness and placed the gun handle in it. "Take this. I'm sure you will be fine, but just in case, you have a weapon."

"Will you hurry back?"

"As fast as I can," Mueller answered, feeling more like a father than one soldier talking to another.

Vogel mumbled something and Mueller interpreted the noise as the man's affirmation for him to leave. He rose quickly, felt his ribs pull, but fought through the pain and moved toward the door. He thought about saying something to Vogel as he left, but he feared any further discussion might give the private reason to reconsider, so he simply made his exit.

Outside the barn, the sounds of war became more prevalent. On both sides of him he heard the buzz of a machine gun and the crackle of gunfire. He knew that at night every noise was amplified, but he wondered what this Christmas Eve held in store for him. He could never have imagined what was about to unfold.

6. Andre, Elise - Evening Exit

December 24, 20:51 Hours – Eschdorf, Luxembourg

They carefully made their way up the stairs and out of the basement into the cobbler shop. There they peered out the window onto Main Street. Satisfied that all was quiet, they exited to the back of the shop and repeated the process. Seeing no one, Andre and Elise slipped out the back door of the shop and were immediately hit by the bitter cold.

Elise gasped at the frigidness despite being dressed in multiple layers. Andre looked at her sympathetically but still motioned for her to follow. Quietly she consented and they made their way down an alley in back of the shop to its end, where finally they stopped and scanned the area. Andre could see a tank to their left some distance away on Main Street, and soldiers walking a post well ahead of him.

His plan was to head to the right side away from the tank and guards. They would have to traverse a small field and a road that would take them to the edge of a narrow strip of woods which expanded out into a dense forest – the Ardennes. Once there, they would be able to find the trails they had navigated for years. There, about a mile into the woods off one of the lesser known trails, was the family's farmhouse.

Andre thought the difficult part would be getting across the snow-covered field. He thought of dressing in white as the German troops did, to blend in with the ground-cover, but he knew being found by the Germans dressed that way would get them both shot. His plan, if caught, was to say he was looking for medical help, using Elise's pregnancy as a ruse.

At the point he felt most comfortable, Andre helped Elise up and they awkwardly hurried across the field, staying as low as possible as they went. As they traversed the field, Andre expected to hear either a voice yelling for them to halt or a machine pistol more forcefully doing so. Amazingly, neither happened and they found themselves against some brush at the road's edge. Once across, they would be on their way to the farmhouse.

Andre looked over at Elise as they caught their breath resting at the hedge. He could see Elise was struggling to navigate, nine months pregnant and all bundled up for the snow. Andre worried that the trip might have been too much for her after all, but he worried more what staying in the town might mean.

"Is this really necessary?" Elise questioned, breathing through her labored pants.

Andre simply nodded as he surveyed the road in both directions, looking and listening carefully for any sights or sounds. Satisfied all was quiet, he helped Elise up and guided her across the road. They were about to enter the woods when they heard "*Stehen bleiben!*" They stopped immediately, knowing gunfire would follow if they didn't. Andre turned slowly to see two young German soldiers manning a machine gun post in a dense thicket just to his right.

"And where might you be going this frigid night?" one of the soldiers asked in German, his tone sarcastic.

Andre looked at the two men, who seemed to him more like boys than soldiers. "Yes, it is cold indeed," he replied in German, trying to feel out their German loyalty.

The second soldier smiled and began to discuss the weather, but the other interrupted.

"I believe I asked where *you* are going," he said sternly, his tone menacing, quickly pulling them back to the question at hand.

Andre breathed deeply. "My niece is ready to have her baby and with the troops in town there is no place to care for her. We have some friends who live a short distance away--"

"I don't care to hear your stories old man," the guard interrupted. "You realize I could shoot you on sight for breaking curfew. Civilians have been ordered to take shelter in their basements and remain unseen."

The other soldier looked at Elise. "Rolf, it is Christmas. What's the harm?"

The difficult German didn't yield. "Don't be taken in by these people, Jaeger. They are breaking curfew and coming out on a night like this seems quite suspicious to me. How do we know she is really pregnant and not sneaking out to meet other underground agents? Take them back to town and bring them to Hauptmann Decker. I think he would be most interested in questioning them."

36

Jaeger refused. "Rolf, if you want to bring them back, do it yourself. I will not be reprimanded by Hauptmann Decker for leaving my post."

Rolf relented, turning to the shivering civilians, "Return to town now! If I see you on the streets again I will shoot you myself!"

Andre said nothing. He put his arm on Elise's shoulder and guided her across the road without looking back. Once across and in the shadows of the high shrubbery, Andre attempted to steer Elise further along the road. She pulled back and he stopped. They exchanged glances. "You heard him; they'll shoot us if we do not return."

"That's why we'll go farther down, away from their post."

Elise started to reply, but Andre hurried her along, giving her little opportunity to debate. Andre was no fool. He knew without a doubt that if they were caught again, it would not likely go so well.

7. Decker - An Eschdorf Christmas Eve

December 24, 21:01 Hours – Eschdorf, Luxembourg

The Fuehrer Grenadier Brigade was encamped in the town of Eschdorf that Christmas Eve. Billeted in the town hall on Main Street, Hauptmann (Captain) Peter Decker nervously paced as he waited for an American attack. Since the Fuehrer Grenadier Brigade's arrival four days earlier on December 20th, Decker's anxiety had been building over the defense of the town. His troops were not at full strength and spread thin. The Brigade was initially borrowed by the German Seventh Army from the OKW reserve to help secure the southern flank. This meant digging in and holding German positions along the Sure River, but the Seventh Army needed its flank extended to include positions south of the river, so the brigade was also deployed throughout Bourscheid and Eschdorf as far south as Arsdorf.

A formidable unit, the Fuehrer Grenadier Brigade contained a battalion of forty Mark IV and Panther tanks, one battalion of mobile infantry, and a rifle battalion. Sadly for Decker, at the time he had only a few tanks and the rifle battalion with which to defend the village. The remainder of his brigade was spread across Bourscheid and Arsdorf.

Decker was also concerned about the morale of his troops. For the last two days, since the twenty-second of December, the village came within range of the American Artillery and Eschdorf seemed to be constantly in danger of shelling. This was always unsettling to the men and Decker wondered how much "fight" was left in them.

Then of course there were the civilians. Most of them had left the town before his troops arrived, but a fair number remained, largely because they had nowhere else to go. Roughly one hundred eighty civilians had stayed, taking refuge in their basements. In one basement alone there were some twenty-four inhabitants.

Decker was uneasy that some of these locals were providing information to the Americans, helping their artillery target areas in the town. He also worried that his army's strength and defensive positions

38

were being compromised. His paranoia resulted in a call to the German security to investigate. That meant a visit from the dreaded SS or Gestapo, who were situated in a nearby town with one of the Panzer units. With callous efficiency the men in black arrived to "round up and question" civilians thought to be a security risk. They checked papers and took those they suspected might be tied to the resistance.

Sitting at a large desk in a room off the main entrance of the town hall, Decker ran a hand through his thick jet-black hair while he inhaled deeply from his third consecutive cigarette. He took his tired, blood-shot eyes off a map he was studying to fix on the burning glow stick as if admiring it. In fact he was, wondering what it was about nicotine that seemed to calm him when his world seemed like it found its way to his gut and was spinning inside it. The phone rang, breaking the fixation, and he sucked deeply, knowing the phone never meant anything good.

"Decker," he announced blandly, knowing it had to be one of only a few who had his private line.

"Peter," the voice bellowed through the other end. "Merry Christmas!"

"Oh, yes, Merry Christmas," Decker replied casually, distinguishing the voice as that of his major, Karl Bauer.

"What's wrong Peter?" Bauer asked, recognizing his Captain's less than enthusiastic demeanor.

"You tell me, Major?" Decker took another long drag to brace himself for news he was certain he wouldn't care to hear. Bauer was being much too casual for Decker's liking. The man had called him by his first name before, but never twice in succession. Bauer was usually business first. Decker wondered if he had been drinking, after all, it was Christmas Eve. It would be just like Bauer to be celebrating the holiday out of harm's way, while *he* braced for an American attack.

"Peter," he said again, making Decker's stomach twist in need of another drag. "I call you to personally wish you a Merry Christmas and you seem like you're not at all glad to talk to me."

"No, no," Decker said, now in recovery mode. "I was just sitting here, studying a map of my perimeter defenses. Is there more you can give me? Tanks, I need the rest of my tanks to truly secure this town."

"Come now Decker," Bauer said, the business side of him quickly returning. You have your orders and know what means you have at your disposal to carry them out. We are all doing what we can to hold our lines until the Luftwaffe can break through and supply us. "

Decker stifled a laugh, couldn't believe that Bauer still believed all the propaganda that Hermann Goering was spewing about his air force, the Luftwaffe, owning the skies again. Decker wanted to scream that he'd give a year's salary to see Eschdorf air-lifted supplies to feed his troops and help thwart the American attack. Instead he choked back any words, snuffing out his cigarette and reaching into his jacket pocket for another, like a well-oiled mechanical chain-smoking robot.

"I understand Herr, Major," he uttered, after inhaling on newly lit tobacco, suddenly just wanting to be done with the call. "Is there anything else?"

"Information from some probing patrols leads me to believe you'll have a quiet night, but early tomorrow I expect the enemy to attack. Have you heard anything from your posts?"

"No, Herr Major," Decker stated. "Nothing has come in at this time although I expect to hear something over the next hour or so when the posts are relieved and I get their reports."

"Good!" Bauer exclaimed in an almost overstated voice that convinced Decker his superior must have been enjoying some libations. "Are you ready for the Americans?"

Decker again sucked hard on his cigarette, thought it had become protocol now every time Bauer spoke. "As I told you Herr Major, we have some areas on the perimeter that I could use additional panzers. But we shall do what we can."

"You will do more than that, Peter. You will hold that town and beat back any American advance. As I told you, the Luftwaffe will provide air support at first light. By tomorrow night you will be enjoying a well-deserved Christmas dinner that I will personally see is delivered to you and your men. Do you understand? "

Another drag, "Yes sir."

"Merry Christmas, Peter... and Heil Hitler."

"Merry Christmas, Heil...," the phone went dead, Bauer ending the conversation.

Decker stared at his maps for the umpteenth time, his head encircled by the cloud of hovering, stale smoke. Did he really have until tomorrow to prepare the town for the American attack? His posts would be reporting, he'd see what information was available then. If the posts reported nothing perhaps he could celebrate Christmas Eve with an hour's sleep.

8. Roehm - Outpost K-6

December 24, 21:10 Hours – Ardennes Forest, Roadside

Grenadier Josef Roehm was cold, tired and hungry as he looked out into the black night. He stared into the nothingness as if waiting for a ghost to appear. In fact, he was. Josef and nine of his fellow soldiers from the Fuehrer Grenadier Brigade were waiting for much needed supplies promised days ago. For several days, they had been manning the roadside outpost with limited ammunition, sparse rations and insufficient blankets and coverings for the frigid conditions.

His Unteroffizier (Corporal) had told him earlier to be on the lookout, that the supplies were en route, but thus far nothing had materialized out of the dreary, still darkness.

Josef questioned why he was even stationed at the remote outpost. The officers were painting a happy picture of German tanks rolling through the limited American resistance, the Allies now chaotically retreating. If that was true, why was he here and not sleeping in a warm bed in one of those rolled over towns? He had heard the sounds of war all day and it didn't seem to him that the Americans were running. From what he heard, they were fighting.

"Grenadier Roehm," a voice came from behind and he stifled the urge to jump. He turned to see Unteroffizier Meier, his corporal, approaching. Meier was smiling as he walked up in the makeshift trench. He seemed amused that he was able to startle the private.

"Unteroffizier," Roehm nodded, not wishing to acknowledge any alarm on his part.

"I like a man with quick reflexes," Meier teased.

Roehm stared ahead, thought about responding to the comment, but instead said, "Where are they?"

"The Americans? They are out there, perhaps coming this way," Meier answered dryly.

Roehm hated it when Meier played his little word games, but in this instance perhaps he was right. "Do you think they ambushed our supplies, Unteroffizier?"

Meier reached up and placed a hand on the logged timbers that roofed their dugout. "It is war. Anything is possible during war, Grenadier."

Roehm looked at Meier but said nothing. Josef then gazed back, beyond his Unteroffizier, toward the remaining men in the dugout, to see if they were listening. But in the dim environment, he could only see shadows of men, either resting, eating from their few remaining rations, or watching another area. Getting not even a glance back, he returned his eyes to the empty road ahead, his disappointment voiced in his silence.

Meier was cold and hungry too. He wanted those supplies to arrive as much as Roehm or any of the men. "I'll get on the Feldfunk and see if I can get a message through," he finally said, patting Roehm's shoulder and calling for Schroder, the radio man.

The "Feldfunk-Sprecher b" was the German equivalent of the American walkie-talkie. The radios had their limits, as wireless communication in the Ardennes was difficult and in the best of conditions the range of the device was about one mile. To communicate with Eschdorf from their location was a two-step process. First, they would contact a radio detection truck, located within range near the town of Heiderscheidergrund. The truck would pick up their signal, verify it, and then transmit their message to Eschdorf. The process would work in reverse to get them a reply.

Roehm looked back and saw Schroder tuning the receiver as he prepared to transmit. "Thank you, Unteroffizier," Roehm called out softly, feeling only a small fraction less helpless than he did moments before.

Meier sighed and in perfect alignment with his character, gently replied back, "By the time that message is received in Eschdorf we will either have our supplies or be celebrating Christmas with the American Army."

9. Andre, Elise – A Dangerous Wait

December 24, 21:11 Hours – Outside of Eschdorf, Luxembourg

After returning to the village side of the road at the guard's order, Andre and Elise paced roughly a hundred yards and rounded a bend to their current location. They were well out of site from the guard post that had stopped them, but had no guarantee who else might be in wait. They still had to cross the road to find entry in the woods and the paths that would navigate them home. Elise couldn't remember being more uncomfortable; the cold, her pregnancy, thoughts of this stress on the baby, all adding to her misery and concern. But given it all she knew her uncle was one of the most capable men she had ever known. If he felt this was best, it must be so. Deep within, she knew too, that her uncle's blood coursed through her veins and with it the same resolve and determination he had to succeed.

The two sat quietly, shaking and shivering in the brush, waiting and listening, trying to assure themselves there were no additional sentries situated at their new crossing site. What startled them however, wasn't across the road, it was on the road. Suddenly, from the black emptiness just to their left an engine roared to life. There was no mistaking the heavy, mechanized sound of a starting panzer. Elise gasped and Andre fought to remain in control as the ground vibrated and a menacing sound penetrated the eerie quiet in deep unsettling tones.

"Where did it come from?" Elise managed, shaking now more from fear than from cold.

"It must have been on the road all along," Andre offered.

"Let's go back, we can't cross here with a tank in front of us," Elise pleaded.

Before Andre could answer, voices were heard on the road, shouting over the gurgling tank's engine.

"Stay down, and remain quiet," he muttered. "Breathe into you coat so it's not visible."

44

The yelling continued – a discussion between one of the soldiers on the ground and the tank commander. Soon other voices were joining the conversation. Andre strained his ear to listen. The Germans seemed to be discussing where the tank should be positioned as part of a guard post.

"If we stay close to the hedge we can make it back," Elise whispered.

"What ist los?" a voice boomed out from the open space directly in front of them not thirty feet away.

Elise muffled a scream and both she and Andre involuntarily shuddered.

"Don't move, stay calm," Andre uttered close to Elise's face, hoping the voice wasn't directed at them and that the darkness would keep them concealed and alive.

The voice obviously belonged to an officer, as all other dialog among the soldiers ceased with his presence. Andre sighed in relief as it was obvious the man was addressing the men around the tank. The officer passed Andre and Elise so close they could clearly see his uniform coat with lapels pulled up to protect against the cold. The slightest glance to his right would have revealed the awkwardly clumped pair wedged into the brush and crushed any chance of leaving Eschdorf. Fortunately, the German lieutenant had other matters on his mind and kept his focus straight ahead.

With a few more steps and seconds that felt like minutes he crossed an opening in the hedge and joined the other men. Andre and Elise knew they had cheated death.

The Lieutenant barked some orders and the tank lurched forward. The vibration and clanking became so loud it was hard to believe the heavy tank wasn't about to crush them both. Andre was concerned that the lieutenant would return the way he came but knew they had no choice but to remain where they were. His plan thus far had been a disaster and he asked his brother's soul to forgive him for putting Elise and her baby in such danger. Still – he was convinced it was better taking the chance than remaining in the town.

The mammoth panzer clamored past them slowly with its entourage including the German lieutenant. With only a hedge between them and the enemy, Elise and Andre felt exposed and vulnerable. They held each other tight and prayed as every second reduced their immediate peril. As the ground stopped rattling and the engine noise reduced to a tremor Elise sighed deeply. "Uncle, that was too close!"

"That was not pleasant, I'll grant you that."

"What now?"

"We wait."

"Wait? For what?"

"To make sure no one is lurking."

"Uncle I'm so cold. And... the baby – I must think of the baby."

"Yes – be patient, just a few more minutes. Now let's listen and make sure no one else is out there. Then we can begin our adventure."

The words forced the corner of Elise's mouth up into something approaching a smile. "Trust me uncle, I've had all the adventure I can stand already tonight!"

10. Conley - Lost and Alone

December 24, 21:22 Hours – Ardennes Forest, Luxembourg

Conley was now lost and so cold he thought his teeth would chatter out of his numb and unfeeling mouth. He staggered around an oddly shaped tree, its trunk starting straight but then curving low to the ground before shooting up, thick and tall. Conley gave it a curious look, continuing to put one heavy and almost limp foot in front of the other, negotiating the deep snow. Conley knew the general direction he needed to travel in order to reconnect with his lines, but in the inky black of a forest night, it was difficult to know for sure the exact direction to pursue. He had lost his compass and tried to use the moon and stars to navigate but he still questioned if he was making real progress or wandering aimlessly. Conley knew he'd feel better if he could just find the road and follow it.

The unrelenting frigid air penetrated him deeply. His boots seemed like logs he could hardly lift to take another step. His body was like a mannequin that swiveled in slow, robotic movements. Conley worked to stay focused on his surroundings, knowing that to become complacent would likely result in death. He tried to recall the map that Morgan had shared with the squad before they left on patrol. There was a main road on the map that zigged and zagged but eventually led to Eschdorf. If he could connect with this road and follow it he'd likely find the point where his patrol started. He would be taking a chance following the road. He knew it was more dangerous to do so, but easier to mark his progress. It was all meaningless however, unless he could actually find the damn road.

Conley heard a German MG-42 rapping some distance away and a new strategy formed in his weary and exhausted mind. He tried to determine the direction of the shooting. American troops were at the other end of the gun he heard and returning fire. Conley knew in the vicinity of the shooting he'd likely find friendly troops. He abandoned his plan to find the road and trudged an uneven path through the snow, sometimes waist deep, using his ears like a compass to point him at the chattering machine

47

gun. Trying to follow a noise in the night woods is like trying to track a leaf in the wind, always changing direction. Just when he thought he was locked in on the course of the sound, it came to him in a new direction. Conley adjusted his path several times, feeling like he was closing in on the recurring sound.

Then he saw it. At first he thought it couldn't be possible, but as it formed like flesh from its shadow there was no doubt. It was the odd shaped tree he had passed some time ago. The realization that Conley had been walking in circles trying desperately to trace the audible machine gun hit him like a brick shot from a canon. Frustration overwhelmed him, immediately draining him of his remaining energy. He stopped and studied the tree, still unbelieving. "Shit…," he screamed out as he dropped in the snow, exhausted and bewildered.

He lay there staring at the funny looking tree, panting in sweat and yet numbly cold. His body was spent and his mind a wash of thoughts, most telling him to give up. *Is this it*? he asked himself. *Do I die right here*?

Conley let his eyes shut. He knew that he was flirting with death, but what use was living anyway? Half his body had no feeling, perhaps freezing to death was painless. It certainly couldn't be any worse than this.

*

If death came, it came quickly. He was suddenly back home playing in the snow. A twelve year old Billy Conley lying in the fort he and his best friend Charlie Sullivan had painstakingly made, packing layer after layer of wet snow together in a circle that spanned about six feet in diameter. The snow that had fallen that day was perfect, wet enough to pack solidly, but dry enough to stay in place. At his feet were a number of almost perfect snowballs, a formidable arsenal should they be needed. Charlie had just been called home and young Billy was now alone enjoying what remained of a rare canceled school day, due to the foot of freshly fallen snow. Life was good.

Young Bill sat up, contemplating what to do next, now that Charlie was gone. He spied someone walking in the distance, through the soft flakes that still fell on that white winter's day. He recognized the walk, it was Helen Kincaid. Helen was in his class and lived up the street. She was kind of cute, although Billy would never admit that to anyone, not even Charlie. He knew that Helen would be passing right by his fort.

How better to get her attention than to ambush her with the battery of snowballs he had sitting there, waiting for a target.

Billy laid low in wait as Helen made her way up the sidewalk. When she was within range he stood up and heaved. The first missed, but he was ready with another and then another. The third snowball hit her shoulder. Helen stopped abruptly and stared at him as though sizing him up.

"Hi Helen," Billy said, almost in a mocking tone.

"Billy Conley!" she replied, now in full understanding of who her assailant was.

"You better run," Billy taunted. "I'm going to blast you!"

Billy was surprised when Helen did not run. In fact she just stood there, out in the open, an easy target. He cocked his arm, ready to fire again and repeated, "You better run!"

When Helen did nothing but stand her ground, he let the snowball fly. It felt good leaving his hand and soared on target. It would hit her.

He stood in amazement as Helen actually turned to face the incoming projectile. With deft hands she caught it and in a flash whipped it back at him. Too dumbfounded to move it smacked him right in the chest, knocking him back on his rump. Billy tried to piece together what had just happened. As he struggled to his feet another snowball caught him in the arm and spun him around. He noted the force of her throws. Billy' never knew a girl who could chuck like that. He awkwardly threw back at her, but she was moving now, playing the game. Helen had found some cover behind a parked car, and was packing another snowball. This was not how this was supposed to go. Billy had more than met his match.

It was then his mind started to piece together Helen's story. She was coach Kincaid's daughter and he suddenly remembered seeing her at the boy's baseball practice. Those boys were thirteen year olds and here she was, a year younger, and holding her own with them. He wasn't even old enough or good enough to play in that league. Billy wished he'd had thought of that before deciding to pick a snowball fight with her.

*

An eye opened and Conley saw a partial moon and a single dim star. How long had he been in dreamland he wondered. It couldn't have been long because he didn't feel any more frozen, although as numb as he was, how could he tell? He regained focus on the twinkling faint light, fixed far above him. While it wasn't shining bright, it reminded him that it was Christmas Eve and he used the thought of Christmas to force himself up. His mind returned home to his family. What were they doing for Christmas? Would they celebrate the holidays differently with him at war? Did they have a candle in the window, letting everyone know their son was a soldier and at war? As these questions pulsed through his brain, Conley awkwardly found his footing and brushed off the snow that clung to his jacket. His first steps were difficult, but slowly Conley regained his rhythm and settled on a direction he felt would lead him toward the gunfire.

He walked robotically, like a zombie staggering along with no purpose or intent. Conley staggered out of woods and into open space without actually realizing it. He had stumbled upon the road but his mechanical movements and emotionless mind only processed that fact after a number of steps. Even then the realization came because the deep snow gave way to packed, solid and more slippery ground under foot. The discovery of the road jolted Conley back and a small sense of relief settled in, knowing he had found a viable path. Following it should lead him toward his unit if he was careful and could keep from being seen. However, Conley found it difficult to navigate the road in a stealth manner. In fact he found it quite unnerving. Despite the close tree-line, which blocked most of the quarter moon, his dark uniform cast a long shadow against the white snow-covered road. He regretted not taking a minute to pull the snow parker off the Kraut he killed back by the machine gun nest. Now every noise he heard: the constant buzzing of the MG-42, sporadic gunfire in the distance, even the sounds of nature, reminded him how exposed he was out on the road. Each became a challenge for him not to duck for cover.

Conley made his way sluggishly, weaving along the slick snowy road. He picked up the scent of something burning: an oily, mechanized smell. Soon after, Conley saw a dark outline and a faint flickering light. He dropped back to the trees, crouching down, looking and listening in an attempt to discern what lay ahead. When he was unable to make out the shady silhouette, he rose slightly and cautiously approached, maintaining a distance along the trees, wishing he could silence the crumpling of snow under his boots. As his body pulsed with shakes, Conley wondered if it was the cold or fear that was more in control of him. Moving closer, the outline materialized into that of a vehicle. Conley recognized the vehicle as a German half-track laying on its side, smoldering. He thought perhaps it had taken a hit from an American bazooka team and hoped those GIs might still be around.

He glanced upward and spied the solitary star. The thought of Christmas again flooded his mind. *Ironic*, he thought. *Please lead me back*, he prayed silently, hoping this star, like the one in Bethlehem so many years ago, might lead him to peace and refuge.

He considered bypassing the half-track, but the thought that fellow GI's might be nearby pressed him to move closer. As he carefully approached the vehicle, he could see a body lying in the snow about five yards in front of it. He stopped abruptly and studied the form. It was German and appeared lifeless. In the frigid air a man would need to be a magician to pull off playing dead face first in the snow. But he knew it had been done before so he felt it necessary to ensure the enemy was indeed dead. His Sergeant used to kick the enemy hard in the ribs – if they didn't flinch it was a good bet they were dead. That approach was good enough for Conley.

Conley cautiously approached the motionless soldier, his eyes darting from the lifeless form to the half-track and back again. He came up on the German and planted his boot solidly in the man's mid-section, his gun at the ready, should there be a response. There was none. In fact the body was partially frozen. Satisfied the German was dead, he returned his focus toward the half-track. He saw the flickering of flame that had all but burned itself out in the engine compartment. The scarce light that remained of the fire gave little away. *There must have been more than one soldier in the half-track*, Conley pondered. He had found one who could do him no harm, but where were the others?

11. Mueller - Flirting with Danger

December 24, 21:24 Hours – Ardennes Forest, Luxembourg

Mueller was pleased to find the Sd. Kfz 7 half-track still intact although a small fire was still burning in the engine compartment. The vehicle had supplies strapped in the third seat which had come undone and rolled out due to the impact with the mine. Mueller found one of the displaced packages on the ground just behind the half-track. His first thought was to drag the heavy package to the barn using a makeshift sled he might be able to fashion from a seat, but he quickly dismissed the idea. His ribs hurt too much to pull it along and he didn't plan on spending that much time in the barn. Instead Mueller pulled his trench knife and cut the straps that wrapped the supplies. Pulling out rations of cheese, bread and sausage, Mueller looked out onto the empty void of road around him feeling exposed and somewhat like a common thief. Hands full of provisions, he lumbered to the half-track and unceremoniously dropped them at its base.

The built-in storage compartments of the half-track were located on its sides, so in a turned position the stowage partition was facing up. Mueller used an inverted seat as a step to gain access to the compartment. He reached out, feeling the burn in his ribs, and worked to open the compartment.

The small fire was burning itself out in the forward part of the vehicle and created an eerie scene. The shadows cast by the few remaining flames played tricks, and dancing images appeared everywhere, most with long arms and large weapons that turned out to be tree limbs upon investigation. The latch was difficult to release and the distractions created by these obscurities made it harder. It was designed to open horizontally, not vertically, as it currently faced in the upturned position.

Mueller constantly checked around him as the meandering light softly flickered nearby. He was hopeful that any risk of the flames catching a fuel line and exploding had past, but he remembered an occasion where fellow soldiers were confident a fire had burned out in a similar situation only to have the vehicle detonate. He tried to push that recollection from his mind.

As he pulled on the latch, Mueller noticed a grenade in his belt. He could only smile and shake his head. It was a reminder that death was never far away. After working the latch fore and aft, it finally released, the compartment access cover swinging open.

Reaching in, Mueller was able to find and retrieve the blankets and medical kit. Stepping down from his makeshift ladder, he placed the items at the base of the half-track against one of the turned seats near the food rations. After again eyeing the gloominess around him and satisfied that all was quiet, Mueller climbed back up to search for the flashlight. His ribs throbbed in pain with each reach and step up the improvised access to the top side of the half-track. Nothing was visible in the storage compartment, and Mueller's only option was to feel for the metal-cased light. Mueller's hand found the cylindrical casing, but when the vehicle turned, it had become wedged in the compartment. He tried to muscle it out but the flashlight was firmly locked in place.

A noise somewhere nearby startled him. Mueller spun, nearly losing his balance, straining to see what the darkness would not give away. He reached instinctively for his Lugar, feeling only the empty holster. Mueller remembered then he had left it with Johann. How senseless he had been to give his weapon to a man who was blinded. Mueller knew he had given Vogel the gun to calm the man's fears. It was why Vogel allowed him to leave the barn for the blankets.

But it was naïve to think that Vogel could use the weapon given his condition. The mistake could cost Mueller his life. There was the MP40 but Mueller's machine pistol was draped over his back and not easy to access perched on the side of the vehicle. If the enemy was out there, they would kill him and then find Johann in the barn and kill his wounded comrade too.

He peered around the vehicle yet another time looking for any sign of movement that might have contributed to the noise he had heard, but nothing revealed itself in the murky forest. Mueller strained his ears, now calling on another of his senses to help discern, but the only audible sound was his own chest pounding a rhythm faster than he would have preferred.

Mueller cautioned himself that to ignore even the smallest of sounds, given his precarious position on the half-track, could have dire consequences. What drove him more was knowing the faster he could free the light and get off the road the safer he'd be. So he accepted the risk and returned to the task of freeing the light in the compartment of the tipped vehicle. If Mueller did not realize how close danger existed, he would soon find out.

12. Wheaton - Back at G Company

December 24, 21:25 Hours – Outside of Heirheck, Luxembourg

George or G Company had been in reserve, ordered to guard the right flank that Christmas Eve day. With help from an H Company mortar barrage, Easy and Fox Companies fought to push the Germans out of Hierheck.

After the long day of bloody fighting and with Hierheck under American control, the Second Battalion of which G Company was comprised, moved up the road and took positions on the small town's south side. It was from here that the order had come for a squad to check the area towards the northeast to ensure the right flank was secure. It was the patrol that Conley was part of and whom the remainder of G Company anxiously waited to return.

Normally G Company's reserve status for Hierheck would make them a lead in the attack on Eschdorf. However, the Captain of G Company took sick and a newly appointed Lieutenant had been given temporary command. Possibly concerned about the young Lieutenant leading the attack, G Company was again placed in reserve for the assault on Eschdorf.

The planned approach was for E Company to advance into Eschdorf via the East side of the town, as F Company attacked from the West. The pincer type assault was to kick off at 1:00 AM that Christmas morning, a little more than three and a half hours away. As "reserve", G Company would be held back to support either attack as needed. If all went well they would be used to perform "mop-up" operations after the town had been taken. That meant flushing out any remnants of German resistance holding out or hiding in basements, attics or otherwise not accounted for during the initial assault.

Roger Wheaton, one of the G Company lieutenants, had reported up the chain of command that Sergeant Morgan's patrol had not returned. Concerned that Morgan's squad had been ambushed, he was also worried that E Company might be heading into heavy enemy concentrations when they attacked through the same direction later that night.

"Any word on Morgan?" he asked, entering a small stable where his men were taking turns evading the bone-chilling cold that imprinted itself on any soul outdoors this Christmas Eve night. The blank stares gave him his answer. Wheaton sighed and returned to the frigid night air, heading toward the area where the remainder of his troops waited for orders to assemble in support of the 1:00 AM Eschdorf attack.

As he approached he could hear the clear chatter of a German machine gun. In the little available light he looked around the road's bend and could see a frozen ditch adjacent to the road where his men had taken shelter. The men were pinned by intermittent machine gun fire that ripped up the road and sides of the ditch like a meat grinder, showering them with snow and frozen bits of earth.

"How long has this been going on?" Wheaton asked Will Kline, one of his Sergeants who came out to the relative safety of the bend to greet him.

"About thirty minutes now, Lieutenant. Been on and off in sixty second bursts letting us know they're watching. The bastards are just messing with us but they're getting the men jumpy."

"Can't we do something about it? Give them some return fire, maybe shut them up?"

"I'd like that sir, but we're not sure where the Krauts are firing from. We'd be shooting kind of blind."

"Get a fifty up here. Make sure the gunner has good cover and start peppering that son of a bitch back. Might shut him up."

"Yes, sir," Kline said.

Wheaton shivered. "It's cold as a witch's tit out here. If that machine gun keeps us pinned down we'll all be frostbitten before the attack on the town kicks off."

"I'm rotating the men out to the stable sir," Kline answered meekly.

"I know," Wheaton said. "Not good enough. Have the men keep moving, flexing arms and legs, fingers and toes. Have them take turns crawling the ditch if necessary but keep them moving. Until the fighting starts, the cold is our biggest enemy."

Kline nodded his understanding.

"One more thing," Wheaton continued. "I need...,"

Suddenly night turned into day as a blinding sheet of light flashed to their left. It was followed by a huge explosion that rattled the ground and propelled ragged pieces of burning hot metal in every direction. Wheaton and Kline both hit the ground brusquely. "Anyone hit," Kline called out.

Before anyone could answer another flash lit up the night, this one behind most of the men and closer to the stable. The ground rumbled again in protest and almost immediately it was followed by calls of "medic!"

"Damn Eighty-Eights," Wheaton grunted as he rose to a low squat, not certain the shelling was over. "Faster than the speed of sound – can't hear them coming in."

Kline had heard it before, had lived it too many times. "What else did you need, Lieutenant?" he asked, ignoring Wheaton's mini artillery lecture as he too pulled himself off the frozen earth.

Wheaton caught his cue, "I need a runner to get a message to Command."

"Johnson," Kline called out over some shouts behind them where the second shell had landed. "The lieutenant needs a runner." The private acknowledged Kline with a nod, then crawled out of the ditch. Staying low he awkwardly ran to where Wheaton and Kline were positioned, his tight, stiff, chilled muscles resulting in his clumsy movement.

"Thanks for volunteering," Kline said with a smile as the private approached. Johnson met the comment with a less than enthusiastic stare.

Turning toward Wheaton the man said, "Private Johnson, sir."

Wheaton started to relay his message to Johnson when a noise from behind interrupted him. It was a young nervous private.

"Lieutenant Wheaton? Message for Lieutenant Wheaton."

"I'm Wheaton."

"Colonel Hamilton would like a word sir."

Wheaton and Johnson exchanged glances. "Looks like I'll be delivering my own message." Wheaton dismissed Johnson.

Wheaton looked to Kline, "Get a fifty set up and returning fire."

"On it, Lieutenant."

"Also get me an injury report on those eighty-eights."

"Yes sir."

"I'll be back as soon as I can."

With that Wheaton looked toward the young G.I. who had summoned him and together they started toward Command.

*

The Battalion Command Post was a battered but standing house in Hierheck. Wheaton walked in and immediately felt captured by the warmth that enveloped him. The change in environment from frosty to almost humid made his head sway momentarily, but he quickly adjusted, allowing the warmth to consume him like a warm, comforting blanket, making Wheaton feel human again. His enjoyment was short lived however, as he saw the serious looks about the room all pull toward him. The task force commander, Lieutenant Colonel Paul Hamilton, immediately motioned him over.

"I understand your patrol never made it back?" Hamilton opened the dialog, right to the point.

"They did not, sir," Wheaton replied, the warmth now starting to make him perspire.

Hamilton sighed, looked down at a map. "Show me where you sent them?" he ordered.

Wheaton walked over and oriented himself with the chart. It was marked with a number of notes depicting unit locations and lines outlining various approaches to Eschdorf that Wheaton interpreted as an attack plan. After a few seconds he said, "This was the route I gave them sir," as he drew an arc with his finger from their current position around the northeast side of Eschdorf, up and into its surrounding woods.

Hamilton frowned. "I have E Company positioned to attack that east side about two hours from now. I don't want to send them in blind."

"I agree sir," Wheaton nodded.

A Captain Chambers, one of Hamilton aides made his way over. "There was a firefight heard an hour or so ago in the woods up that way," he chimed in. "That could have been Wheaton's patrol."

"There has also been penetration in those woods from the 80th Infantry Division. The shooting that was heard could have been them." Hamilton said as a matter of fact.

"That's correct," Captain Chambers agreed. "The 319 Infantry Regiment, sir."

Hamilton turned, brought himself eye to eye with the Captain. "Doug, get Captain Donahue from the 319th on the horn. Ask him if all his patrols are accounted for."

"Right away, sir." Chambers left to carry out the order.

Hamilton walked away from the table, let out a long sigh. "Too many damn questions and not enough answers," he said to no one in particular. "We're going into Eschdorf in two hours and we don't know what's waiting for us around the town's perimeter. That's got to change."

All eyes were upon the Lieutenant Colonel now and the silence in the room was deafening. Wheaton felt as though the room was on fire, felt self-conscious as the warmth revealed in a pungent way the days he had not been able to properly bathe.

Hamilton suddenly spun, turned his attention back to the sweating lieutenant. "Let me know as soon as your boys return."

Hamilton's gaze moved off Wheaton to Morris, one of his staff officers. "John," he called his staff by their first names, "I want an armored patrol from the 735th Tank Battalion to see just what the hell's out on this flank. Have them coordinate with Lieutenant Wheaton."

Morris said nothing, just tilted his head, a known acknowledgement between him and his Colonel, and left for the radio room.

"That is all," Hamilton said to Wheaton.

"Yes sir, thank you sir," Wheaton replied.

"Oh, one more thing," Hamilton exclaimed.

"Sir?"

"Depending on how this all goes, I may need to send G Company into Eschdorf."

"I understand, sir." Wheaton said, as enthusiastically as he could.

"Have your men ready to move," Hamilton ordered.

"They'll be ready sir."

Hamilton looked at him as though sizing him up. Wheaton suddenly felt self-conscious again. "Good luck," the Lieutenant Colonel offered.

"Thank you sir."

Wheaton turned and left, the cold air enveloping him like an ice pellet blanket. Initially it was refreshing, closing his open pores and wicking away the sweat. But within seconds Wheaton felt himself shivering almost uncontrollably, the frigid temperatures drawing away his body heat. He fought through the shaking, turning his attention to what had just happened. Wheaton was glad that Hamilton shared his concern about E Company attacking across an unsecured flank, and relieved that the Colonel was sending out a team to recon the area. Something had prevented Morgan's patrol from finding its way back – something that might stop E Company too if not accounted for.

He found himself still trembling but knew it was more thoughts of what might have happened to Morgan's squad than the cold. Hopefully the armored patrol Hamilton was sending out could provide some quick answers. It had to. There was also the thought of sending G Company into Eschdorf and it was a sobering one. If that machine gun hammering the road was any indication of what waited in Eschdorf, it would be a bloody Christmas indeed.

13. Conley, Mueller - First Contact

December 24, 21:28 Hours – Ardennes Forest, Luxembourg

Conley suddenly spotted another body off to his right out of the corner of his eye. He stopped abruptly and surveyed the area, his gut stitched, his chest pounding now in double-time. Approaching the body cautiously, Conley kept an eye on the half-track fearful someone might be hiding nearby. He could see the front of the vehicle but the darkness prevented him from eyeing inside or the back end from his current position. Similar to the first German he found, this man also appeared lifeless, lying crumpled on his side. Not taking chances, Conley crouched by the body and drove the butt of the Thompson hard into the soldier's mid-section. Even through the German's heavy overcoat, he could hear ribs crack in violent protest, no match for the force he applied. Nothing! Conley again noted the body wasn't fully frozen. The death was fresh. Whatever happened here happened not long ago.

Conley's mind played out different scenarios as to what might have occurred. He still harbored hope that it was a bazooka team that ambushed the half-track. Based on the half frozen dead German, the Bazooka squad might still be around. Perhaps they took the remaining half-track crew prisoner and were marching them back to the lines now. If he continued along the road he might find them. Conley caught himself playing the "what if" game and remembered some advice Morgan had given the squad. *In war, overthinking a situation will get you killed more times than not*, he had warned. *Analysis paralysis*, Morgan called it. Conley knew if Morgan were there he'd tell him to make decisions based on what he knew, not on how he'd like it to be. That meant he'd have to do a closer inspection of the half-track to determine what really happened. Until then his main concern was securing the area around him.

Conley knelt further over the body to check the division emblem on the dead soldier's sleeve. His curiosity would unknowingly save his life. By dropping low, Conley took himself out of the line of sight of Mueller, looking out in search from atop the half-track after hearing the dull thud of the Thompson smashing flesh and bone.

Conley rolled the German on his back and noted the Fuehrer Grenadier Brigade insignia on the uniform sleeve. He assumed it was this division that occupied Eschdorf and whom he would be fighting when he got back to his unit - if he got back. The dead German looked about Conley's age, maybe a little older. He wondered about the man, not his personal life, but as a soldier of the Fuehrer Grenadier Brigade. Conley had been told that this brigade was an elite combat unit, originally assigned to guard Adolph Hitler's East Prussian Wolfsschanze or "Wolf's Lair" Headquarters. Conley imagined hardened, well trained and well equipped troops that fought savagely. They won't take prisoners and won't be taken prisoner he reasoned. Fanatics – likely to fight to the last man. He shivered at the thought of vicious house to house fighting in Eschdorf. He'd have to get his M1 back, perhaps use his bayonet training to flush those Kraut bastards out of every house and cellar in that God forsaken town. His bayonet encounter an hour or so ago flooded his mind and he suddenly wanted to retch. That, and the sound of his chest, doing triplets through his field jacket, brought him back to his Sergeant's advice. *Too much thinking*, he scolded himself. *Get on with it*!

So far, Conley had found two of the enemy, dead. How many had traveled in the vehicle? It could have been two or more. The vehicle could probably carry up to six or eight men. Conley knew he needed to check the half-track and stop making assumptions that could cost him his life. Conley cautiously rose to a crouch position, brought his weapon up and approached the vehicle, trying to stay low to the ground. As he came level with the vehicle, he could see movement; a shadow in the larger shadow the half-track presented. The triplets his chest played were now a full blown drum solo. He felt his breaths coming in short spurts and his body convulsing, almost to the point of panic. After all he had been through this night, Conley wondered why this shook him as it did. *Stop thinking*, Conley screeched silently at himself, and with that his nerves settled a bit.

A darkened form appeared to be working atop of the turned half-track. Conley tried to level the Thompson in his shaking hands and made a wide arc, angling his approach so he would come in from behind.

His mind now locked on a different dialog. *Pull the trigger! Pull the damn trigger*, a voice kept churning in his head, but he couldn't yet tell whether the form was friend or foe.

Conley continued his approach, closing the gap in the darkness, his finger tensing on the Thompson's trigger.

Of course he's a Kraut, his instincts badgered him. *Who else would be out here rifling through that damn thing? Kill the bastard!*

As Conley walked closer, the shape slowly became defined. First the boots, then the uniform told him the man in front of him was the enemy. The unyielding voice in his head now screamed for him to pull the trigger and his finger responded by applying added pressure.

Conley wondered what was so important to fully engross the German, and that curiosity resulted in a few additional steps forward.

*

Mueller gripped at the flashlight, the icy steel of its handle penetrating his bare hands to the bone. He fought through the throbbing, but no matter how hard Mueller pulled to free it, it would not budge. He tried hitting it with his closed fist but that too had little effect; it was really stuck.

Recognizing how valuable a light could be in the dark barn, Mueller doubled his efforts to liberate it. Beads of sweat trickled across his brow. Grabbing the flashlight handle with both hands and with feet braced against the metal floor and seat, he jerked and pulled furiously to secure leverage. Finally, Mueller felt it give a bit and he stopped and took a breath. It was then the realization struck that working as feverishly as he had, had caused a momentary loss of awareness. Now refocused, instincts kicked in, and Mueller felt the presence of someone behind him. There was no doubt it was the enemy and that any sudden move would surely mean death.

*

Conley took another step closer. Rather suddenly, the man stopped his activity, sensing a presence. Conley watched as the man's hands slowly extended from his sides and rose as his head gradually and cautiously turned in his direction.

63

14. Decker - No Way Out

December 24, 21:29 Hours – Eschdorf, German Headquarters

Hauptmann Decker exhaled a plume of smoke, the ash from his cigarette dangling, as he paced the room in his patented, nervous style. The captain was listening to his radioman in conversation with the field and what he heard was making the hair on his neck stiffen like a quill on a porcupine. He forced one foot in front of the next in an anxious stroll, waiting, but said nothing until the radio buzzed static signifying the end of the conversation. Then Decker made his inquires.

"Who was that?" he quizzed dryly in German.

"Sector East Machine Gun post, Hauptmann," the man replied.

"And...?" Decker's impatience was beginning to show through.

"Sector east post was attacked by an American patrol earlier tonight. No survivors. The relief post came upon a lone American soldier when they arrived, but he escaped into the woods."

Decker said nothing, just continued to pace, arms clasped behind his back, head down and eyes focused on the floor. His mind was calculating everything he'd just heard, trying to digest it, spit out the answers. The elucidation he sought had nothing to do with the action in the woods, but instead how the incident could be explained so it had no ramifications on him. Everything Decker did was with a single purpose, maintaining his image as a competent German officer. It seemed these days, as the tides of war turned against Germany, every line officer was scrutinized, every decision made viewed under a microscope, every failure brought to the attention of the senior leaders, who were undergoing scrutiny of their own. The pressure fell upon them heavily and mercilessly with many sent to the Russian Front for anything less than success. Some officers were even shot under trumped-up charges for situations in which they never could have succeeded. It all flowed down to men like Decker, who had to execute sometimes impossible orders. The elite, powerful division Decker had been given to wage battle at the onset was now divided up across a number of towns in the southern sector. As a result Decker was left with the unenviable task of holding Eschdorf with a fraction of men and equipment he felt necessary to keep the town in German hands. In addition, weapons, ammunition, food were running low with no resupply in sight. And now, posts he had situated to protect his flanks were being overrun by American patrols.

Decker knew that losing Eschdorf would secure him a one-way ticket on the Siberian Express, a slang expression used to depict the Russian Front. Despite knowing he was up against a well-supplied and strong American contingency, his instincts for survival drove him to succeed none-the-less. They also fed his paranoia which led to some questionable decisions, such as bringing in the Gestapo to interrogate civilians about resistance activity. Looking back he knew such moves would get him shot if he were taken prisoner once word from the locals got back to the Americans. And it would, for word always got back!

With his options limited, Decker had to find a path to success or die trying.

After close to a minute of silent pacing, his head rose. "We have a well camouflaged, heavily armed post and the element of surprise. Still we are destroyed by an American patrol... I don't understand!

Decker looked at the radioman and slammed his fist on the table, "Details, I need details!"

"There are none, Hauptmann."

Decker shook his head, took a breath and tried to regain his composure. "Have we heard from Mueller? He should have arrived by now and be on his return trip."

"No Hauptmann, no word, although the post Mueller was ordered to is outside our radio range."

Hauptmann Decker nodded in resignation. "Keep me posted on any messages that come in," he ordered.

"Yes sir."

Decker felt control slipping away. Too many things were happening that plucked at his nerves like a Spanish guitar solo. The thought of the holidays suddenly entered his mind and with it thoughts of Christmas past. For a brief moment he found himself home with his parents and brothers laughing and singing. They were good times he thought would never end.

The moment passed too quickly and Decker found himself staring at the floor again, his stomach knotted up like a noose hanging from a gallows. He felt with certainty if he didn't somehow hold Eschdorf the knot in his chest would find its way around his neck.

"Merry Christmas," he said in cold tones to no one in particular. "Merry Christmas!"

15. Conley, Mueller – Harsh Encounter

December 24, 21:30 Hours – Ardennes Forest, Luxembourg

Mueller stood, hands up, his back fully exposed to the enemy. He had been totally engrossed trying to free the flashlight and had lost his awareness. Mueller was furious at his stupidity knowing the gaffe might cost him his life. He pushed that aside for the moment knowing it was only what he did *now* that would determine his fate.

Mueller's mind raced in a life or death effort to find a way out. He considered turning quickly while swinging the machine pistol from his back, but Mueller knew he'd be shot before the gun got half way around. Then there was the grenade tucked in his belt. Maybe he could quietly pull it out, arm it and lob it over his head? No, that would take too long.

Guilt relentlessly pulled at him for the number of amateurish mistakes he had made and Muller fought to stay focused on simply staying alive given the grave situation. Given his position balanced on the tilted seat, Mueller was vulnerable with few options available. He didn't have to move, however, to know behind him was an American soldier with a gun. Mueller figured the man was part of a patrol probing German defenses around Eschdorf and perhaps even looking for a prisoner to pump for information. He cursed silently knowing he had made securing a prisoner very easy for the Americans if that was their motive.

But Mueller had also heard about a massacre of American captives from Decker just a few days ago, his Captain warning him that the G.I.'s were incensed by the senseless slaughter and had shot a number of prisoners as retribution. The sobering thought left Mueller unsure of what the man at the other end of the gun had in mind.

While he had very limited alternatives at his disposal, Mueller did have one card to play. Slowly angling his head Mueller hoped that speaking calm words might mitigate his earlier stupidity at not staying alert and maybe save his life.

16. Andre, Elise – Escape

December 24, 21:31 Hours – Outside of Eschdorf, Luxembourg

Andre and Elise sat quietly, shaking and shivering in the brush, as they waited and listened. It had been disconcertingly quiet since the incident with the tank and Andre was feeling comfortable that they could make it across. He reminded himself that the same feeling persisted the first time and they'd almost gotten killed. So once more he stole a look, first around him, them across the road. Andre knew all too well that within the quiet there was no guarantee that nothing menacing lay in wait, hidden in the woods, on the far side of the road.

Elise was now more uncomfortable and anxious to cross.

"Uncle, I'm freezing," she expressed apprehensively. "My teeth are chattering and I've all but lost feeling in my hands and feet."

"This can't be good for the baby," she added.

"I know! I know! You're a brave girl, Elise," Andre tried to sound reassuring. "Please be patient. I only want to make sure this time there are no surprises on the other side. We were lucky the guards were not hardened like some and let us go. That isn't likely to happen a second time if we get caught breaking curfew."

Elise pleaded. "Uncle, I'm just so uncomfortable... and tired. I don't know if I can make it to the farmhouse even if we get across the road." Andre quietly pulled out from the hedge and took a final look around the immediate vicinity then across the dark road. Still hearing and seeing nothing, he dropped back into the hedge and pulled up close to Elise.

"Now we go," he whispered as he stood partway up and helped her to her feet. Elise felt numb all over, and she wondered if her legs would support her as she stepped forward. She wrestled with her unfeeling body, heavy legs buckling a bit, causing her to sway. Andre quickly steadied her, providing assistance to prevent her falling back into the brush. Concern flooded his mind that Elise might not be capable of reaching the farmhouse.

Together, arm in arm, they awkwardly navigated the hedge before waddling across the road and collapsing into the brush on the other side. They sat there sucking in the frosty air, feeling it sting their lungs, fluttering hearts gradually settling back to a rhythmic beat. When they could hear over the pounding of their chests, they listened for any indication of being observed.

A minute passed, then another. It appeared all was quiet. Andre pointed towards the woods, motioning Elise toward the farm. She grabbed a tree branch and with Andre's help began pulling herself up from the ground. As she did however, Andre heard voices on the road and pulled her back down. She landed on him in a clump and for a moment both giggled, feeling a bit like clumsy kids. Realizing there was no humor should they be caught, they quickly separated. Andre peered along the road as best he could but could not see anything. He *was* able to discern that the voices were getting louder and heading in their direction.

"We should wait until they pass," Andre started to whisper, but when he turned, Elise was up and moving into the woods. Too cold to argue, Andre shivered, looked back toward the road and quickly followed her.

17. Conley, Mueller – Formal Introduction

December 24, 21:31 Hours – Ardennes Forest, Luxembourg

Conley had leveled his Thompson toward the back of the German's mid-section and his finger began applying the pressure that would end the man's life. Conley had every intention of shooting the enemy soldier, but the man spoke and gave him reason to pause. In perfect English, Mueller said, "Please don't shoot, I am your prisoner."

Conley's finger eased and he looked at the form before him, suddenly unsure of what to do. "You speak English well for a Kraut," Conley replied, more as a reflex than thought.

"I spent significant time in America before the war," Mueller slowly turned his head trying to glimpse his captor, ignoring the Kraut reference and simply hoping to keep the man on the other end of the gun from shooting him. With his footing not secure on the half-tracks inverted bench seat and in the darkness, Mueller wasn't able to angle his head enough to see the G.I. holding him.

Conley noticed the machine pistol slung over Mueller's shoulder and realized that despite the perfect English he spoke, the man before him was the enemy. He stepped back from Mueller, keeping the Thompson leveled. "Slowly step down, turn around and face me," he demanded, hoping his voice had an authority he didn't feel. Mueller was happy to oblige - any position was better than balancing on the upturned seat, totally vulnerable to the American. He tried not to grimace as his ribs burned in response to his every movement.

"Nice and slow," Conley cautioned, still wondering why he hadn't shot the enemy soldier.

Mueller needed no incentive to comply. His painful ribs only allowed slow movements so he was able to exit the vehicle without making Conley aware of his injury. As Mueller stepped down he surveyed the area for other American soldiers but saw none. He found it curious that this man was alone and wondered if it was why he hadn't been shot dead off the half-track. That was a good omen and something Mueller filed away. He slowly turned to face Conley, noticing in the dim light that the soldier in front of him appeared to be very young. Mueller thought the American's youth could work to his advantage, but also noted the G.I. was solidly built like himself, although perhaps an inch or two shorter. With his ribs a liability, Mueller knew it would be difficult to overpower the American strength against strength. As a seasoned soldier though, he was keenly aware that strength was only one factor that contributed to winning in the trenches. More important than strength was technique and opportunity. Mueller felt confident if he could just keep from getting shot in the next few minutes the opportunity would arise, he was less sure his ribs would support the execution of technique. Mueller knew the one advantage he held was experience and believed that to be his trump card. He was throwing down that card now to stay alive.

Conley noted the potato masher in Mueller's belt along with a trench knife, holster, cartridges and pouch. "Remove your belt with your left hand and let it drop in front of you," he commanded, still debating the value of keeping this German alive. Conley reminded himself this wasn't a game and trying to play the part of his sergeant or someone he wasn't was likely to get him killed. "Now!" he heard himself say as the thought somehow faded into space.

Mueller looked down and slowly brought his left hand to his belt. Being right handed he fumbled a bit, but that was what Conley wanted him to do – to use his non-dominant hand. He had seen his Sergeant use this technique once before and Conley thought it a good approach to keep the German off-balance and unable to use his stronger and more dexterous arm, should he wish to attempt something. Conley of course had no way of knowing if the German was right or left handed, but was able to make an educated guess based on the location of Mueller's holster.

Mueller thought about his options; throwing his belt at the American, but knew he'd be shot before he could launch it. Even if he could, the American had correctly guessed; he was right handed and Conley made him handle the belt in his left hand. He awkwardly worked his left hand to unbuckle the belt and let it fall, along with the grenade that had been tucked in. Mueller figured he'd have to wait to make his bid against the American. Each minute alive was time leading to opportunity, he thought.

"Turn back around slowly, hands up," Conley said, his voice deepening again.

Mueller turned as asked and faced the half-track once again. He started to consider if he'd be shot in the back, then felt Conley's hand slip under the strap of his MP40 and slide it over his head and arm in a quick, single move. He glanced over at Conley and could see the Thompson still aligned with his upper body. Mueller was impressed. Conley had removed his weapon with one hand, while keeping the Thompson trained on him with the other. Conley tossed the machine pistol into a snowy bush off to the side.

"Your holster is empty," Conley growled insinuatingly as he looked back at Mueller's belt lying in the snow.

Mueller said nothing.

"Where is your Lugar?" Conley rephrased impatiently.

"I don't know," Mueller replied. "It must have fallen out when the half-track rolled on its side."

Conley didn't believe him. He wasn't sure why he was even talking to this man. He should have dropped him when he first came upon him. "Lean against the half-track," he ordered.

Mueller hesitated, trying to rationalize Conley's next move.

"Do it!" Conley said, pushing Mueller hard from behind.

Mueller stumbled, pain exploding from his rib cage. He reached out to avoid collision with the vehicle. Conley used Mueller's vulnerability to his advantage, searching him quickly as he leaned, arms extended against the interior of the turned half-track. Satisfied that the Lugar was not stashed somewhere in Mueller's uniform and that he didn't have a knife or other concealed weapon, Conley stepped back. "OK," he said simply.

Mueller tried to clear his head as pain shot through his ribcage and lungs from Conley's hard push. He turned slowly and faced Conley. Mueller was miffed. This young American had been trained well. He had made no mistakes in their short engagement. Mueller was counting on that to change. At the moment however, he knew he was no match for the American. His ribs felt like he had just been jabbed with a hot poker. Mueller knew he'd have to be smart to turn the tables. He tried his best not to let the American know about his injured ribs and wait for the right moment.

"What were you looking for?" Conley demanded, glancing up at the half-track to where he had found Mueller.

"I have a dying man in a barn up the road." Glancing beyond Conley, he continued, "I pulled out the blankets and medical kit and was trying to retrieve a flashlight."

Conley studied Mueller for a number of seconds trying to determine if the man spoke the truth. He contemplated climbing atop the half-track himself to see if it really was a flashlight or something else that Mueller was after. The flashlight didn't interest him; there was no need, he carried one in his gear. But the thought of visiting the barn did intrigue him, if only for a short while to thaw his bone-chilled body and get this Kraut to reveal exactly where he was.

Mueller stood there shivering and pondered about Vogel as he waited for the American to decide the next move. *My wounded Private must be wondering what's happened*, he thought. *He may think I abandoned him.* He wanted to move the process along – get Conley to take him to the barn. There he could provide Vogel with some basic care and perhaps recover the Lugar and kill this American. He debated if Vogel was still alive, the man had been critically wounded. Mueller knew the clock was ticking, possibly marking off the last seconds of Vogel's life. He wanted to leave for the barn now, but didn't want to seem too eager and give the American any reason to change his mind.

"What is your name, Private?" Mueller heard himself ask, guessing at Conley's rank based on his youth.

The question interrupted Conley's thoughts. "I'll ask the questions!" he replied bluntly.

"If you prefer," Mueller said, wanting to keep the American talking, hoping to hurry things along.

"What happened to your vehicle?" Conley queried.

"Mine."

Conley gave a slight nod. "How many traveled with you?"

"Three others," Mueller said.

"And you... you were in charge?"

"Yes, I am Unterfeldwebel Mueller," he said. "Sergeant Mueller in your army."

Conley tried to piece together Mueller's story to discern if there were holes in it. It seemed plausible. Conley felt his body quiver as the icy breeze swept across him.

"Grab the blankets and medical kit," he said, letting his depleted senses and tired, numb body drive his decision.

Mueller nodded and started over to the half-track.

Conley watched him closely. "Slowly," he cautioned with a slight wave of the Thompson.

Mueller turned, took a few steps to the side of the half-track and retrieved the blankets and medical kit under Conley's watchful eye.

"Where is this barn?" Conley asked.

"About a quarter mile farther up the road," Mueller replied.

"That is a road?"

"Yeah, it's narrow initially, but opens up."

"OK, move!" Conley said, waving the Thompson.

Mueller wanted to ask about the flashlight, but thought better of it. Perhaps he could use the darkness to his advantage. Quietly, he started past Conley, toward the opening in the trees that defined the road, blankets and medical kit under his arm. Conley followed a safe distance behind, his Thompson pointed in Mueller's direction.

As he walked, Mueller felt more confident that Conley would not shoot him in cold blood and that if he waited it out, he would get his chance to either kill the American or escape. He would have to be careful however, Conley was about his size, younger, and in Mueller's injured condition he was no match for the American. Thus far, Conley had done everything right, aside from not killing him, but Mueller looked at Conley's youth and felt certain he would misstep. Then Mueller would strike. Until then, Mueller could only help his cause by playing up to the young American GI.

Mueller's confidence however, was misplaced.

Conley, for his part, didn't know why he hadn't shot Mueller at the half-track. Even though Mueller spoke English, Conley reasoned that was no reason to keep him alive. Mueller was the enemy and Conley had no illusions that he could be a dangerous man.

Had Conley spared the German as an act of charity because it was Christmas? He didn't think so. He had spent the earlier part of the night killing Germans. Was it because he didn't want to be alone? He couldn't rationalize that, knowing this man would likely kill him given half a chance. So why was he walking with this Kraut? Why was he on his way to a barn to care for another Kraut, moving perhaps further away from his lines?

Conley hurt all over and what didn't hurt was numb. He was dog tired, drained mentally and physically. Was the cold affecting his ability to think straight? His mind screamed how crazy the scenario was, and he felt it needed to end here and now. He brought the gun up on the shadow that walked in front of him. It was now or never. His finger closed on the trigger.

18. Wheaton – The Plan

December 24, 21:40 Hours – Outside of Hierheck, Luxembourg

Since returning from Company Command, Wheaton had spent the better part of the last hour in the ditch crawling back and forth with machine gun fire ringing over his head. He continued checking his men for frostbite and reminding them to stay down but to move their joints to keep from freezing up. *What a fucking unbelievable way to spend Christmas Eve*, he thought.

The men kept asking to break to the stable for some warmth, but Wheaton could only send them in small numbers at a time and for a short stay. They needed to be ready to move in little to no time and hold defense positions should the Germans mount a counter-attack from Eschdorf. The ditch afforded them cover and a quick exit if needed. Also given the intermittent bombardment, the Germans lobbing in two or three eighty-eight millimeter shells every hour, Wheaton couldn't chance a direct hit on the stable with a lot of his men in it. So he kept the stable visits brief, a quick warmup then back to the ditch.

"Wheaton, Lieutenant Wheaton," his name was being shouted from somewhere in back. It got drowned out in the machine gun chatter and it took the men passing his name along the line to reach him. Once informed, he scurried back through the ditch as best he could, always reminding the men he passed to keep moving and working their joints.

Wheaton found a tank commander in the stable waiting for him.

"Lieutenant Wheaton," Wheaton said in introduction as he approached the man.

"Sergeant Lindquist, 735th Tank Battalion."

"Heard you were looking for me?"

"Yes sir. I have orders to assemble an armored patrol to search for the foot patrol you sent out earlier tonight."

"Good luck. That fucking gun has us bogged down at the moment. Soon as you show the mug of your Sherman I'm sure you'll draw some eighty-eight fire. Those Kraut bastards been peppering us all night."

Lindquist smiled. "We have a local from Hierheck, a farmer who tells us there's an unmarked road that will detour us from the main roads. Says he'll accompany us himself. I'd like to review the route you think your men may have taken."

"Happy to show you," Wheaton said, pulling a battered piece of map from his pocket. "Just need some god damn light to see."

Lindquist motioned, "Follow me, sir."

Wheaton followed the tank commander behind the stable and down the murky road a ways until he heard engines turning. The engines belonged to two Sherman tanks and a half-track. Lindquist led Wheaton in the back of the canvas-covered half-track. The interior was dank and stank of stale cigarette smoke, but was warmer than outside. Wheaton went to sit on the bench seat but found it was occupied by a solider laying across it.

Lindquist laughed. "Smitty, wake up and make some room for the Lieutenant."

Smitty grunted what Wheaton thought was an apology, sat up and leaned his lanky frame in the corner away from the two men. As far as Wheaton could tell, he completed the whole exercise without waking up.

Lindquist flipped on a small light that made Wheaton squint, but his eyes soon adjusted and he laid out his map on the table. The two men reviewed the area that Wheaton had designated for Patrol. When he was done Lindquist let out a long sigh.

"It'll be tough trying to find your boys. Plus Command wants to take Eschdorf starting at 0100 hours. If the fucking Krauts are out there they'll have the element of surprise and they'll be ready. But we'll give it a try."

Wheaton knew Lindquist's assignment was as difficult as it got. He was taking his tanks and half-track in no-man's land and with all hell breaking loose in about an hour and a half. Wheaton also knew the effort wasn't strictly to find his men. Hamilton wanted to know just what awaited E Company when they moved into attack positions. Either way he knew Lindquist had drawn the short straw with this job.

"Good luck," he said sincerely.

Lindquist smiled, "Thank you, sir. Merry fucking Christmas!"

19. Conley, Mueller – Deadly Walk

December 24, 21:40 Hours – Ardennes Forest, Luxembourg

The Thompson ignited and a spray of 45 caliber bullets left the muzzle. For a reason Conley didn't understand, he tweaked his arm as he fired and the burst tore up the ground just to Mueller's right side. Mueller dropped to the snow, feeling his ribs almost explode out of his chest, not from a bullet, but from his reaction to the gunfire. Conley stood there embarrassed while Mueller lay there in astonishment, his ears ringing, ribs on fire and snow finding the seams in his uniform.

It took but a second for the shock to escalate into outrage. Mueller's rage exploded like a caged animal. His head spun at Conley but he knew the boundaries in which he could act without another pull on the trigger. Instead he held a scream deep in his lungs. A litany of fury wanted to explode outward, but he kept his composure. His gaze fixed on Conley and even in the darkness it was evident Mueller had accepted death as a consequence of war. The thought sent a shiver through Conley's already trembling body.

After the silent exchange of glaring stares, Mueller pulled himself up, suddenly too incensed to feel his burning ribs. In the awkwardness that followed only the rapid breath of both men was visible in the little light of the three-quarter moon. Mueller's mind was awash of mixed feelings. His anger began to give way to inquisitiveness regarding why Conley pulled the trigger. The sudden change in the American's demeanor was unnerving but curious. Was this man trying to kill him and in the last second lost his nerve? It seemed the most plausible explanation to Mueller. Perhaps it was good to know that his enemy couldn't shoot him even when he tried. Mueller wanted to believe that but knew he couldn't count on it. He'd seen emotions change on a dime and knew as long as he was Conley's prisoner, his life would be held in the balance.

Conley had played the pros and cons of keeping Mueller alive. He came to the realization that Mueller could help him get back to his lines.

He knew he was in this transition zone between the American and German positions, but he didn't know exactly where. Just a half mile in the wrong direction could mean capture or death, and he felt he was already in German-held territory. He wanted to use the barn to warm up and eat a K-ration. If Mueller could inadvertently help him determine his exact location that would be a bonus. Then he could map out the safest route back to his lines and be on his way. "Finger's numb, twitched the trigger," Conley finally said in an attempt to save face.

Mueller said nothing, simply collected the blankets, medical kit and food stores, which had been strewn about when he fell. The men's eyes again collided, the silence screaming between them. Mueller resumed walking toward the barn.

Conley's youth and inexperience were clearly evident, even to him. The last thing he needed was for Mueller to see through his fear and indecisiveness. Conley tried to think how Sergeant Morgan would have handled the situation. *Morgan would have shot Mueller at the half-track*, Conley believed. *But he would have also known the way back to our lines.* Conley remembered something Morgan had told him when they first met. *You've got to use whatever resources are available to you. It's the only way to survive this war.* Conley thought of Mueller as a resource to finding his way back. Partially because of embarrassment, partially because he needed Mueller, Conley played a different card. He opened a dialog.

"Where did you spend time in the states?" Conley asked, the words sounding strange because his mouth was dry, his lips half frozen and because of the situation.

Mueller was still furious and conversation with the American did not appeal to him. Still, he knew he needed a dialog to gain further trust with the American to avoid another occurrence of gunfire and to eventually turn the tables on the young G.I.

"Boston area... I was a medical student at Harvard."

This resonated with Conley. He had a flashback to Harvard Square and an incident involving Helen Kincaid when both were freshmen in high-school. He had just separated from his friends after watching a movie and was about to bike it home, when he saw Helen. Conley remembered seeing her quite upset and in a heavy discussion with a guy he didn't recognize. He felt that Helen could take care of herself, remembering well the snowball incident, but this was a very different scenario. He watched from a distance until the boy pushed Helen hard. She went back into a parked car and slid down a bit before regaining her balance. Young Conley had seen enough. He peddled over, jumping off the bike long before it stopped and put himself into the other boy's face. As he did he realized the guy was somewhat bigger than he looked from across the street.

"What are you doing, pushing a girl?" Conley barked at the surprised teenager.

"What's it to you?" the boy replied, no fear evident.

"She's a friend and you're a jerk! You don't hit girls!"

"Fuck you," the boy replied and he reached out to grab young Conley's shirt.

The grab never happened. Conley let loose with two lefts and a right that crunched when it connected with the teenager's nose and sent the boy to the ground, blood quickly staining his shirt.

Conley was ready for more but the boy never looked up, instead holding his broken nose trying to stem the blood.

"Are you OK?" he asked, turning to Helen.

"Yes, now I am," she replied, obviously grateful for his assistance. "Where did you learn to fight like that?"

"Golden Gloves," Conley said. He had never won anything in the boxing ring, but he certainly knew how to block and throw a punch.

It was the start of a nice friendship with Helen Kincaid. One he hoped would become more...

He kept that all to himself and simply asked Mueller, "Are you a doctor?"

"No."

"Medic?"

"No."

Mueller wasn't sure whether to continue. He looked back at Conley but could see little more than an outline of his face. "I was in my second year of medical school when my father got ill and I was called home. Then the war broke out and I was conscripted into service."

"Into the infantry?" Conley asked in bewilderment. "With two years training and a shortage of medical help on the front?"

"Yes," Mueller replied. "I didn't make it known. I felt it was better to be armed in combat than to gamble my life with a red cross stitched on my sleeve."

They walked in silence until they came to the burned structure of the house. Mueller stopped for a moment as did Conley behind him.

Mueller turned. "The barn is just ahead."

"Has it also been blown to timbers?"

"No... untouched, strangely enough."

Conley considered that and thought how odd it was that one house could be in such stark contrast to its nearby neighbor. It was an irony he had seen played out so many times during his short two months of war.

"How much farther to the barn?" Conley inquired.

"It's just ahead on the left."

The men walked on. Conley did not like the location of the demolished farmhouse and barn. It seemed to him a likely place for an ambush. The thought froze him for a second. *What if Mueller was leading him to a barn where German troops were encamped? What if this man, his enemy, was setting him up?* He could see the silhouette of the barn now. He thought about turning and running, but with the cold numbing his legs, he physically didn't think he could. He'd have to play this out.

Mueller interrupted Conley's thoughts. "We should be quiet; if Private Vogel hears us speaking English he will panic."

"Does he have a weapon?"

"No," Mueller lied, knowing Vogel had his Lugar. "He was blinded when our half-track hit the mine."

Mueller started to move forward but stopped again and turned back toward Conley, who instinctively raised his Thompson a bit. "I'd like to enter the barn first and explain the situation to the wounded private. He is young and very nervous."

Conley considered what Mueller proposed. He tried to play it out different ways and evaluate the safest scenario.

"We'll both go in the barn," he started. I'll stay at the doorway and provide light."

"You have a flashlight?" Mueller asked, now understanding why Conley made no effort to retrieve the light at the half-track.

Conley produced a small flashlight from his pocket and nodded. "Let's go."

Mueller moved forward, the two of them walking the rest of the way to the barn without further words between them.

As they approached the barn, they heard gunfire not too far away. Mueller whispered to Conley, "That is an MG-42."

"Yes," Conley said quietly in return. "Answered by an American BAR... It is possible we could have company soon."

Mueller turned and faced Conley, "I trust there will no more accidents with your weapon. Depending on who finds us, we could become each other's prisoner."

Conley could only nod. He knew Mueller was right.

20. Andre, Elise - Dangerous Woods

December 24, 21:40 Hours – Ardennes Forest, Luxembourg

Andre and Elise slowly navigated their way through the dense forest. It had been arduous, nothing like they remembered from earlier days when these same woods where their playground. They stopped often to rest, winded, their muscles protesting each step forward. Andre was second guessing his decision to make this trip with Elise but she was a gutsy young woman who, once committed, was driven to succeed. Andre couldn't remember a colder night, but they stayed relatively warm, plowing through the fluffy, thick snow, continuous movement one of their few allies.

These woods that were so familiar, had been like an old friend, on this night seemed to have turned against them as they labored in the deep snow. Elise, thinking of her unborn baby, knew she had to keep moving and forced herself to do so, even though she felt twinges of what she thought could be labor pains.

They remained silent, trudging along the path as best they could. Suddenly to their left a machine gun ignited and they both fell to the ground, the thick snow almost burying them. The machine gun was quickly answered by other weapons and a grenade.

Relieved the firing was not aimed at them; Andre nodded at Elise and pointed to the right, away from the shooting. The exhausted woman struggled to find her feet. About half way up, she lost her footing and fell in a heap. The snow found its way everywhere, and the cold and wet drained Elise's energy and the determination that had been her focus just moments before. She looked over to Andre who was quickly by her side.

"Uncle, I can't do this!" she said, her exhaustion clearly visible in the dim light of the moon.

"You must," Andre said calmly, resting a hand on the back of her coat.

Elise was cradling her stomach with her freezing hands.

"I'm so tired and cold! I am covered with snow! I should never have left the basement!"

"We are close Elise," Andre continued in the same calm voice. "Your baby needs you to be strong. We have come this far, you don't want to die by freezing to death. Come, I will help you up, and we will be at the house in ten minutes."

Elise knew the estimate was ambitious but knew she couldn't give up on her unborn baby. The fierce resolve she had had just moments before returned as if she had been stuck by a bolt. She nodded and with Andre's help was able to get back on her feet. Once up, the two civilians re-routed themselves through the thicker woods, away from the firing to lessen the threat of detection.

Despite being wet, chilled to the bone and very afraid, Elise still saw the beauty in the snow-covered woods around her. She had always felt a kinship with nature and she tried to use that intimate relationship to guide her as she trudged step after step. Elise took solace that these woods, her woods, had not been ravaged by artillery as so much of the area had been. She had no illusions however, that it might not hold true tomorrow, so Elise took each step as though it might be her last opportunity to do so.

More gunfire crackled in the distance, disturbing the calm Elise was beginning to feel. She stopped and spun her head as an explosion flashed the darkness bright for a moment off to her left. In the murky silence that followed, Elise felt a mild nudge from Andre, a gentle prompt to keep moving forward.

For Elise the reminder also had other connotations. It was an awakening to what they were really doing – fleeing the German army during a time of war. A war that had stalked its way to their door and had infiltrated their lives. More than that it was like a disease consuming them one by one. A sudden sensation of helplessness washed over her as the snow had done moments before. Elise fought the mood, would not let herself be a victim, at least not of her own making. She felt a sense of anger and defiance welling up within her, felt her baby kick as if giving his or her support. Suddenly she had purpose and with it a new burst of energy. Elise picked up her pace knowing the barn was not too far away. She even put some space between herself and Andre, who could only smile, a tear forming in his eye. *My brother would be proud*, he though as he hastened to catch up.

21. Conley, Mueller – The Barn

December 24, 21:50 Hours – Ardennes Forest, Luxembourg

Mueller entered the barn calling Vogel's name softly while Conley crouched just inside the door. He hesitated at turning on the flashlight, knowing it illuminated him as an easy target in the dark, but did so anyway aiming it at Mueller, his Thompson ready. In the dim light it shed, Conley could see a German lying in the hay as Mueller approached him. Mueller tried to rouse his compatriot but was unable to do so. He placed his head close to Vogel's, listening for breathing. Conley knew the drill well and assumed the man was dead.

Conley then ran the light in a wide sweep of the barn. He quickly found the room was divided by what looked to be a large stone fireplace in the barn's center. He could see no opening though and could only assume the hearth faced toward the rear of the barn.

As soon as Conley's light fell away from him, Mueller began searching around Vogel's body for the Lugar. His hands dusted the hay around the dead man, but could not locate the weapon. Mueller saw the beam's light circling back toward him and cursed to himself as he stopped searching, looking up into the light.

"He's dead," Mueller called out to Conley.

Conley had already concluded that. He said nothing, gave a slight nod in the dark Mueller would never see.

Mueller rose and looked around in the sparse light Conley's flashlight cast. Mueller took a step toward the back of the barn and suddenly fell over. Seeing Mueller go down, Conley uncoiled from his crouched position, stood, and cautiously walked over, refocusing the light and his Thompson out in front of him.

"Damn," Mueller moaned, rubbing his ribs.

Conley approached, first shining the light on Vogel, the man's face a bloody mess, the makeshift bandages that Mueller applied earlier doing little to hide the damage. Swinging the light back up Conley found Mueller on his feet. Conley stepped back from the German Sergeant then directed the light toward where he had fallen. He was startled to find the object Mueller tripped over was a frozen American GI. The man had a huge red stain on the back of his field jacket and had likely crawled in wounded, then died.

"Wonder what else is in here," Mueller said casually.

Neither man paid much attention to the dead GI. Both knew there was nothing that could be done for the frozen corpse and had seen too much death to be startled by the sight.

Conley swept the light around the back side of the barn. He verified what he had initially seen was a fireplace in the center of the barn with a hearth that faced to the back. On each end of the fireplace were waist high shelves and under them bins stacked with wood and tools. The fireplace and attached ends were impressive and divided the barn into forward and aft sections. Moving the light against the back of the barn revealed stalls that appeared to once house livestock. They were empty now except for a large, old, two-wheeled cart in the center stall.

Mueller took in the interior and was as impressed as Conley. He said nothing about it, instead stating, "I'll move the bodies so we don't trip over them again."

Conley looked at Mueller trying to determine if he had an alternative motive. "Alright," he responded hesitantly.

Mueller carefully negotiated his way back to Vogel's body in the shadow cast by the flashlight, careful not to fall again over the corpse. Once next to Vogel, Mueller felt around the body for the Lugar but again couldn't locate the weapon. He was incredulous as to where it could be and getting frustrated that he couldn't find it. Seeing Conley's light arcing back in his direction, Mueller decided he would first move the American body then come back for Vogel to give himself another chance to search for the weapon. Perhaps the American had a weapon easier to locate.

Mueller rose and looked at the light flashing at him. "I'm going to move them to that end stall."

"OK," Conley agreed.

Conley provided light and Mueller took the two steps over to the American corpse and found his frozen collar. He wanted to frisk the GI in hopes he harbored a weapon, but with Conley supervising he had no opportunity to do so. His ribs protested as he dragged the dead soldier.

Mueller hoped Conley didn't see him wincing in pain. He deposited the corpse in the back of the stall.

Once Mueller was in the stall, Conley shifted the light and began exploring an adjacent stall. In the darkness, Mueller ran his hands over the American but could find nothing, not even a cartridge belt.

Mueller thought about taking advantage of the dark and jumping Conley, but knew his ribs would place him at a strong disadvantage against the young, strong American. Instead he found his way back to Vogel and again searched him, frantically looking for the Lugar.

Finally, on Vogel's left side, down along the man's leg, his hand found what he had been searching for. He looked over toward Conley on the other side of the fireplace to see the light swinging back in his direction. He locked his hand on the object and clearly identified it as the Lugar.

Conley was now rounding the edge of the fireplace wall and his beam searched to locate him in the darkness. Mueller knew he didn't have time to prepare the gun for firing so he quickly pulled the gun out from under Vogel and stuffed it inside his uniform.

He managed this just as the light found him. There was a moment of silence as both men stood there staring at each other. Mueller thought this might be it, that Conley had seen him with the weapon. If the circumstances were reversed, he would have dropped Conley where he stood. A second passed, then another. *Too much time* Mueller thought. He waited for the muzzle flash.

22. Elise, Andre – A Long Trek

December 24, 21:45 Hours – Ardennes Forest, Luxembourg

Andre and Elise were nearing exhaustion as they labored through the deep snow. The spark that pushed Elise to drive forward after her fall, had been extinguished by an area of dense forest heavy with snow. Despite the tree cover that buffered the ground from direct snowfall, the snow drifts still registered at hip level in some places making the going difficult, strenuous and very slow. The firing was well behind them now, although the echoes through the night woods made it sound much closer. They searched for the re-emergence of the trail, which had been detoured to distance themselves from the fighting. Elise and Andre knew they were close but the snow and dark night made the path challenging to find. Both knew that if they were to lose their way, it would be fatal. For Elise, she knew her death would count for two.

The shadows ahead opened up. Adrenaline shot through Elise like electricity surging to a light bulb. The trail lie just ahead – that had to be it. Like a cheetah who suddenly picked up the scent of a gazelle, her spent legs found new life. She calculated where they would be intercepting the trail. While not totally sure in this black abyss, which gave the forest chameleon-like qualities at night, she believed they were only minutes away from the farmhouse. Her pace quickened as she steered her way through the trees and thickets toward the opening she believed was the trail. The separation between the trees was now just ahead. A few more arduous swings of her legs and Elise would be back on the trail. She looked back to see if her uncle was keeping pace – he was. Elise quickly rounded a tree, then another, so focused on finding the path that for the moment nothing else mattered. There it was, the path. One more tree and some brush to slog through. Elise grabbed the last tree and spun herself around it, almost giddy at the thought she was nearly home. Her spin however, came to an abrupt stop as she careened directly into a German soldier poised against some brush.

The collision sent her backwards into Andre's arms, who had come up behind her. They both went down again feeling the icy embrace of the snow. Elise shook hysterically and emitted a muffled scream, her mouth numb from cold. The soldier appeared to lunge at them, but like an uprooted tree, fell forward, stiffly landing just to her side.

Andre stole a look at the German. It would be catastrophic if they were found here. His mind panicked, desperate to craft a scenario that might buy them their lives. But as the seconds ticked he realized the soldier was not moving. The German was dead.

They lay there, their breath forming small clouds as they gulped in and rapidly exhaled the frigid night air.

Andre turned to Elise, her woollen coat now crusted in snow. "Are you OK my dear?" he asked, his voice almost a moan, his gut twisted in a hard knot.

Elise didn't immediately answer. She continued breathing deeply, in and out, trying to let her rattled nerves settle, reaching deeply into reserves she didn't know she had, hoping not to scream. Only after a while did she look up at Andre.

Still shaking and with tears in her eyes she said, "Another meeting like this and I'm going to have this baby out here."

Andre said nothing as he helped Elise awkwardly to her feet and dusted the snow from her clothing. The reality that he was playing a callous game with her life and that of her baby's suddenly struck like a hammer. He had grossly underestimated this trip, somehow minimizing the snow, cold and Elise's condition. The deep, black night and possibility of encountering Germans had also been conveniently left out of the equation. *No*, he reminded himself, *it was always part of the calculated risk*; a risk he still believed was their best bet for survival. With that the optimist in him returned.

"We're almost there," Andre said hopefully. "We need to get you to the farmhouse and in front of a warm fire."

Elise had only half heard her uncle, her eyes still fixed on the dead German. "Where do you think he came from?"

"Perhaps a sniper who was shot out of the trees and landed in that bush," Andre said, his breath still coming in quick gasps.

"If he is here, who is to say there are not more Germans at the farmhouse?" Elise blurted out as though the thought just entered her mind.

"A real possibility," Andre answered honestly. "Let's go find out for ourselves."

With that Andre dusted the snow from himself and off the bag he had draped around his shoulder. He examined it to ensure everything was intact. Then Andre treaded over snow and brush to the dead German, bent over and tried to remove the man's sidearm. It might come in handy although he knew if found on him it could be a death warrant. It was a moot point. The gun was frozen solid in place and would not budge.

Not wanting to spend any more time in the woods than needed, Andre stood and motioned for Elise to follow. They stepped awkwardly over the dead soldier and onto the snowy path. It was narrow and devoid of light, except for the little that reflected off the snow. None-the-less, they knew it as well as they did each other and where it would lead. As they began down the weaving trail, Elise realized that despite falling in the snow, she was no longer cold. A meeting like this had a way of accelerating blood flow through the body and warming it quickly. Still, she hoped to stay clear of any similar encounters.

23. Conley, Mueller – Night Noises

December 24, 21:55 Hours – Ardennes Forest, Luxembourg

The seconds ticked and Mueller waited for Conley to shoot, sensing he had caught him stashing a weapon he said he didn't have. After what seemed an eternity, Mueller heard Conley speak.

"What's taking so long? I thought you were moving your soldier to the back of the barn?"

"Yes," Mueller said quickly, rising to his feet in relief he had not been seen. He still had life, and he vowed he would not be as careless again. His ribs throbbed and Mueller doubted he could move the soldier at that moment. He knew he should wrap his chest but he didn't want to give anything away to the American. He needed a diversion to buy some time. "Did you hear that?" he said, feigning that he heard a noise outside the barn.

"No, what?" Conley answered, suddenly concerned.

They stood there in silence, listening.

"I thought I heard something...outside," Mueller reiterated in a hush whisper.

Conley said nothing, just continued to listen. He turned away from Mueller, shifting his attention and his gun toward the door. Conley wondered whether he should switch off his flashlight. Any rays that filtered through the barn or under the door would give them away, but he didn't want to lose sight of Mueller in the dark. So they stood, his flashlight dimly illuminating the doorway, and waited.

As they stood there, Mueller couldn't understand why the American was at the barn. He felt Conley could have already found his lines if he had not diverted as he had. The man had done many things right but leaving Mueller alive and not seeking his own lines was a big mistake and Mueller felt the time was now to make him pay.

He reached into his coat, placed his hand on the Lugar and considered how easy it would be to pull the weapon from his coat and shoot the

American. Holding the flashlight, Conley presented a silhouette that would be hard to miss at the close distance.

Conley seemed to be reading his mind, however, for in that moment he turned back to Mueller, the light and his Thompson following, pointing directly at the German. "I don't hear anything," he exclaimed softly.

"No, nothing," Mueller answered, quickly extracting his hand from the weapon.

Conley dismissed the noise or absence of it and stepped back, turning toward the fireplace. He spun the light to the fireplace for a moment then back to Mueller. "I've never seen a barn like this with a big central fireplace. What do you make of it?"

Mueller was happy to engage in conversation at that moment. It meant giving the burning in his ribs time to subside. He made his way toward the back of the fireplace facing Conley, "This barn was likely a blacksmith shop."

"That would make sense," Conley agreed. "There seems to be a number of blacksmithing tools along with wood and kindling for the fireplace."

Mueller nodded. It wouldn't be long now he surmised. The American was becoming careless. He would soon pay with his life.

"All this wood," Conley continued. "I'm surprised no one's used it for a fire."

"To do so would mean an Artillery barrage maybe from both our armies," Mueller replied quickly. "This barn could end up looking a lot like the house."

Conley said nothing. The quiet that followed was interrupted by the subtle sound of voices. The sound was faint, but enough to filter through the night and thin walls of the barn. In fact it seemed to Conley that he heard sobbing. Both men stopped and exchanged quick glances in the dimness. With the gun muzzle, Conley motioned Mueller to the far side of the fireplace and placed himself at the other end. Conley swung his Thompson over the top of the side wall ready to unload his clip if warranted. After a brief look that Mueller was where he was supposed to be, Conley dosed the light.

In the ensuing darkness, Mueller immediately pulled his Lugar. Both men contemplated their options. They would have to see who entered then play their hand. Together they waited alone.

24. Elise and Andre – The Lost and Found

December 24, 22:04 Hours – Ardennes Forest Barn

Andre and Elise stared at the house, or what was left of it. Neither said anything, just sullenly gazed at the burned timbers, lost in thought at once used to be. Their minds were a flood of emotion in that moment, strong resentment rising like a tidal wave for both the Americans and Germans, whoever was responsible for this devastation. For Elise, seeing the burned shell of her family house was the spark that ignited all the passion she had kept in check since they had started out that night. The feeling of helplessness she fought off in the woods struck again with such intensity that Elise crumpled up in the snow, legs becoming like putty, unable to support her. Her anger was so intense that Elise could not form tears but she pounded the snowy ground again and again.

"No, No, this can't be happening!" Elise cried out in anguish.

It was only when Andre embraced her that her fury gave way to anguish and a parade of tears marched down her cheeks.

Andre said nothing, simply because there was nothing he could say. He let Elise cry.

In a cruel irony the charred remains of the farmhouse contrasted sharply with the frosty chill that stung at their bodies as they sat in the snow exposed to the elements. Long gone was the adrenaline rush from their encounter with the dead German in the woods and the excitement of finding the trail.

Elise's mind filled with memories of the home she grew up in. Simple things like sitting on the large porch in the summer eating ice cream and watching the stars. She looked in the emptiness and recalled chasing fireflies with her cousins. And... of course, dad... always working, tending the livestock or vegetable garden, but never too busy to take a moment to laugh or play with her. It seemed long ago, yet the images seemed so vivid it could have been yesterday. How she missed those carefree days and all the memories this house personified. Seeing her home in ruins ached like the second passing of her parents.

"What do we do now?" Elise asked through streaking tears.

"Let's check the barn," Andre said

Beyond this, Elise felt strange in a way she never had before. She wondered if it was the cold, the shock of seeing the burned house, the exhausting walk, the baby or all in combination. She began to feel pangs of pain, and wondered if it was the onset of contractions.

They rose as one and walked the path toward the barn also of the same mind. What if the barn too was nothing but charred embers? What then? Neither spoke, not wanting to deal with the possible reality that the barn might be destroyed. Andre took solace in believing he had seen the top of the structure from the path to the house, but he couldn't be sure and wanted to elicit no false hope. He was concerned about his niece, both her health and that of her unborn child. They had endured a lot that night and without shelter from the brutal elements he did not like the scenario that would result.

As they rounded the bend along the narrow path, they saw it. A shadow they knew well, silhouetted against the dark backdrop of snowy trees in back and open pasture on its side. Standing unscathed, looking much as it did the last time they visited, the barn welcomed them.

Elise gasped in relief, stopped and squeezed Andre's hand. "Oh my God, it's still whole... untouched," she muttered in a low, hoarse voice.

Andre said nothing, just looked at her and smiled.

Elise found herself fantasizing about the comfort and coziness of the fire Andre would have burning shortly. The first good omen of the night she though. Perhaps the difficult part was behind them. Elise felt a flutter within, thought it excitement – no, more likely the baby.

Andre suddenly slowed, his pace becoming very cautious as they neared the barn. Elise, tired, cold and with the warmth of the barn within reach, looked at him impatiently. She was about to make her feelings known when he brought his finger to his mouth, pointing down. Elise saw them - footprints in the snow – leading to the barn door. The snow was also stained, perhaps with droplets of blood, although it was too dark to tell. Andre bent down, removed a glove and ran his thumb and index finger through it. After bringing his fingers close to inspect, he nodded to her tellingly.

Elise's legs quivered, the exhilaration of finding the barn suddenly tainted. For a moment anger consumed her, the burned house and now intruders in the barn. But as reality returned, Elise thought herself naïve to believe that with war raging, no one would have found the barn and used it for shelter. Perhaps, she imagined, all the wood and limited provisions, placed by her family for times such as this, had been taken and used. She felt panic creeping in, wondering if she had traveled all this way, risking her life and that of her baby, only to die here, never giving her baby a chance.

Andre pulled her from these thoughts, nudging her gently and quietly toward the door. Andre placed his ear against it and for a long moment stood inert, listening for any sound of movement within.

Finally satisfied that all was quiet, he carefully cracked open the door, stopping after a few inches, peering into the darkness and listening again. Still hearing nothing, he slowly pushed it open further and cautiously entered alone. Elise waited outside, shivering, but understood why. Once in, Andre turned, shut the door and in the darkness turned again, reaching high above the door frame. There he found a small gas-fired lantern kept hidden over the years their family owned the farm.

Conley saw the door open and shadows outside. He fought for control, his heart nearly ripping out his chest, watching in confusion as one of the shadows entered then immediately closed the door, becoming lost in the darkness. Conley strained in the blackness trying to make out what was happening. He determined that whoever entered the barn was searching for something over the doorframe. Everything this night had been strange, bordering on bizarre, and Conley's fatigued, weary mind stopped, chose not to make sense of it. He firmed his grip on the Thompson and turned the light toward the door, his thumb posed to illuminate the target before he laid waste to the shadow in front of him. Conley held back when suddenly the door swiveled and his target stepped back outside.

What the f... Conley's mind spun as he struggled to make sense out of this turn in events. The dark forms he saw didn't seem to wear helmets of either army, carry weapons or give the appearance of soldiers. He had been trained not to trust what he couldn't see so he stayed quiet, waiting for what would come next. Thinking of what wasn't visible, Conley turned his attention to Mueller. He wanted to flash the light at the German, ensure Mueller was where he was supposed to be, but knew doing so would give him away. Conley took small comfort in believing that any movements Mueller made he would hear given their close proximity. Conley knew his luck had been stretched thin like a weathered elastic band that could snap at any time. Was his life being held this night by a last few strands of tether?

*

Once Andre had retrieved the lantern, he opened the door and stepped back out into the filtered moonlight. Handing the lamp to Elise, he reached under his coat and deep within his pockets. Finding what he wanted, Andre pulled out a small pouch containing a box of wooden matches. Andre took a long breath, hoping his falls in the snow hadn't dampened the matches and rendered them useless. He struck the match, relieved to see a small flame ignite at its end. Returning into the barn Andre traversed the match in a semi-circle doing a quick survey of the barns interior. The shadowy match light gave him no real view into the barn, but with this minimal assurance, he turned to Elise, who had followed him in, and lit the lamp she had readied.

Elise saw the lantern come to life and a wave of relief surged over her. She closed the door behind her, shaking snow from her coat, happy to be embraced by a damp chill rather than biting cold. Elise sighed, grateful that no one had found the kerosene lamp stashed in the door frame. Another good omen she thought.

Andre adjusted the flame, and with Elise, they turned to get their first good look inside the barn. Immediately they saw it – a body lying in the hay. Elise gasped and Andre froze. Andre's mind raced to the dead German they had literally run into just a short time before. He wished now that he had made more of an effort to retrieve the dead man's Lugar from the frozen, stiff body.

25. Lindquist – Search

December 24, 22:06 Hours – Outside of Hierheck

Lindquist looked again at the crude map. It had roads penciled in where he had not known there to be means of passage. He took the last pull from what once was hot coffee, but now tasted like tepid, flavored mud.

He glanced over at Sal Delminico, who was assigned to drive the half-track that evening. "We need to get this show on the road. Time's a wasting!"

Delminico rubbed his hands together and shot back a curious stare. "Why ya telling me, Sarge? I'm ready to go anytime. Where's this civilian whose going to lead us to the Promised Land?"

Lindquist smirked. "Being briefed, I think. Funny, I'm the guy in charge of this little band of fun seekers and my briefing consisted of being handed this fucking map and a pat on the back."

"How do we know this guy's legit Sarge? I mean he could be a collaborator setting us up for a turkey shoot in front of a Kraut machine gun."

"If we run into Kraut's it won't be because of him. I'm told he's helped the Resistance a number of times, despite having a family, all whom would die painful deaths should he be caught aiding our cause."

The men exchanged glances, no further words needed as both imagined what that could mean.

Moments later Wheaton arrived with Philippe Ruscart. He was the man who would lead them through the back roads, keeping them away from the German artillery sights so they could look for the lost patrol and check the flank. Ruscart, a Luxembourg native, was an older man and even in the thin light his face looked weathered. But despite his age, which Lindquist guessed was seventy or so, he seemed upbeat and anxious to help the American cause.

"This is Philippe Ruscart," Wheaton made the introductions. "Philippe, this is Sergeant Lindquist, in charge of this patrol."

Lindquist introduced Delminico.

The men shook hands.

Lindquist motioned the men to the back of the M3A1 half-track. He wanted to review his map to ensure Ruscart understood their mission. Ruscart entered the half-track back end looking around with a curiosity indicating he had never been in one before. Lindquist had no time for tours and in the dim light of a flashlight quickly walked through the coverage area of the patrol road by road. Lindquist was not thrilled with his Luxembourg guide's command of the English language, but he felt it good enough to get them where they needed to go.

"You will ride in the half-track with Private Delminico," Lindquist instructed. "I will follow in my tank and Corporal Miller, who you should meet momentarily, will follow me in his tank. We'll travel these back roads you drew out to get us around any German artillery and get us to the main road about here," he said pointing.

Just then there was a knock and not waiting for an answer, Josh Miller stuck his head in. "Sarge, they told me I should sit in on this."

Lindquist nodded and introduced Miller to Ruscart as he climbed in. The four men made the back of the half-track a crowed space. They reviewed the plan again, their civilian guide nodding each time he received his instructions. Lindquist hated working with civilians. He felt a personal responsibility for their well-being and despite their best intentions, they often put his men in danger. He knew without a doubt however, that their bravery was unmatched and that they often risked the lives of themselves and their families to contribute, which they had in a huge way. Lindquist was also aware just what Ruscart was risking to help them and that without the aging Luxembourg man guiding his patrol through the *back-door* to get to the main roads, the German eighty-eights would blow his team to pieces.

They headed out shortly after; Delminico and Ruscart leading in the half-track with Delminico's gunner, Smitty, manning the 50 caliber. Lindquist's tank followed with Miller's tank at the back end of the procession.

The vehicles motored over snow and ice. If there was a road below the tracks and tires, it was a well-kept secret. They drove with the most minimum of lights to give little hint of their existence. Driving in the near blackness was slow, tedious and dangerous. Delminico speculated about mines but couldn't really worry about them because all his concentration was needed to keep the half-track from slipping and skidding across the icy surface. On more than one occasion, Delminico felt the vehicle pulling away and starting to skid. It took all he could do to keep the half-track straight.

Despite the weight of the tanks, they found the going just as difficult. Their tracks couldn't penetrate the thick ice and driving became the act of countering each skid to maintain control. Lindquist watched from the turret periscope as his driver fought to navigate the heavy Sherman forward yard by slippery yard.

Ruscart seemed the most relaxed of all the men. Huddled just behind and between Delminico and Smitty, he looked side to side, occasionally pointing small course corrections to keep them on the *road*. To Delminico it all looked like a continuous white carpet in an empty blackness, but he did his best to follow the direction Ruscart provided.

At one point Ruscart motioned for Delminico to slow down. Delminico decelerated the half-track, sliding a bit, and came almost to a stop. Ruscart pointed to his right. Delminico rose from his seat, straining to see through the ink of night. As his eyes focused he could see they were now running parallel to a ravine. Amazed at Ruscart's navigation ability under these conditions, he quickly reached for his radio to warn Lindquist and Miller. His warning however, came just a little too late.

26. Andre, Elise – The Meeting

December 24, 22:10 Hours – Ardennes Forest Barn

With the lantern in front of him, Andre cautiously stepped toward the body, lying motionless on the ground.

Conley and Mueller watched from their vantage points, unsure about their next moves. Each had planned out their moves for different contingencies. If the entrants were German, Conley planned to open fire with the Thompson. He couldn't take the chance that Mueller would yell out and allow the enemy to take cover before he could shoot. He'd then turn the gun on Mueller and leave to find his lines. He thought for a second that he'd be shooting Mueller in cold-blood, but he justified it by acknowledging that Mueller was the enemy and he should have already done so at the half-track.

It was fear and cold that put him in this dire situation and Conley knew he should have figured out his location from the road. Had he done that instead of panicking, he'd be back with his unit by now.

Conley's strategy, of course, lacked the knowledge of one very important piece of information – that Mueller had a weapon. That factor was key in Mueller's blueprint to survival.

Mueller had planned to shoot Conley if the entering party were his German comrades. He would need to be quick to ensure Conley didn't fire before him. If he lost the draw, he knew fellow soldiers would be killed, with him likely being shot as well.

If those entering the barn were Americans, he had very limited options. Then he'd ditch the Lugar, surrender, and the war would truly be over for him. He would be a prisoner of war but with any luck he would survive the war.

Neither man had planned on civilians entering the barn. In that moment of recognition, both felt uncertainty. There was helplessness in not knowing what to do.

A number of thoughts went through Conley's head in those seconds of indecision. Were these people sympathetic to the Germans? This part of

Luxembourg was close to the German border. It was very possible civilians were siding with the Germans. Perhaps some of their children even served in the German army.

However, it seemed odd that on this cold, Christmas Eve, non-combatants were roaming the woods and looking for shelter. Could they be with the *Resistance*? Were they running from the Germans? Not knowing what to do or say, he simply stepped out from behind the fireplace, his Thompson leveled. "He's dead," he uttered.

Elise screamed at his sudden presence, and Andre turned toward him abruptly, almost dropping the lantern.

Mueller cursed silently as he struggled to evaluate the situation himself. He was relieved it wasn't the American army in the barn, but there was a certain amount of complication when civilians entered the canopy of war. He had seen much suffering endured by inhabitants from town to town, inflicted by both sides. Through it all he was never quite sure where the allegiance of civilians was actually placed. He recalled looking at towns through binoculars to see the American flag waving only to find his country's flag flying when he entered. Whatever it takes to stay alive, he rationalized.

Mueller looked across toward Conley, but the fireplace blocked his line of vision. Mueller knew his options were limited for the moment. In frustration he tucked the gun back in his uniform and forced himself up, his ribs pulling as he did. Mueller then walked out from the other end of the barn adding to the already tense and confused atmosphere. Andre, hearing him and seeing another shadow, swung the lantern back toward the left side of the barn. As Mueller stepped out Andre and Elise tried to process what was happening. An American soldier to their right and a German soldier to their left. It seemed surreal and was all too much for Elise. She dropped to one knee.

"Elise," Andre cried out, seeing his niece falter.

"I'm alright uncle, this is just...,"

Conley tried to gauge the situation. He studied the woman and could see she appeared very pregnant to him, but it was hard to tell bundled up.

"Who are you?" Conley inquired firmly, keeping the gun steady.

Andre looked back, more at the gun than at him. "We, well my niece... She is the owner of this property."

Conley wasn't buying. He had too many thoughts running through his mind at the moment to be easily taken in. "And you decided on this frigid night to visit your barn?" he questioned, sarcastically.

"No!" Andre answered immediately. "We were headed to the house, but it has been demolished. We need a place for my niece to have her baby."

Mueller was also struggling with the story. He too was trying to discern the true reason for the unexpected visit.

"A woman in your condition should be under a doctor's care, back in town," Mueller spoke, doubt evident in his voice.

"Yes, yes, normally that would be true," Andre countered, trying to reconcile the unusual circumstance that he was being questioned by both an American and a German. "However, the war will shortly find Eschdorf. Tonight or sometime very soon, the Americans will come, and the Germans are preparing to fight. The town will be ravished by war very soon. How can I allow Elise to have her baby under such conditions?" He paused. "I also didn't like what I saw there," his voice trailed off.

"What do you mean?" Conley asked, a little less edge in his voice.

Andre looked at Mueller noting the German uniform, then back at Conley. Conley nodded, "Go ahead."

Andre signed. "The German Captain in Eschdorf . . . he is . . . obsessed with the thought that those of us townspeople who didn't evacuate are all in collaboration with the Allies. He called the SS in and they randomly pulled people for... interrogation." Andre paused and altered his voice to make his point, emphasizing the word interrogation.

Andre again looked back toward Mueller, unsure of whether to continue.

Conley looked at Mueller, who was expressionless, then back at Andre. He nodded again at the civilian. "Go on," he said.

Still Andre hesitated. It was Mueller who spoke.

"I am not with the SS," he said softly. "You may speak freely."

Andre still seemed taken aback. With some reluctance, he continued, "Those taken by the Gestapo were never seen again. Word is they were all shot and dumped in a shallow grave close to the river. I feared for Elise's safety and for my own so we slipped out of town to hopefully find safety here at the farm. Of course I did not know the house had been destroyed."

He stopped and looked down. "It hurts me…us…deeply. All that is left now is the barn but more importantly we still have each other. I may die here, but I prefer to die on my family's soil where I can give Elise and her baby their best chance."

Conley could see Elise was crying. He knew people did desperate things in time of war, and this seemed more reasonable than many. He looked curiously at Andre's shoulder pack. "What's in there?" he inquired.

"Supplies to help deliver the baby," Andre said without hesitation. "I will show you."

Before Andre could pull the bag off his shoulder, Elise grimaced as her first real contraction struck. Andre looked around. "Elise, we must find you a place to lie down and be comfortable."

Conley tried to rationalize if this was ploy. If it was it was a good one. Mueller seemed to think it legit.

"There is a cart with hay in the back of the barn. I also have some blankets you can use which should make a warm bed," Mueller offered. With that he turned toward the back of the barn to retrieve the cart.

Andre started to guide Elise in that direction, but Conley stopped him, still trying to verify the couple's legitimacy. "Do you have a weapon?"

"No."

"Should I search you?" Conley reiterated.

"You may if you like," Andre said flatly.

Conley liked the way Andre's focus seemed to be solely on Elise. He wanted to believe the man but hoped he wasn't a fool for doing so.

Mueller was working the cart out of the stall. The wooden wagon looked a bit rickety but would have to do. It laid out about six feet, supported by large wooden wheels with spokes on each side that Muller guessed were about two feet in diameter. The sides of the cart were build out with containment rails and just forward of the wheels two struts hung to keep the wagon balanced. Two long tapered arms extended from the front of the card to allow it to be pulled by man or attached to livestock. Mueller stood grasping the handle of each arm, wrestling the cart forward. His progress was slow, his ribs throbbed and his mind wandered. He needed a new plan; pulling his Lugar and shooting the

American was no longer an option. Perhaps with the civilians here he could escape and make his way back to town. Yes, he could use them as a distraction and sneak out. He just needed the opportunity.

"Ahhh!" Elise screamed and bent over, a gripping pain immobilizing her.

Their progress stopped, Andre held Elise up as best he could, in wait of the cart. Conley dashed around the corner of the fireplace to check on it and Mueller.

"Need help with that?" Conley asked and before Mueller could answer, he slung his Thompson over his shoulder and jumped beside the German, grabbing one of the handles to help him drag it out of the stall.

They were just about to exit the stall with the cart when Andre instructed "Leave it there please," as he carried Elise around the corner of the fireplace and toward the men.

"Here?" Conley questioned, looking at the cart's location at the end of stall.

"Yes," Andre reiterated. "It's protected from the front of the barn, affords Elise some privacy, is next to the fireplace and provides all around access."

Conley looked at Andre and said nothing. It was obvious to him that the man had given this more thought than he.

Mueller turned to Conley. "I will get the blankets."

Conley nodded and Mueller exited to the front part of the barn. Soon Mueller was kneeling next to Vogel's body, the blankets stacked where he had left them next to the dead man. *An opening to escape*, he thought. *They would never chase after me; this woman is their main concern.*

But inexplicably, he gathered the blankets and hurried them to the trio. One blanket was laid out over hay on the cart floor like bedding, while the other blanket served to wrap the mother to be. Once she was more comfortable, Andre strolled in front of the fireplace.

"Elise, dear, I'll have you nice and warm in no time." With that, Andre reached for some kindling but found Conley in his way.

"I'm afraid I can't let you do that," Conley said.

Andre looked at him, some understanding in his eyes. "Are you afraid I'll give away your position with a fire?" he asked.

"Worse than that! I'm afraid you'll be sending smoke signals for a raining of shells."

Andre's eyes opened wide. "Do you think use of the fireplace at the house is what led to its destruction?"

"Anything is possible," Mueller chimed in.

"Uncle," Elise cried. "How will we stay warm without a fire? How will we keep my baby warm?" She began to sob.

Andre made his way back to Elise and began consoling her. Another contraction hit, her body shaking as she bellowed out again in pain.

Mueller and Conley walked off to the side of the stone hearth. "Should we chance it," Conley asked, looking at the fireplace.

"Only if necessary," Mueller replied. "She should be warm with the blankets and there is a lot of hay if additional warmth is needed. I would suggest seeing how she does with that first."

"I have some morphine," Conley offered. "Can you give morphine to a pregnant woman?"

Mueller shrugged, "I don't know."

The contraction passed and they closed around the cart talking to distract Elise, as much as anyone can distract someone close to delivering a baby.

Conley noticed that Elise's eyes were a vivid blue. "Are you comfortable?" he asked her.

She nodded yes, and he saw her bright eyes shutter. He could see that she was an attractive woman and despite her pregnancy and all that she had been through, still maintained a very feminine glow. Her eyes closed slightly, and suddenly she looked to him, very tired. Conley stepped back from the cart and nodded for Andre to do likewise.

"The woods are a constant battle zone," Conley said almost as a whisper. "What did you see on your way here?"

"No soldiers that were alive," Andre answered. "But we did hear much gunfire deeper in the forest."

Conley looked at him seriously, "Yes, it sounds to me that the war this night is making its way closer."

"That would be unfortunate," Andre retorted.

"Perhaps I should take a look around," Conley added. "See just how close the war is and maybe determine who is doing all the shooting." Conley spied Mueller overhearing his conversation with Andre and wondered what Mueller would do if he left to patrol the area. Conley realized he would have to stay in the immediate area if he stepped outside the barn. Otherwise he figured Mueller would leave, head back to town and probably return with a squad of troops. If he were in Mueller's position, that's what he would do.

"Tell me something," Andre asked, catching Conley in thought. "Is there some kind of Christmas truce in place, or are the two of you opting to become citizens of Luxembourg?"

Conley looked at Mueller and both shared a half-hearted smile. "Something like that," Conley shared lightly.

Elise cried out again and the men went over to comfort her. Andre lifted the blankets and checked on Elise's progress. "The baby is on the way," he announced.

Conley felt a conflict rising within. He had planned to use the barn to warm up and the German to help him orientate himself as to his location. He had accomplished that and should have already left for his lines. Staying with these civilians was a nice gesture, but one that could get him killed. Conley struggled with how to exit gracefully. He heard himself making small talk with Andre.

"You said this is your property?"

"Actually, it is my brother's," Andre replied. "Elise's dad built the house and this barn a number of years back. Elise grew up on this farm. My family used to visit every holiday, and all of us worked the land each summer. Even when the Germans first came in 1940, Elise and her family were able to live here and farm their land. It wasn't until earlier this year, just before the Allies first liberated this area, that the Germans herded us to town. And now that they have reclaimed this area they have forbidden civilians from leaving the town, have strict curfews about even being outside. Ah – but until then this was our Shangri-La! We had so many special times here."

Elise smiled, remembering, even while tears were streaking down her face.

Mueller chimed in, "Your brother . . . is he alive?"

"No," Andre said, his expression solemn. "He and Elise's mother were killed in shelling not far from here, only a few months ago, an unfortunate consequence of the Allied liberation. A number of other civilians suffered a similar fate. All for nothing now that the Germans have returned and the town must be liberated again. You see now why I felt the need to leave…," his voice trailed off.

Conley nodded, the pieces of Andre and Elise's story starting to fit together in a gloomy puzzle. Sadly, Conley knew it was a fate shared by many civilians during times of war. Talk of Elise's family lead Conley to wonder if she had a husband. He assumed the man was also a victim of the war, or he would have been with her this night.

The group remained silent for a number of seconds, each lost in their own thoughts. Finally Mueller stepped back from the cart. "Excuse me, I have yet to move Private Vogel." He looked over to Conley who gave him a nod. With that, Mueller exited around the fireplace to the front part of the barn. There, with Conley casually keeping watch, he found Vogel's body. With aching ribs, he slowly dragged Vogel to the far stall, placing him next to the American he previously moved.

"Ahhh!" Elise cried in pain as another contraction hit her hard.

Andre brought his face in close. "Breathe Elise, breathe."

Elise tried to focus on her uncle and follow his instructions, but found it difficult given the severity of her discomfort. Conley came over to the other side of the cart. He wanted to do something, anything to help, but felt powerless.

He brought his hand up to stroke Elise's hair, but hesitated. Elise seemed to sense his awkwardness and for a moment her steely blue eyes locked on his. Through her pain she managed a faint smile and smiling back Conley reached out, first gently touching her brow then letting his fingers run slowly along her flowing hair. It was a moment Conley would remember.

Mueller was kneeling next to his dead compatriot in the back of the far stall. His mind was racing. He knew he had missed a number of opportunities to kill the American and escape; that he should have done so long ago. After Andre's story detailing the disturbing behavior of the SS and German army, he felt to do anything now would only lend credibility to what they all believed.

Perhaps now was his chance to quietly slip away. Elise had the attention of Andre and Conley; he could be far in the woods before they even noticed he was gone. The American was a good man, but was foolish to think he could stay in this barn for long without consequence. It was a matter of time before a patrol saw the barn and used it to warm up. This was still German territory as far as Mueller knew. It would serve Mueller no good to stay as well. With the town a short distance away, he would be thought a deserter should he be found catering to civilians. Mueller got up and walked out of the stall. Andre and Conley were still fully absorbed with Elise. He passed by the fireplace to the front side of the barn and in the dim light took a long look at the door. Across the backside of the fireplace Mueller could hear them talking. No one seemed to miss him. *It's now or never*, he thought. Mueller pivoted his body, took a quick step toward the door.

27. Ryan, Tiny, Tucker – Retreat

December 24, 22:15 Hours – Ardennes Forest, Luxembourg

The firefight had been swift and violent, the American patrol surprising a German outpost. The fallout, however, resulted in additional nearby German troops who were in strength giving chase. In a series of separate actions, the American squad had been reduced from twelve to three, with the Germans still in pursuit. The American privates, running for their lives, were all young, frightened and cold. One of the men, Tucker, was wounded, his thigh ripped apart by a machine gun burst. The disabled G.I. was carried by Tiny - a huge bull of a man whose nickname was ironic. The third soldier, Ryan, nervously led them away from the pursuit.

The men stopped to catch their breath, puffs of steam rising in the frigid air as they gulped and inhaled. They huddled under a tree, Tiny resting Tucker against its base. A check of the crude tourniquet around Tucker's leg showed it had loosened and was seeping blood.

Tiny pulled on the make-shift wrap, a belt, to remove the slack. Tucker grimaced. Gunfire was heard not too far behind, the enemy search party blindly peppering the woods with machine gun fire. A stray bullet found a tree branch nearby and it cracked as it snapped. They all dropped in the snow, taking cover.

"Son of a bitch," Tucker scowled in pain as Tiny fell across him.

"Sorry buddy," Tiny replied meekly. He looked over to Ryan, "Sniper?"

"No, don't think so. But let's not hang around to find out."

The men found their feet. Tiny scooped up Tucker easily and tried to adjust him on his back so he was comfortable.

"Leave me," Tucker pleaded. "I'm slowing you down."

"Not happening," Ryan replied. "You know what just happened in Malamney. Those Kraut bastards slaughtered nearly 100 of our boys. Machine gunned them in a field in cold blood. The Heinie's aren't taking prisoners and we're not about to give them any to add to their count. "

Ryan looked at Tiny. "You ready?"

Tiny nodded.

"OK, let's put some distance between us and them Nazi sons of bitches."

28. Lindquist – Back roads

December 24, 22:21 Hours – Outside of Heirheck, Luxembourg

Lindquist's radio buzzed at the same time he saw the deep gorge just to his right. He yelled down to his driver, "hard left and stop," bellowing the same instruction over the voice box for Miller to do the same behind him. His driver complied immediately but as Lindquist turned to check on Miller out the rear viewport, he caught the shadow of Miller's tank sliding off the edge and down into the ravine.

Miller had seen the gorge about the same time that Lindquist had. He was a millisecond slower to react and in that fraction of a second, his tank's right-side track lost its edge along the top of the ravine. He yelled to his driver as Lindquist's message broadcast but the tank was already careening down the gulley.

Joe Hogan, Miller's driver, felt the thread leave the road and immediately went into damage control. He steered the Sherman as best he could down the 6-foot gorge, struggling to keep the tank on an angle. His actions kept the tank from rolling over but it slid ungracefully to the bottom of the ravine. The men in the Sherman were shaken and rattled, but otherwise unharmed.

Lindquist opened the hatch, pulling himself out into the cold air, and with difficulty gave chase as Miller's Sherman skidded to a stop. The angled side of the gully, packed solid with icy-snow, was too steep and slick and Lindquist awkwardly slid down on his butt. Wet and dishevelled, he found Miller checking on his crew when he arrived and climbed up to the turret.

"Everyone OK?" Lindquist asked as he saw Miller pop out of the hatch.

"Son of a bitch," was Miller's initial reply.

"Anyone hurt?" Lindquist persisted.

"No, shaken up like a turd in a blender, but OK," Miller said. "Why didn't that shithead civilian warn us about this . . . hole in the ground?" he added, perturbed.

"Sarge, Miller, everything OK?" Delminico yelled down from the top of the gulch.

"I've got a thirty ton tank stuck at the bottom of this butt-hole of a pit, how's that OK?" Miller yelled back up.

"Can we tow him out, Sarge?" Delminico asked, trying to stay positive.

Lindquist thought for a second. "I don't think we can get the traction we need. We'd have a better chance of us ending up down here too than getting him out."

"Son of a bitch," Miller moaned again.

29. Mueller, Andre – The Chance

December 24, 22:25 Hours – Ardennes Forest Barn

Mueller had taken a single step in the direction of the door when Andre suddenly appeared from the other side of the fireplace. Mueller froze like a statute, the two men exchanging glances. There was an awkward silence that followed as they each waited for the other to say something, do something. Mueller felt it obvious to Andre that he was making for the door, an effort to escape. *Would Andre call him on it, would he tell Conley? And... what would Conley do? The American had already proven himself to be unstable. With the civilian there did Conley need him anymore? Would Conley have the nerve to actually kill him? Would Andre let him?* There were so many questions that only Andre's actions would answer. The silence continued in the dimly lit space of the barn, both men standing, staring.

Whatever Andre had been thinking in that moment, he kept it to himself.

"I'm told you have a medical kit," Andre finally said.

Mueller hesitated as if the words needed time to sink in; they were not what he was expecting.

"Yes, ah, I do." He looked behind him in the thin light. "I left it over here, somewhere." Mueller got down on his hands and knees and spent a few moments feeling around the hay before he located the kit.

"Here it is," he said in an almost jubilant tone, although the words sounded even to him more theatrical than necessary.

He looked up to hand the kit to Andre, but the man had left and was back with Elise.

Mueller thought about what had happened. *He knows*, he reasoned. *He knows and he's giving me an opportunity to leave if I want to.* Again, Mueller looked at the door in the dim light then at the medical kit in his hand. Part of him hated that he could not leave, that he had a conscience about people he didn't even know, one of them the enemy in a time of war. The Russian Front had taught him that to hesitate at any opportunity was to die, and Mueller wondered if he had not already signed his own death warrant.

But Mueller also knew if he left, he'd be haunted by doing so, always wondering about the lives of these innocent people he could have helped. The American he was indifferent about, but he could tell Conley also cared for the well-being of the civilians to the point that he left Mueller virtually free and unwatched.

Conflicted but convinced at what he must do, Mueller slowly rose to his feet and walked the kit around the fireplace to Andre.

"I hear you have had medical training," Andre said as he approached. "Are you a doctor?"

Mueller's eye locked on Andre's. In that moment of exchange Mueller could have sworn he saw Andre's eyes twinkle in the faint light, almost smiling that he did not leave.

"Not really," Mueller replied, pulling his eyes from Andre's and shaking his head. "I was a medical student but was called home and never able to finish my studies." Mueller paused. "I have never delivered a baby."

Andre looked at the man and smiled. "Don't worry. I've delivered six children, including Elise."

Conley's eyes widened, "Perhaps *you* are the doctor?"

"No," Andre told him. "But on a farm, one has to make do with what one has. Beyond those six children, I have assisted with the birth of a variety of farm animals."

"He is a professional delivery service," Elise chimed in, stifling the pain of a just passed contraction.

Her response elicited a number of smiles.

Andre lifted the blanket and checked on Elise's condition.

"Not much longer now," he told her lovingly. "You could have a Christmas baby if he hurries about it."

Elise looked at him lovingly. "Now dear Uncle Andre, you're the only one convinced this baby is a boy."

Andre smiled. "Well, if it keeps us waiting much longer I may come around to agreeing it's a girl."

Again grins were exchanged.

Conley looked around the barn. "You must have many memories of this place."

"Yes," Andre replied, "especially during this time of year. The family always spent Christmas at this farm. As I said, Elise grew up here; this was her home. Each year, on this very day, the 24th of December, Elise, her cousins, her dad and I would head into the woods to find a tall sturdy tree. Elise's dad would cut it down and all of us would spend the day decorating and getting ready for Christmas day. On the holiday we were always together, opening gifts and eating the fabulous meals the women would prepare. We had so many good times, year after year. It seemed those days would last forever. And then, of course, the war came and everything changed. Now, everything is gone! Everything but my sweet Elise . . ,"

Elise began sobbing and Andre realized he had picked a most inopportune time to reminisce. He moved up close, wrapped his arm around her and offered her soft words of consolation.

Conley and Mueller felt ill at ease. Mueller spoke more in an attempt to ease Elise's sobbing than because he wanted to.

"When I was younger, every Christmas season, I would go hunting with my dad. We'd shoot numerous fowl and prepare the birds for a holiday feast. On Christmas, our entire family would gather and eat and sing songs all through the day. It is what I remember most about growing up."

Conley tried to picture a young Mueller spending time with his dad hunting. He had a hard time seeing Mueller as anything but a German soldier. *Maybe that is a good thing*, he thought.

In the silence that followed, Conley realized that the group waited for him to share memories of his Christmas' past. He thought of his family's tradition of attending midnight mass, but his mind keyed in on a much more recent memory. "For the past two years, my family has visited the Boston Commons each Christmas season for the lighting of a massive Christmas tree. The tree is donated by one of the New England towns and is forty feet tall. When all those lights illuminate it's the most amazing sight."

Mueller looked at Conley nodding. "I know the Common you speak of. I have been there."

Andre looked at Mueller incredulously. Knowing nothing of Mueller's past, he was about to ask how, when Elise grimaced in pain, grabbing the sides of the cart serving as her bed.

All attention returned to Elise. Andre checked again under the blanket as Elise fought through the difficult contraction. "The baby is close," he said. "We should get prepared."

Andre looked toward the fireplace. "Gentleman, all risk aside, we really must build a fire. The baby will need warmth and we will need to boil water and sanitize a knife to cut the cord. The wood is dry and should burn clean. I don't believe we have a choice."

Conley and Mueller exchanged glances, both thinking of the potential danger. When they looked back toward Andre he was busy at work. He opened his small pack and removed some towels and rags. Then he opened the medical kit Mueller had provided, removing a small scalpel, whose blade he placed on one of the rags atop the stone mantel. Andre then popped into one of the stalls, then another, before exiting with a bucket.

He started toward the door with the bucket, then stopped and turned. "Gentlemen, again, we can't wait any longer! Can one of you get a fire started and the other stay with Elise until I return? I'm going to gather some snow to boil. Mueller turned toward the wood, leaving Conley to tend to Elise. As Mueller took some of the stacked wood and kindling and placed it in the fireplace, he wondered if he could do anything to minimize the smoke. With the barn this close to town and battle lines less than well defined, he felt he'd be placing a smoke bulls-eye over the place. He watched Andre exit the door and admired him. Andre didn't seem to let any of the circumstances lessen his spirit. Mueller filed that thought away and got to work building the fire.

30. Ryan, Tiny, Tucker – Contact

December 24, 22:40 Hours – Ardennes Forest, Luxembourg

As Ryan surveyed the dark woods, the sky ahead seemed to lighten up. Cautiously moving ahead, the trio saw that the woods ended and in front of them laid an open pasture, covered in snow. They stopped for a moment to catch their breath and discuss crossing.

"What do you think?" Ryan asked.

"You know me, I never like crossing anything that is open," Tiny replied.

"Could be mined as well," Ryan added.

"Let's hug the edge of the woods around the perimeter of the field," Tiny suggested.

"Good idea. Ryan turned to Tucker, who was on Tiny's back, his arms wrapped around the big man's shoulders. Tucker had one leg draped around Tiny's waist, with his wounded leg hanging limply.

"You doing OK?" Ryan asked.

Tucker said nothing, just grunted, Ryan took a look at the belt tourniquet. It had loosened again and Tucker was losing more blood.

"Tuck, buddy, the belt's loosened up. I'm going to tighten it. It's gonna hurt," Ryan warned.

He pulled the belt tight, but other than another grunt, Tucker offered little else.

Ryan looked up at Tiny and moved in close to the big man.

"We need to find somewhere to stop and get him bandaged up better. He's getting weak, lost a lot of blood."

"Maybe on the other side of the field," Tiny offered. "From there we'll get a view of anything coming our way with ample time to move out if we need to."

"OK," Ryan agreed. "Ready to go?"

"Lead on."

They headed out hugging the woods line along the edge of the forest. After covering about half of the pasture from its wooded edge, Ryan looked ahead and saw what appeared to be the silhouette of a building ahead.

He stopped. "Do you see that?"

"Where?"

"There," Ryan said, pointing toward the shape.

"What is it, a barn?" Tiny asked.

"I think so," Ryan replied.

As they approached, what had at first been only a shadow soon materialized into an actual structure. Suddenly a dim light appeared. Ryan and Tiny hit the ground, Tiny losing his grip on Tucker who fell on top of him, then rolled off with a moan. Ryan pulled his M1 up, ready to fire. A second later a dark figure emerged from the light. Although the outline was mostly shadow, Ryan could see long boots and concluded they were not those of a fellow American soldier. Without hesitation he aimed and pulled the trigger three times. He watched as the body fell over in the crystalized snow.

"What the fuck you do that for?" Tiny reprimanded.

"He was a Kraut," Ryan said nonchalantly.

"What if there are fifty more in the barn, you moron?" Tiny continued. "We need to get Tucker help. We can't be fighting off the German army while he's bleeding to death."

"Alright, alright, I wasn't thinking about that," Ryan conceded. "We'll hit the woods if any Krauts come out."

Tiny checked on Tucker. He lay shivering, his eyes open, staring above into the dark void of sky. Tiny wondered if he was thinking about death – his own. Tucker's skin felt cold and looked overtly pale in the dim moonlight.

"We're near a barn," Tiny whispered to the empty face.

Tucker gave no indication he heard any of what Tiny uttered. His eyes maintained their ghostly stare into the night. Tiny didn't like what he saw but knew they'd have to see what was happening in the barn before they could move him there. Tiny returned to Ryan, dropping next to him in a heap.

"He's unresponsive… I think he's dying," he said, low and slow.

Ryan looked back in Tucker's direction but said nothing.

"See anything?" Tiny continued, nudging his chin forward.

"Not yet," Ryan replied, turning his gaze toward the barn. "Waiting game now."

It was indeed. Two men were slowly dying in the snow, one with them and the other just outside the barn.

31. Roehm, Gunn - Outpost K-6

December 24, 22:47 Hours – Ardennes Forest, Roadside

The timbers of the dugout shook gently from the vibration, as though a giant bee buzzed nearby. The origin of the sound was an approaching vehicle coming up the blackened road. To Grenadier Josef Roehm it resonated like a symphony orchestra, a sweet sound to his frostbitten ears.

"It's here," Roehm shouted in his excitement, forgetting for a moment where he was, military decorum, and that men were trying to sleep.

"Shut up you stupid fuck," came one German reply.

Other less than grateful comments followed as the other occupants of the dugout, who were trying to rest, responded to the rude awakening.

"What is the commotion here?" Unteroffizier Meier asked, walking over from the Feldfunk radio.

"The supplies are here, Unteroffizier," Roehm said gleefully. He was now perched at the edge of the dugout. "I will guide them in."

Roehm ran up the crudely fashioned steps and out the dugout before Meier could reply. The Corporal was furious with the private, and wanted to yell to stop the man, but something held him back from responding. By now the approaching vehicle was nearing the dugout and the rattling of the timbers was more pronounced than it should have been. The vehicle approaching was not the half-track they were expecting, it was a tank.

"Americans!" Meier blurted out, not fully sure but not willing to take a chance. "Weapons… get to your weapons."

Meier looked to the far end of the dugout but really couldn't see that far. "Get on the Feldfunk…,"

*

Grenadier Roehm had ran out into the darkness and onto the road. Hunger, cold, tiredness and the lack of training had led the young soldier to make a serious mistake. As the Sherman M4A4 tank rounded the bend and its silhouette became defined, Roehm recognized the error he made.

120

He turned to run, but his dark shadow on a background of white outlined him like an ink spot on a lightly colored canvas.

*

Inside the Sherman, the motion was observed.

"You see that?" Ellis, the gunner, asked. "Should I take him out?"

"No... wait," the tank commander, appropriately named Rudy Gunn replied.

"Let him run away. Probably lead us right to his little group of Kraut friends." They watched in anticipation as the scared Grenadier raced back to the dugout.

*

In the dugout Meier took it all in helplessly as it unfolded. "Run the other way!" he tried to instruct Roehm, but the panicked soldier could not hear him over the engine noise. Meier realized there was no chance Roehm would change course. For a moment he thought the dugout might remain unseen in the murky black of night. It was well camouflaged and the night was very dark. But Meier was seasoned enough to know that the Americans had not fired because they could see Roehm and as soon as he left their sight they would know where he was taking cover and where other men were doing likewise.

Meier looked over at the men in the dugout. Tense and on their weapons they looked at him, waiting for the order to fire. He could have them open up and perhaps give Roehm some cover to make it back to the dugout.

Then what? They were no match for a Sherman tank. They could surrender but would the Americans take prisoners? Meier's options were few, but his time had run out.

Roehm was but two strides away from the dugout steps.

*

Gunn, too, had a front row seat to Roehm's blunder. He did a quick recon of the area around the tank, then followed the German lumbering desperately towards the roadside.

"Wait for my command," Gunn instructed. "Then open up with both machine guns and let's put a shell in there as well."

"Better hope those bastards don't have a panzer-thrust," Ellis commented. "They could be setting us up."

A panzer-thrust was a German version of a bazooka. It was a very effective anti-tank weapon, especially at close range. Gunn had thought about this as well, but tried to push it from his mind. The German in his viewport reacted too quickly and ran like a duck, someone who had been sitting around in an icebox for a while. He didn't think this was a setup. He'd know soon enough if his tank ignited around him.

"Now! Fire, fire, fire!" Gunn yelled as the German hit the steps and his shadow started to descend into the dugout.

With that the machine guns on the Sherman erupted, as did the 75mm gun turret.

*

For a moment, Meier thought that Roehm would make it as he hit the steps. But Meier watched helplessly as the Sherman's machine guns unloaded, twisting Roehm's body as a bullet slammed through him, literally ripping the man in half. Almost immediately following, there was a large flash as a high explosive shell ripped through the outer part of the dugout. Pieces of timber splintered the air along with dirt, dust and snow as though a mini tornado had struck them.

"Return fire!" Meier ordered instinctively over the screams and groans of the wounded. Those that could tried to comply. His leg felt wet and he noticed he had been hit in the thigh by shrapnel. He cursed.

An MG-42 machine gun was the only heavy caliber weapon the outpost had and it's bullets just thumped off the tank.

"Keep firing!" Meier commanded as he grabbed two grenades and limped to the far end of the dugout.

"The tank is pulling back," one of his men observed.

"He's repositioning for a better shot!" Meier yelled back as he exited the dugout. He crossed the road as quickly as he could, hoping he hadn't been detected by the tank. His hopes sank as the tank unleashed another salvo, but fortunately its aim was off. The shell exploded in the woods just above the dugout.

*

"Something just crossed the road," Moyer, the assistant driver of Gunn's tank reported.

"The bastards are trying to flank us," Gunn noted.

"Sarge – make sure that hatch is secured," Ellis warned.

122

"Don't go pussy on me now," Gunn replied. "You know me better than that."

Gunn looked through one of the side viewports but could only see darkness. "OK, let's put another shell or two into that Kraut ice shelter to silence it and get the fuck out of here!"

*

Meier found the going difficult. His leg throbbed and he was losing too much blood, the wound deeper than he had thought. He stopped and wrapped his thigh with his belt. As he resumed his flanking maneuver, Meier saw a flash, night turning to day for a second, as thunder shook the ground, the explosion deafening. With it the firing from the dugout ceased.

Was that it? he wondered. *Were his men all dead?* For a moment rage consumed him. The tank pulled forward again, it was now almost in front of him. Meier pulled the cap from the potato masher grenade and pulling his bad leg along, determinedly made his way toward the Sherman. He hoped they would open the hatch to check out their work. Then they would pay.

As Meier was getting close the tank leaped ahead. *The bastards are leaving,* Meier thought in a panic. He now stood exposed in the open road, the tank ahead of him, moving off. With two good legs he could have caught it, but he knew he had no chance hobbling. In utter frustration he pulled the string on the masher and heaved it at the tank. It landed short, exploding harmlessly on the road.

"Stop!" Meier screamed as the Sherman made its way down the road, away from him. He knew full well his silhouette stood out on the open road and that he'd be an easy target – Meier didn't care. He hoped the tank would see him and reverse, thinking they could pick him up as a prisoner. Meier however, had no intention of being taken captive, he had embraced death if only to honor the men he had just seen blown to a hellish grave. He was now engaged in a personal war. Meier had another grenade left, he wanted a chance to use it.

*

"What the fuck," Ellis said, startled by the blast in back of the tank.

Gunn took a look out the rear port. "There's a fucking Kraut standing in the road back there. Guess he hasn't had enough – stupid bastard."

Gunn turned the turret so it was facing behind the tank. He looked at the dark object standing in the road defiantly, sighed and opened up with the M4A4's turret machine gun.

"Merry Christmas, you stupid fucking Kraut," he said sarcastically as he watched the shadow crumple to the ground.

32. Conley, Ryan – Bad Impression

December 24, 22:51 Hours – Ardennes Forest Barn

Conley was uncomfortable holding Elise's hand. First, she was squeezing it very hard and secondly, he had never comforted a women giving birth before. He was anxious for Andre to return.

Three loud cracks sobered his thoughts.

"Those are from an M1," Mueller said in a concerned tone.

"Yes," Conley replied, pulling his hand from Elise's grip and moving toward the door as he unslung the Thompson from his back.

"Andre, Andre!" Elise screamed.

Mueller put down the log he was preparing for the fire and hurried to Elise's side as Conley rushed by him.

Conley cautiously cracked the door open but stayed in the dim light so as not to create a shadow. He could see Andre lying in the snow about ten feet in front and to his right. From the door frame he called softly to Andre but got no response. He was certain, as had been Mueller, that the weapon that fired was an M1. Conley gambled that the soldier on the other end was an American GI.

"You just shot a civilian!" he screamed out.

"And who are you?" a voice bellowed back promptly in reply.

"Conley, 328th Infantry Regiment, G-Company," he answered.

"Prove it," Ryan called back.

Conley heard Elise's wail from the barn, a combination of not knowing what had happened to Andre and a strong contraction. Conley sighed, furious at a faceless voice at the end of a gun that was too quick to fire, that put so little value on human life. He drew a quick breath, keenly aware he needed to stay calm to stay alive. Conley was tired of playing this game but knew lives depended on him.

"Listen to me!" he yelled, trying to sound more convincing than he felt. "There is a woman here trying to give birth! You just shot her uncle! I'm walking out to check on him and then going back into the barn to check on her! I'll let you read my fucking dog-tags if you want, but I need to help them now!"

He slung his weapon back over his shoulder and moved slowly out toward Andre. He wasn't sure how persuasive he'd been, but figured he'd know soon enough if he heard the bark of an M1.

Ryan watched him from a distance, a little miffed at the abruptness of the conversation and tone of Conley. He positioned his M1, taking aim.

Tiny placed a hand on Ryan's M1 and with subtle pressure moved it down away from its target. "Hear that! You already shot a noncombatant, you gonna start shooting fellow GI's too!"

Ryan was taken aback. "Just trying to keep us alive, pal."

"I'll take my chances this time," Tiny said as he rose up from the snow. "Cover me but don't do any more stupid shit!"

As Tiny carefully made his way toward the barn, Conley was hunched over Andre. The man was still breathing, but drawing air in labored gasps. Conley reached in his own pockets, searching to find a morphine syrette.

"I can see you are a good man," Andre uttered softly through difficult breaths as Conley crouched in the snow. Each word formed on his lips before he arduously sputtered them out. "Please... take care... of my Elise."

Conley could only nod, but it wasn't enough for Andre. He repeated through coughs, blood trickling from the corner of his mouth, "Please take care of my Elise...she has no one now."

Conley nodded again. "I will," he said, as he fumbled the syrette out of his pocket.

"Stay with her... until she and the baby are safe." Andre coughed, choking, more blood seeping. "Promise me."

Conley looked into Andre's dying eyes. "I promise you I will protect her and her baby with my life," he said, hoping the emotion of the moment didn't later make him a liar. He went on preparing to administer the syrette.

Now it was Andre's turn to nod. He did so and Conley thought he saw the man smile as his eyes closed, his last breath complete. Conley wondered if Andre had waited until he heard what he wanted to hear before giving in to death.

Conley heard footsteps and turned to see a large man with an M1 pointed at him approaching. Tiny came up on Conley and looked over his shoulder at the corpse lying prone in the snow.

"Damn!" he uttered. "That crazy bastard's shooting noncombatants now!" He looked back toward Ryan and waved his hand that it was OK to come down.

Turning back to Conley he said, "I'm sorry about this. We've seen our whole fucking squad get shot up and Ryan, well that poor bastard's trigger happy. I'm Anderson, everyone calls me Tiny."

Conley thought the name strange for a man his size but wasn't in a mood to talk about it. "Conley," was all he said.

Ryan came up struggling with Tucker on his back and Tiny helped him the last ten yards. Elise screamed in the barn as another contraction hit. Voices were heard, one of them Mueller's, speaking to Elise in German.

Ryan reacted, immediately putting his M1 to Conley's head. "What the hell is that about, soldier?"

Conley turned to Ryan, the gun now right between his eyes. He was mad as hell at Ryan, wanted to explode, but knew he couldn't. The man shot first and had a gun in his face; he was capable of killing him and not blinking. "There's another civilian in there, the niece of the man you just killed. She's about to have a baby."

"And the other voice," Ryan challenged, no acknowledgement of the noncombatant he had just shot dead.

"A German, his name is Mueller. He's a…,"

"Seems to be a good night for killing Germans!" Ryan growled menacingly. He nodded at Tiny and the men moved quickly towards the barn, Ryan leading with his weapon, Tiny with Tucker again on his back.

33. Mueller, Elise – Waiting

December 24, 22:53 Hours – Ardennes Forest Barn

"No! No! Andre... Uncle Andre!" Elise screeched at hearing Conley bellow out to the American G.I.'s what they had just done. She struggled to rise from the cart, Mueller needing both hands on her shoulders to hold her back.

"Please, it would be dangerous for you to be on your feet and more so to be outside. The American will check on Andre. I bet your uncle is only wounded," Mueller sympathized, knowing it was a lie.

Elise sat back still sobbing, her face wet with tears. She looked at Mueller, wanting to believe him. "So much killing," she said softly through her sniffling. "I am tired of so much killing." Elise allowed Mueller to reset the blanket around her. As he did another strong contraction raked her body.

"Breathe Elise, breathe deeply," Mueller coached.

Elise looked at him, uncertainty in her eyes. In that moment, Mueller thought she looked very weary. He had seen that look in men who were on the verge of giving up, sometimes giving into death. Too tired, hungry, hurt... too weak to continue. Mueller knew the mind gave out long before the body.

"Will yourself," he said to her. "Will yourself to breathe. For your baby, breathe Elise, breathe deeply."

As was her way, Elise's eyes spoke before she reacted. The steely blue returned and with it her resolve. She leaned forward, forced in the air and pushed it out several times, her body convulsing with the pain. After several hard breaths Elise collapsed back on the cart, spent.

"That was a bad one Unterfeldwebel," she said in German.

Mueller nodded. "Yes indeed." He looked at his watch. Her contractions were coming in short intervals. Andre was right, the baby would arrive soon.

There was talking outside the barn, in English, muffled, words Mueller couldn't make out. He wondered what they were discussing... Andre perhaps… perhaps him. Mueller was concerned that Andre was dead, if not, given the frigid night he would have been brought in the barn immediately for care. Conley knew Mueller had medical training, he would not have waited to act. Unless… the other G.I.'s were giving him a difficult time.

Mueller tried to listen more intently, but still couldn't discern any conversation between the American soldiers. He thought he would relocate just inside the door, give himself a better listening post. He turned to Elise, "Let me see what's going on out there."

"Be careful," she warned. "Andre, please check on Uncle Andre."

Mueller stood upright and turned. He was about to turn the corner around the fireplace when Elise grunted, stiffened and cried out in pain.

"Aaaaaaaaaaaaahhhhhhhhhhhhhhh," she thundered, spinning Mueller in his tracks.

He immediately returned to her, "Breathe," he coached again.

"Sooo bad," she groaned her reply.

"Breathe," Mueller reiterated, soft but firmly.

"I'm trying! I have nothing left!" Elise screamed out in German.

"Will yourself," Mueller yelled at her, also in German, remembering she responded well to this request during her last contraction.

Slowly the pain subsided, a combination of Mueller's words and Elise's breathing in response to those words. Moments later she lay there, panting, her chest rising and falling rhythmically, her hand firmly locked in Mueller's.

"You are a strong woman," he said.

Elise smiled at him, her eyes igniting the dimly lit space. She opened her mouth to speak, but before words materialized, the voices outside the barn got loud. The last words they heard were barked loudly and threateningly. Their eyes locked at hearing… *a good night for killing Germans.*

34. Decker – Needing Answers

December 24, 22:56 Hours – Eschdorf, German Headquarters

Hauptmann Decker was receiving numerous reports now about American movements around Hierheck, the small town just south of Eschdorf. The Allies had taken the town earlier in the day. In his mind, Decker could see the American officers planning their attack from the town, and in so doing, positioning their troops. He thought it warranted another review of his defensive positions and summoned one of his officers to retrieve his map from the back room.

The radio again jumped to life. *Another report about American troop movements*, he thought. *How did they amass so much firepower in such a short time?* He looked over to Krieger, his radio man. "More American troop movements?" he asked in anticipation of the report.

"No, Herr Hauptmann," Krieger replied. "This is from our transmission unit outside of Heiderscheidergrund. Roadside outpost K-6 reports Mueller's supply truck never arrived."

"Damn!" Hauptmann yelled. "First the Sector East post and now this. The Americans have regrouped. This is not good news."

Krieger knew enough to offer nothing and remained mute.

An adjutant came over. "Your map, Herr Hauptmann."

Decker took the maps, saying nothing, and walked to a small table at the far end of the room. After placing the map across the table, he fumbled in his uniform for a cigarette to steady himself. Decker put it to his lips, lit it and took his customary long draw. Exhaling a smoky cloud around him, he bent over the table studying the map. It was a few minutes before Decker rose and looked toward Krieger, who maintained eye contact only with the radio. "Contact Panzer Unit Five, Lieutenant Wolf," Decker instructed. "Hurry, be quick about it," he added forcefully.

Hauptmann Decker walked decidedly to the doorway of the next room and yelled for his adjutant, a small wiry man, Lieutenant Albert Zimmermann.

Zimmermann entered, a nervous look about him. Decker walked him to the table and brought him quickly up to speed. "What are your orders, Herr Hauptman?" Zimmermann inquired, his body seemingly in constant motion.

Before Decker could answer, Krieger interrupted, "Lieutenant Wolf is on the line, Herr Hauptmann."

Decker shifted his gaze from his awkward adjutant toward Krieger. He quickly strode to the radio where he took control of the headset and microphone. He spoke at length with Wolf, describing the situation. After an extended dialog, Decker ended with "Thank you, Lieutenant" and the customary "Heil Hitler."

When he was done, Decker handed the radio equipment back to Krieger and returned to Zimmerman who was himself reviewing the map. Zimmerman snapped to attention as Decker approached. Decker thought his adjutant looked and acted like a small puppy – a little too eager to please, but not really sure what to do.

Decker initially said nothing, just stared at the map for some time before turning to Zimmermann. "Albert, I need two armored half-tracks and a squad of men to be ready to travel in 15 minutes."

"Yes sir," Zimmermann replied immediately, although his mind was churning trying to decide which squad he would nominate for the duty and where he would pull the vehicles.

Decker continued. "Lieutenant Wolf will be here shortly with some of his men to lead the squad. There are two objectives of this patrol. First, retrace Mueller's route and find him, his men and his vehicle. Second, eliminate any American resistance along the way. Do you understand?"

Zimmermann nodded. He understood fully, except for the biggest question that remained on his mind. "Do you wish for me to accompany the patrol, Herr Hauptmann?" he asked almost sheepishly.

"No, I need you here with me. Lieutenant Wolf is fully capable of leading this patrol himself."

"Thank you, Herr Hauptmann," Zimmermann replied.

Decker looked at his adjutant and wondered if he was being thanked for acknowledging his need of the man, or for not sending him on the patrol.

35. Ryan, Mueller – Meet and Greet

December 24, 23:03 Hours – Ardennes Forest Barn

Ryan stepped in the barn with his gun leveled, seeking out Mueller, who he found crouched by the cart, next to Elise. He immediately stuck the muzzle of his weapon into Mueller's ribs, pushing him away from Elise toward the far side of the barn.

Mueller had hoped Conley explained his presence, but was not surprised based on the last words he heard outside the barn. Still he was agitated by Ryan's use of excessive force. "What is this?" Mueller called out, grimacing, his ribs protesting the steel pressed against them as Ryan forced him away from the cart.

"Please!" Elise pleaded in desperation, "I need him... he's helping me."

Ryan ignored Elise's pleas and shoved Mueller hard to the floor once they were around the fireplace, the man wincing as he went down.

"So you speak English," Ryan blurted out to Mueller. "I'm not impressed, you Kraut bastard."

Conley, who lagged behind, heard Ryan's voice and found him with his M1 in Mueller's face. Seeing this, Conley slung his own Thompson from behind his back and aimed it at Ryan as he came around the other side of the fireplace.

"What the hell do you think you're doing? You shoot a civilian and now you think you can come in here and kill in cold blood!"

Ryan looked at him and shifted his weapon from Mueller to Conley. Conley stole a quick glance at Tiny, hoping the man would act as a voice of reason. To his dismay, he noticed Tiny's gun was now also pointing at him.

"What are you, a Kraut lover?" Ryan said sarcastically. "Don't you know what these bastards have done to our boys? They massacred almost a hundred GIs in Malmedy just a few days ago. These sons of bitches aren't taking prisoners, why should we?"

Mueller sat there quietly but had already positioned his hand on his Lugar inside his uniform. He cursed himself for allowing this to happen. *So many chances I had*, he thought, and *now it is too late.* He had no choice now but to let the talk play out and hope he managed to stay alive.

Conley stared at Ryan. He knew men like him, men who had seen too many of their buddies killed and had lost all reason of right and wrong. To Ryan it was all black and white. The Germans were bad, no exceptions, and they all must die. Conley didn't know Mueller's political leanings. For all he knew the man was a devoted Nazi. But he did know that he needed the German and his medical knowledge to help Elise deliver her child into the world. He'd do what he could to keep Mueller alive.

"I can give you two good reasons not to kill him," Conley argued. "First, the man is a medic."

Ryan glanced down at Mueller then back at Conley, "He's no medic, he's infantry."

"He's not a uniformed medic, but he's medically trained. He could actually help your wounded man, if you let him. He's also going to deliver that woman's baby. Unless *you* feel some responsibility to help, seeing you killed her uncle who was originally going to do it."

At that, Elise burst into tears and Conley realized for her it was the confirmation of Andre's death. For seconds the men stood in silence, guns leveled, staring at each other.

Finally Tiny broke the quiet. "Let him be," he called across the floor to Ryan. "Maybe he can help Tucker as well. Been enough killing around this barn tonight."

Ryan dropped his gaze on Conley and looked over at Tiny. He stepped back and lowered his weapon, pointing it back toward Mueller. The German was ready to draw the Lugar but didn't think Ryan would shoot based on his sudden change in demeanor.

"OK," Ryan said, looking at Tiny. "Bring Tucker over."

Looking at Mueller he glared, "But if he dies, I'll blow your fucking Nazi brains all over this barn!"

Conley thought about responding but held back. He had won a small victory and he was happy with that. He lowered his Thompson, slung it over his back and hurried over to Elise.

"I'm sorry," he said as softly as he could. He tried his best to comfort her, but her sobs shortly turned to moans as another contraction racked her body.

After it had passed, she turned to him and said simply, "The baby is here."

Conley looked into her deep blue eyes and sighed.

"Check," she said.

Conley hesitated, clearly jostled. He stole a glance at Mueller, but the German was now busy tending to Tucker under Ryan's watchful eye.

"Please check," Elise pleaded, knowing that birth was soon to happen.

Conley reached for the flashlight at the edge of the cart, slowly raised the blanket's edge, and peaked awkwardly. Peering underneath he saw she was correct - birth was imminent, and Conley thought he could see the baby's head at the opening.

"You're right, the baby is coming."

Suddenly he remembered that Andre had left to bring back snow to boil. He kept his focus on Elise but raised his voice, trying to sound authoritative so Ryan and company could hear. "Be right back. We need snow to boil for sterile water."

Elise nodded, her blue eyes watering up, and Conley wondered if the tears were more for the pain of childbirth or for Andre.

Turning toward Mueller and looking at Tucker, he asked, "How is he?"

Ryan and Tiny looked at Mueller curiously. Mueller answered, "Lost a lot of blood but I've applied a new tourniquet. It seemed to stop further bleeding for now."

"Nice work," said Conley, not really knowing what else to say. He stepped toward the door. "Tiny can you tend the fire? We'll need it to boil some water."

No one said anything. Tiny looked over to Ryan. For a moment there was an uncomfortable silence and Conley wondered if this would be another battle of wills. Ryan gave Tiny the slightest of nods and the big man began to move toward the fireplace. Conley slipped out the door. *What a night*, he thought. *What else can happen?* He'd soon find out.

36. Lindquist – New Plan

December 24, 23:15 Hours – Outside of Hierheck

Lindquist had a new set of orders – he and his half-track would proceed on the patrol alone. Meanwhile, Miller and his crew were ordered to stay with the disabled tank until help could be dispatched. That help would be slow in coming given the priority to take Eschdorf in an hour and forty-five minutes. Command wasn't happy for the time lost either in locating G Companies lost patrol or locating enemy positions on the East flank. They especially weren't pleased about a tank out of action.

Miller had words for Ruscart but the man could only apologize in broken English. Given the frozen earth and darkness of night he had to work with, the Luxembourg civilian had done a pretty good job in getting them this far.

Lindquist looked over to Miller as he stood by his tank. "Keep the tank buttoned up and your eyes open. No telling who's out there. The Engineers will find you soon and haul you out."

Miller, still distraught over the incident, looked at Lindquist with tired eyes. "It'll take hours for the Engineers to show. Soon as the dawn breaks, some Kraut bastard with binoculars will see this tank sitting here from one of those buildings in town. You know what happens then…,"

Lindquist nodded, knowing Miller was right. "Don't let that happen. If you're still here when it starts getting light, hoof it back to camp. Otherwise, you're right, someone will notice and start lobbing shells at you."

"Shit Sarge, hate to destroy the tank?" Miller said, knowing it would be necessary should he have to leave.

"Yup, we can't take a chance on a fully functioning Sherman finding its way into Kraut hands. They find a way to get it out of this ditch, they could drive that sucker right into camp and blow us all to hell before we realized it was the enemy."

"Son of a bitch," Miller responded. Lindquist picked up that it was Miller's favorite phrase.

"Good luck." Lindquist called out.

Miller said nothing, just looked at him with that same dejected look he'd had for the past half-hour.

Lindquist then headed for his own tank, motioned for Delminico to move out and shouted down the hatch for his driver to follow.

37. Decker, Wolf – In Search of Mueller

December 24, 23:30 Hours – Eschdorf, German Headquarters

The half-tracks sat, engines idling, outside German Command in Eschdorf as Hauptmann Decker stood shivering, waiting for Untersturmführer Wolf. He checked his watch to note the time. He was punctual, Wolf was the late one - but then, SS men always seem to play by a different set of rules. Decker lit a cigarette, let it fill his lungs as he inhaled, felt warm for a moment, settled, as though it held some ironic healing power, then blew a puff of white smoke into the frigid, dry air. It seemed to linger a moment before drifting off.

He heard an engine noise and turned to see a Kubelwagen approaching. The Kubelwagen was for the Germans what the jeep was to the Allies – an "all purpose" vehicle known for its durability and reliability. Decker crushed his cigarette under his boot as the vehicle drove up and stopped abruptly. Wolf jumped out from the passenger seat and, after adjusting his long black trench coat, looked at Decker as if sizing up a date for his daughter. "Heil Hitler," he said casually, not waiting for Decker's reply before walking over to the half-tracks.

Decker wanted to dress down Wolf for his lack of etiquette in addressing a superior officer. Like most officers however, he did not wish to get on the wrong side of the SS, so he let it pass.

"Is all in order?" Decker asked.

"It will do," Wolf replied. "Who is your man in charge of this patrol?" Wolf's words sounded more like an order than a question.

Decker wrapped his fist on the side of the half-track they stood near. "Unteroffizer – Corporal Brandt," he called out.

A second later the door opened and Brandt exited the vehicle. "Jawohl," Brandt said as he stood at attention.

Wolf stepped in front of Decker and addressed the young soldier. "Here are your orders Unteroffizer. First, you will proceed along the Eschdorf to Heiderscheidergrund roadway until you find the Kfz 7 half-track that left here earlier this evening. You shall contact me by radio as soon as you come across it for further orders. Do you understand?"

"Jawohl," Brandt replied. "Herr Untersturmführer, what if Americans are on the road?"

"You will kill them of course," Wolf said flatly.

"Jawohl!"

"Raus!" Wolf ordered.

The soldier quickly found his way back inside the half-track, revved the engine and left, followed by the second half-track.

Decker didn't like the looseness of Wolf's plan. With an American attack imminent he felt Wolf was not accounting for a number of situations the men might find. He was second guessing himself for not assigning Zimmermann to the patrol. His adjutant's nervousness would have at least provided some caution.

"Are you sure that road isn't held by the Americans?" Decker questioned.

"I'm guessing it is," Wolf answered casually. "Just ten minutes ago I was informed that Outpost K-6 was under attack. Their radio transmission was abruptly cut-off so I am assuming the Americans took the outpost and are at this minute approaching Eschdorf from that direction."

He could see Decker was uncomfortable. "Herr Hauptmann," he continued, "I am leaving to pick up some insurance to deal with any American presence on that road. You have no need to worry. You're only concern is maintaining control of this town."

Decker had no idea what Wolf meant by *insurance*. He hoped Wolf had access to tanks but doubted that was the case. Wolf gave him no more information. Decker was more than annoyed with what amounted to Wolf reissuing his orders. He knew holding the town was his responsibility, didn't need the SS also holding him responsible. Decker felt it was part of a play, staged to make him the fall guy. Still he held back, said nothing.

"Heil Hitler," Wolf said with a passing hand. The SS man quickly walked back to his Kubelwagen, conveyed something to his driver and was away.

Decker suddenly felt the cold again. He reached under his coat, found his cigarettes and lighter, lit up and slowly made his way back to his post.

38. Conley – Unwanted Visitors

December 24, 23:41 Hours – Outside Ardennes Forest Barn

Conley stepped outside and immediately picked up the scent of smoke emanating from the fireplace. It was mild but enough that anyone in the area could detect it. The good news was that the slight breeze was pushing the remnants of the fire in the best possible direction, opposite the town, away from the road and away from the thickest of the woods where he had heard gunfire earlier. He couldn't say with certainty that the soot would remain undetected as it traveled out in front of the barn. But, given what he knew, it was the safest direction for it to pass.

He looked at poor Andre lying motionless in the snow. Conley felt badly leaving the man there to become another frozen corpse, but he had limited options and now wasn't the time to consider them anyway. He spied the bucket just beyond Andre's body and went over to retrieve it. As Conley reached for the bucket, the sound of a dog's bark echoed nearby. Startled by the barking animal he instinctively dropped to the ground, making himself as small as possible in the snow. Conley's eyes pried the darkness, desperately trying to locate the source. A quick look revealed nothing, but a second pass depicted the outline of the dog and two German soldiers. They appeared to be tracking footprints in the snow.

The dog was growing excited as the scent became stronger closer to the barn. Perhaps the animal was now picking up Conley's scent. The German's seemed focused on tracking the ground, and Conley didn't believe they had yet seen the barn. They obviously hadn't picked up on the ash from the fire and Conley gave silent thanks that it was not moving in that direction.

Conley slowly raised the barrel of his Thompson, wondering if this range was still too far to generate accurate fire. He decided to wait until they got closer.

Suddenly the door swung open, spilling light over Conley and Andre's body. Tiny started out the door but stopped at seeing Conley on the ground. "What's going on?" he said. "You OK?"

Conley flinched when the light spilt over him. "Krauts! Shut the fucking door and get down," he screamed as quietly as he could.

Tiny reacted quickly for a big man, jumping out the door and closing it behind him.

It was too late however, the Germans had seen the flicker of light, ducked down and released the dog.

"Krauts? Where?" Tiny blurted out, trying to read the darkness, his eyes struggling to adjust to the dim light.

Conley saw the dog rapidly approaching and knew that shooting the dog would give away his position, which was exactly what the German's wanted.

"Shoot the dog!" Conley shouted to Tiny, who was far less exposed than he, covered by the corner of the barn. It was obvious, however, Tiny didn't know where to look.

"What, where?" Tiny repeated, eye's darting all around, trying to pick up movement in the eerie night.

Conley knew he had no choice. "Son of a bitch!" he screamed out as he fired a burst at the dog, then pointed the barrel up and continued the burst toward the woods where he had last seen the enemy.

His burst stopped the dog but his bullets missed their mark in the woods. Immediately there were shots fired in return, ripping up the ground immediately in front of him. Conley knew he was vulnerable lying in open space. A bullet nearly found him, tearing up the ground inches from his head and showering him with dirt, snow and ice. It was time to move.

"Cover me!" Conley yelled to Tiny, clamping his finger on the trigger sending out a volley of fire from the Thompson and rolling backward to the shelter of a tree. It wasn't much but it was better than the dark silhouette on the white apron of ground he had presented. He lay catching his breath and watching the woods as the shooting stopped without visible targets.

"What the fuck's going on out there?" Ryan muttered, opening the door a crack.

"Keep that door shut!" Conley shouted, not wanting more complications.

"We've got this," Tiny said in such a calm demeanor that Ryan said no more and closed the door.

Conley was impressed with Tiny. He made a mental note to use Tiny to help keep Ryan under control should he need to.

The seconds ticked off as the Germans and Americans played a game of cat and mouse, each waiting for the other to move.

Finally Conley saw it, a shadow dancing in the night against a black backdrop. Before he could react however, Tiny's M1 barked twice. He watched as the shadow collapsed to the ground, but he couldn't tell if the German had been hit or was simply dropping for cover. Conley wasted no time. He had a visual location on one of the enemy soldiers and fired a long burst.

Conley felt satisfied that at least one of the German's was down. Suddenly the second shadow stirred, intent on retreating in the woods. Again Tiny was quick on the trigger and mowed him down with another three rounds.

Then there was nothing, just a still quiet as the smoke from their weapons slowly wafted into the clear night sky.

The awkward silence was broken as Elise wailed out in pain from inside the barn.

"Sounds like she's ready to have that baby," Tiny said so nonchalantly, Conley would have thought they were at a bar discussing sports over a beer.

"We gotta check those Krauts," Conley replied, remembering a rule his Sergeant had drilled into him, that a wounded Kraut can still be a deadly Kraut.

Tiny rose. "On it. Give me cover," he said, slowly making his way to the woods to check that the Germans were really out of action. They were. On the way back he even checked the dog.

When he returned Tiny nodded to Conley.

"Baby time," Tiny said in his casual tone.

Conley wished he felt as relaxed as Tiny sounded. His mind suddenly became flooded with thoughts all painting pictures of tragic scenes. The enemy was nearby – he had just witnessed how close. Ryan seemed to be losing his personal war and Conley wondered how long it'd be before he snapped. Mueller must be in fear for his life and surely would leave if Ryan didn't kill him first. And then Elise – he had made a promise to care for her and deliver her baby… The thought of Elise pulled Conley back, away from the vines of doubt that for those moments immobilized him. He signed, quickly surveyed the dreary darkness around him, grabbed the bucket, ran it through some fresh snow and walked into the barn.

39. Lindquist – Complications

December 24, 23:45 Hours – Back roads outside Heirheck

The snow covering the icy ground started to resemble more of a path now as shallow gulleys appeared on both sides and trees became more plentiful along the edge of the poorly defined passage. The vehicles had made slow but steady progress after leaving Miller, stopping a number of times to investigate where Lindquist thought it worth checking.

Ruscart proved his worth as a scout, guiding them through the dark and treacherous pathway. As Lindquist checked his map, he noted they should be intersecting the main road anytime now.

Suddenly Lindquist saw Delminico's half-track skidding to a stop. He was about to yell down the hatch for his driver to do the same, but didn't as he felt the heavy Sherman already maneuvering to a halt.

Lindquist's radio buzzed. Delminico's voice was terse and Lindquist felt the man's sense of urgency. "Sarge, there's a tree across the road. Classic road-block if ever I saw one."

"Shit! Back her up," Lindquist bellowed to his driver, spinning toward the rear viewport, searching for anything that might indicate an ambush. The tank responded sluggishly as it struggled on the icy terrain. Lindquist wanted to put a little distance between him and the half-track, to allow the Sherman's machine guns and turret more maneuverability. He knew though that moving backwards with no real vision could easily result in his tank slipping down the gulley, making him a sitting duck.

Lindquist stopped the tank after a few feet and spun the Sherman's turret around. He hoped the turret would intimidate whoever was out there, while giving him a 360 degree look out his main viewport. Nothing but black was visible and for the moment all was silent.

In the half-track, Delminico had Ruscart drop in his seat so the man was literally curled up on the floor. Smitty was at the fifty caliber and ready to rain bullets on anything that moved.

Lindquist didn't like the situation at all. He was hemmed in with no maneuvering space on a narrow icy road with culverts on each side. He couldn't move forward without removing that tree and wasn't sure he could do so without blowing it out of the way. Even at that, Delminico was in front of him and he couldn't simply drive around the half-track to get a shot.

That wasn't the worst part. Lindquist felt certain that in the woods nearby the enemy was waiting for him to make a move, perhaps to remove the tree. Or, a panzer-thrust, (German bazooka) was being moved into position to knock out his tank and ambush his patrol.

Both ways his options seemed limited and outcome doubtful. *Get on with it*, he thought to himself, wondering why the quiet ensued. But the seconds ticked on with only the silence to show for them.

*

In the woods, along both sides of Lindquist's patrol, the Germans watched and waited. They had their orders and knew the plan they needed to execute. Unteroffizier (Corporal) Helmut Schmidt shivered as he waited, wondering if their idea would come to fruition or if he and his fellow Grenadiers would soon be dead. He saw the turret of the American tank turn in search of his men and it stopped facing him, leading him to guess if it spied them. Perhaps a sliver of moonlight caught a buckle or gun muzzle and reflected back to the tank. It really didn't matter. All Schmidt knew was that he was looking down the barrel of an American tank and his life could be snuffed out in a second should the tank unleash a shell from where it sat.

He knew they had waited long enough. It was past time. He needed to act now.

40. Conley, Ryan – Unexpected Exit

December 24, 23:55 Hours – Ardennes Forest Barn

When Conley returned to Elise, one look told him she was now in full labor. Mueller, who'd finished with Tucker had now moved on to tending to her, as Ryan watched, M1 in hand. Conley placed the bucket on a rack just above the fire to heat the water. Mueller checked his medical kit and readied the few things he had: the last of his gauze, wipes and sulfur powder. He then retrieved the scalpel from atop the fireplace mantel, knelt and ran the blade through one of the smaller flames. Conley watched him and hoped they would only require the scalpel to cut the cord. A complicated birth was the last thing they needed on this night.

Conley checked his watch and noted it was exactly midnight. "Merry Christmas," he called out, but he did not get the reaction he expected.

Instead, Ryan suddenly rose and announced he and his men were leaving. Tiny, who was just settling back by the fire, seemed miffed.

"What? You can't be serious?" he questioned.

"Look… there are Krauts everywhere. Those Heinies you shot ten minutes ago were looking for us. That gunfire was probably heard for miles. In another ten minutes his whole fucking place will be crawling with Krauts." He looked at Conley, "You'll leave with us too if you're smart."

Conley shrugged him off, his gaze on Elise.

"Look, it's your life," Ryan reminded him. "Remember, the fucking Krauts don't take prisoners." Ryan then proceeded to tell him again about the Malmedy massacre, trying to make eye contact with Mueller as he did.

But Mueller knew better than to look over. He kept busy preparing, first checking the scalpel blade then the water and the fire underneath it.

"You should leave," Elise grunted to Conley through her pain.

"I too think you should leave," Mueller conceded. "Should one of the hardened SS Panzer Units find us, they might shoot us all."

Conley waved them off. "I'll take my chances," he said simply, never mentioning the promise he made to Andre.

"OK," Ryan said. "Like I said, it's your life." Looking at Tiny he uttered, "Let's go."

Tiny said nothing, but hoisted Tucker on his back like he was a sack of wheat and nodded at each Conley and Mueller. Then looking at Elise, he said humbly, "Good luck, ma'am."

Ryan and Conley exchanged a quick glance before Ryan headed out of the door. Tiny followed with Tucker on his back. Passing Conley he said, "I admire your principles, but don't get yourself killed."

Conley sighed. "I'll try not to," he said solemnly.

He watched the men leave in search of the U.S. lines.

41. Gunn – The Road

December 25, 00:02 Hours – Ardennes Forest Road

"That fucking road's got to be around here somewhere," Gunn said in frustration.

Greg Farner, the tanks shell loader, looked at the map on Gunn's lap. "We've probably passed it four times. Can't see shit in this black soupy hell."

The tank had indeed passed the road, twice in fact. The first time was on their initial trip, which led them to ill-fated Roehm at Outpost-K6. The second time was after reversing course. Now they had changed direction again and were retracing their route.

"Maybe I should get out and search the area a bit," Gunn thought out loud.

"Then we'd be searching for you," Ellis replied, not a fan of the idea.

"Sarge, something's ahead. A break. I think that may be the road we want," Drabowski, the driver yelled up.

Gunn peered through the viewport. "Yep, I see it. I think that's it. Approach slowly so we don't drive off the road and lose a fucking track."

"The last thing we need is to get stranded here," Ellis commented.

"Yeah, Sarge. What the fuck? I mean, who gives orders for a single tank to travel across enemy territory in the middle of the fucking night?" Farner questioned.

Gunn snickered, "Look guys, what I was told is that a patrol was lost earlier tonight and we're supposed to navigate the road toward Eschdorf and let them find us assuming they're out here. Then we hook up with some other friendlies... a guy name Lindquist, just outside of town and hold the flank during the attack."

"This whole road could be lousing with Krauts," Ellis chimed in. We're the fucking guinea pigs, checking it all out."

"You know it," Farner agreed. "Why do they think that patrol disappeared? Cause of the fucking Krauts, that's why!"

148

"Come on guys," Gunn reasoned. "We get orders, we follow orders – it's that simple."

*

The Mark IV Panzer tank that Wolf dispatched as "insurance" had found Mueller's Kfz 7 half-track and radioed in its position. Wolf ordered the tank to continue up the road in search of any American presence and eliminate it. He would investigate the half-track personally, together with his SS contingent and the men Decker had assigned to him.

Lenert Reimer was the competent Prussian tank commander who had seen a lot of combat in his 22 years. He was just sixteen when he joined the German army and like Mueller had spent time as part of Rommel's much respected and feared Africa Corps. As a loader, gunner, driver and now commander, he held just about every role possible in a tank crew. He, more than any of his current crew, knew the risks involved in navigating a large tank along an icy narrow road. Additionally, after looking at the Kfz 7 half-track, Reimer accurately had determined the cause of its demise was a mine and was not thrilled at the prospect that additional mines could lie in wait for the tank up the road.

Reimer reported his findings regarding the mine but did not question Wolf's orders to proceed ahead up the road in search of Americans. Wolf assured him the road was now clear of mines, the one taking out Mueller's half-track an anomaly. Wolf ranted about incompetence and how heads would roll at the miscue that cost Mueller and the Third Reich a valuable vehicle. Reimer dismissed Wolf as someone who told people what they wanted to hear to shut them up. While he wasn't sure he believed Wolf, Reimer's discipline would not let him disobey or even question an order.

"Keep a close eye ahead," Reimer commanded his driver, mines still monopolizing his thinking.

"We will feel a mine before seeing one," the driver commented, referring to the poor visibility on the road.

"Just keep watch," Reimer reiterated.

*

The Mark IV Panzer and Sherman M4A4 tank both crawled their way along the slick, snowy roadway. Like two turtles they clawed and scratched along the icy curves and slippery straightaways. Neither knew what lie ahead or that every foot of ground gained brought the two steel warriors closer together on a collision course. It was early Christmas morning in the Ardennes Forest. For Rudy Gunn and Lenert Reimer there was no savior in sight.

42. Lindquist – Words to Ponder

December 25, 00:07 Hours – Back roads outside of Heirheck

Lindquist sat and considered what seemed a dire situation for him and his patrol. The silence was deafening as he waited for something to unfold. Like Delminico, he believed the fallen tree was too coincidental to be anything but an ambush in waiting. He only hoped he could fight his way out somehow.

He had sent a short message back to command on his radio, giving his position and what he suspected. He hoped to confirm the ambush once the shots rang out to verify to command that this was in fact German-held ground.

However, it wasn't a shot that ended up breaking the silence; it was a voice.

"Americana! Americana!" he heard coming from the surrounding woods.

Lindquist took a deep breath. *Oh hell*, he thought. *They want us to surrender.*

His radio buzzed: Delminico. "Want me to answer Sarge so you don't have to open up your hatch?"

"Yes," Lindquist replied. He was concerned the Germans might be trying to lure the Americans into unbuttoning the tank. Once no longer secured, nearby Germans would lob in grenades, disabling the tank and killing those inside. With Delminico doing the negotiations, he could keep the tank closed, limiting its exposure and retaining it as a formidable weapon of war.

"What do you want?" he heard Delminico holler out to the Germans from the half-track in his heavy New Jersey, Italian accent.

What they heard next took them all by surprise. No one--not Delminico, Smitty, Lindquist, nor the tank crew - knew exactly how to interpret it. The words lingered in the icy night for a number of seconds.

The voice belonged to Unteroffizier Schmidt, who spoke limited English and hoped he had pieced together a sentence that correctly conveyed his intention. After calling out to the Americans and hearing their reply, he knew the next words he spoke could mean life or death. He replayed the English translation in his head a number of times then spoke, trying to hold back the guttural accent that was his natural dialect.

"Do not shoot, we wish to surrender," Schmidt shouted out, hoping his English was correct.

In the quiet that ensued, Schmidt again repeated the words in his head. He was sure he had said them correctly. His men looked at him, wondering if the pause meant something was wrong. Schmidt yelled out the words a second time to ensure they were heard over the engine noise.

"Did you hear that?" Deliminco relayed to Lindquist in a voice that sounded to him suspicious.

"I heard," Lindquist replied simply.

Lindquist tried to play this new scenario in his head. It made little sense to him so he feared a trap. He had heard of Germans surrendering during this offense, but with Eschdorf so close by, he couldn't rationalize it. He looked to one of his crew he had assigned to a view port facing the far side of the tank.

"Any movement on that side?" he asked. It was possible that the surrender was a diversion to allow other Germans to sneak up from behind.

"None," he was told.

"What do you want me to say?" he heard Deliminco's voice say nervously through the speaker.

"Shit, I don't know. Tell them to drop their weapons and come out of the woods with their hands on their heads."

"Damn," Delminico replied. "OK, here goes."

"Tell Smitty to be ready on that fifty," Lindquist chimed in.

Turning to his own crew, he said, "You guys too. Open up on my order."

Delminico barked out the order to the Germans over the engine noise, still convinced that a hail of bullets would be the return reply.

Unteroffizier Schmidt heard the words and pieced together the meaning in German. Finally, he thought. The reply he was waiting for. Schmidt planned the next sentence in his mind, again hoping his limited English wouldn't get him and his men shot.

They had endured much fighting that day in Heiderschied. Schmidt had watched all of his officers and many of his comrade's die in brutal house-to-house, and sometimes hand-to-hand fighting. As a corporal he found himself the highest ranking survivor among the fifteen soldiers that had somehow managed to evacuate under heavy enemy fire. His small contingency had no food and little ammunition as they made their way in retreat toward Eschdorf. Along the way they were intercepted by an SS officer, who positioned them at the road-block with orders to thwart any attempt by the Americans to advance during the impending battle. Having been given no food or additional ammunition and knowing from the earlier day's fighting the armored strength that the Americans would bring to bear, and with bone-chilling cold permeating their bodies, the young group of men had agreed surrendering a preferable option to death.

"Yes, OK," Schmidt hollered back in reply to Delminico's order to exit the woods, hands on his head. "I need to tell my men on the other side," Schmidt continued, choosing his English words carefully and bellowing out over the idling engines.

He waited for a reply but received none as Delminico and Lindquist tried to determine if Schmidt's plea was legitimate.

With cold and fear limiting his patience, Schmidt shouted across the way to the seven men on the other side of the road. Within seconds they came out from the woods in compliance with his order.

Smitty swung his machine gun toward the movement, then back, not sure if the move was a ploy. But as the shadows emerged, the Americans could see the Germans in compliance with the order – hands on head, no weapons visible. Delminico buzzed the mic, "Sarge, you want me to check this out?"

"Carefully," Lindquist replied.

"Is there any other way?" Delminico mocked, his voice a blend of excitement and nervousness. He looked at Smitty and said, "Cover me," as he pulled his carbine and stepped out of the half-track, watching the last of the Germans emerge from the nearby woods.

In the Sherman, Lindquist was just as bewildered. "Unbelievable," he called out in amazement. He turned to one of his crew, "Give me that tommy," and was handed a Thompson machine gun.

Schmidt and the men around him dropped their weapons, also coming out from their positions in the woods. By the time Lindquist had exited the tank and stood next to Delminico, fifteen German soldiers stood in front of them with their hands interlocked behind their heads.

"Damn," Delminico replied again, looking at Lindquist. "Whose gonna believe this?"

43. Conley, Mueller, Elise – Childbirth

December 25, 00:07 Hours – Ardennes Forest Barn

Childbirth had begun. Both Mueller and Conley coached Elise as she breathed and pushed, the baby's head fully visible in the dim light of the fire and flashlight beam that was starting to wane.

"You're doing great," Mueller reassured her. "Keep pushing."

Elise cried out. "I'm trying, just so tired!"

"Just think… you're having a Christmas baby," Conley added, trying to keep Elise positive.

"But . . . such a . . . sad . . . Christmas," Elise grunted, through labored breaths.

"No," Mueller countered. "Bringing life into the world is never a sad thing.

"But we have no one," Elise groaned, her eyes wide. "My baby . . . has no one."

"That's not true," Conley jumped in, picking up his cue from Mueller, wondering if the German too was trying to convey a message he was struggling to believe. "Your baby has you and you have each other."

The process of birth continued, the baby slowly descending the birth canal. Having run out of things to say, Mueller started singing in German. "Stille Nacht, heilige Nacht, Alles schläft; einsam wacht…,"

Conley started to chuckle, thought how trite, but to his amazement, Elise, through grunts and groans, joined in the singing. She stopped abruptly and with a long distorted moan, pushed out a little being.

Conley had never witnessed such a thing and was awestruck by it, suddenly realizing why it was referred to as the *miracle of birth*. Mueller took some warm wet towels and cleaned the baby, then patted it gently and checked that it was breathing. Mueller then motioned for Conley to get the scalpel and holding the cord taunt, let Conley cut it. Mueller secured the severed end with gauze as best he could.

Elise watched, still breathing heavily from the delivery, happy and sad. She thought of Andre and how close he had come to realizing the dream

155

of having her deliver at the farm. She thought too of her family and prayed that her husband would one day be able to see his child.

Mueller bundled the infant in rags and towels and handed the baby to her mother. "Elise, I'm proud to introduce you to your beautiful daughter."

Elise cried as she took the infant in her arms. Conley put a hand on her shoulder.

"She is beautiful."

The tears flowed. Such a happy time during this holiest of seasons was tempered by the realities of war. Conley found himself thinking of home and the needless loss of life he had witnessed and found his own eyes filling with tears. Mueller too, thought of how close he had come to running away, even killing Conley, and felt a wave of emotion consume him.

"What will you name your daughter?" Conley asked, trying to squelch the distressed atmosphere that seemed to have engulfed the room.

"Anna, after my mother," Elise said without hesitation, her crying suddenly reduced to sniffles.

"A beautiful name," Mueller commented.

"I think she looks like an Anna," Conley added, feeling the mood lighten.

Mueller looked over at Conley with sudden seriousness. "I do think you should leave now, for your own safety. The baby has been born and both child and mother are well. I can manage from here and will assure both are taken care of."

Conley was taken aback from the sudden turn in discussion. He looked over at Elise, who seemed so peaceful with Anna in her arms. The baby too seemed to be resting comfortably. In that instant it was hard to believe there was a war outside the barn. "I don't know," Conley said reluctantly.

"If you leave now you can still catch up with the other Americans and find your lines," Mueller offered.

Conley struggled. He thought of his promise to Andre and wondered if he had fulfilled it. He looked toward Elise. She nodded at him.

"You should go," she agreed. "You are a good man and deserve to survive this war. Leave now while you can."

He looked back to Mueller. "If your army comes, they will brand you a traitor or a coward for not returning to town. With me here you can say you were held prisoner."

Mueller seemed unmoved. "I have the perfect alibi in this little infant. Who can deny a soldier helping a pregnant woman deliver her baby on Christmas Eve?"

Conley was still unconvinced, but their discussion was interrupted by a sudden burst of gunfire nearby. The two men exchanged glances, knowing that the gunfire came from a German machine pistol. Mueller gave a head nod toward the door and Conley knew he must go.

He kissed Elise on the forehead. "Good luck to you and your precious Anna," he said.

She looked at him, fresh tears budding in her eyes, "God go with you. You and Mr. Mueller were my shepherds tonight, guiding me each step of the way."

She kissed him on both cheeks and then lifted Anna up for him to hold. He took the baby awkwardly and placed a very delicate kiss on the child's head, careful that his dirty, stubby unshaven face didn't contact the baby's tender skin. Then he carefully returned the infant to her mother.

He walked over to Mueller. "Take care of her," he said solemnly.

"You only need to worry for yourself now," Mueller said. A few moments passed. "Thanks for sparing my life."

Conley thought of a lot of things he could have said, but in the end he said nothing. He simply nodded, then turned for a quick glance at Elise who was now sobbing quietly. With that he picked up his helmet, slowly ambled to the door, carefully cracking it open only as much as necessary to exit, emitting as little light as possible.

44. Lindquist – Clearing the Road

December 25, 00:17 Hours – Back roads outside Heirheck

Lindquist sized up the Germans in front of him in the dim light of the quarter moon. They were young, scared, dirty, cold, and tired and many nursed wounds. It was obvious to him they endured a lot and had little fight left, but he still wondered why they hadn't chosen to withdraw to Eschdorf.

He would have liked to question the Germans at length, but command had ordered him to send the prisoners down the road toward the American lines and get on with his patrol. They would send an interrogation team out to meet the Germans. In the meantime, the 26th Division would be attacking Eschdorf in less than an hour and Command needed to know if the remaining flank was secure.

Lindquist decided to pull Schmidt over for a quick dialog. He rationalized that Schmidt might talk more freely to him than to an interrogation team.

He motioned Schmidt out of line and walked him into the back of the half-track. He lit a small battery powered lantern and found the German shaking profusely, eye's wide with fear.

"Would you like a smoke?" Lindquist said, offering up a cigarette.

Schmidt took the offering and Lindquist watched the German's hand trembling as he put it to his mouth.

"I just want to talk," Lindquist said, hoping to put the German at ease as he lit the cigarette.

"Yah, OK," Schmidt replied, taking a deep draw. The German did seem less edgy – Lindquist wondered if it was his words or the cigarette.

"How did you get here," Lindquist inquired.

Schmidt hesitated a moment as if contemplating what to say. Lindquist wondered if the German was a name, rank and serial number guy, but the truth was that Schmidt was trying to form the English words in his head.

"We retreated Heiderschied," he finally began.

After another drag, "Retreat to Eschdorf."

There was another long pause before Schmidt continued. "The SS found us. Gave us orders to hold this ground. No food, no bullets, no grenades... just fight until we're all dead."

It was starting to make sense to Lindquist.

"The men... too much dying. We had enough," Schmidt finalized.

"Did you see any American patrols between here and Heiderschied?" Lindquist asked, hoping to get some information on the lost patrol.

"Nein... ah no."

"Thank you," Lindquist said, concluding the dialog. He motioned for Schmidt to extinguish the cigarette, killed the lantern and escorted the German out of the half-track and back to the line-up.

"Jesus," Delminico said softly as he approached. "We're fucking freezing out here and you're having tea time with this guy."

"Got some good intel," Lindquist said. "You're not getting soft on me, are ya?"

"No sir," Delminico replied. "But if I liked the cold that much, I would have joined the infantry instead of driving around in that iron coffin."

Lindquist snickered.

"We need that tree moved, Sarge," Delminico reminded.

Lindquist walked back over to Schmidt, who was back in line with the other captives. Schmidt looked at the American wondering what came next. Was this where the Americans stripped his men of their watches and wallets? Schmidt had seen it done to American prisoners – to the conqueror goes the spoils...

"I need that tree cleared off the road," Lindquist ordered.

Schmidt stifled a smile. "Yah," he answered, relieved that was all Lindquist asked.

Schmidt's men made small work of moving the tree. Task completed, Lindquist gave Schmidt instructions to march his men down the road until an American team picked them up.

Nearby, gunfire reminded Lindquist and his men the war was not far away. He looked at Ruscart. "The main road is close, yes?"

"Yes," Ruscart replied in his broken English. "Less than a quarter mile ahead. I will show you."

"No," Lindquist answered. "Can you find your way back to the American lines?"

"But of course," Ruscart replied. "These roads are my home."

"Please follow the Germans and make sure they return."

"What can I do if they run off?" Ruscart asked. "Will you give me a gun?"

"You won't need a gun," Lindquist began. "These men want to surrender. They have been given a death sentence by their own army. It is safer for them to surrender than to return to Eschdorf."

Ruscart nodded as if he understood. Then suddenly he shook his head. "But I should stay to guide you until your mission is complete."

Lindquist smiled and patted the man's shoulder, "You have been of tremendous help. I expect to engage the enemy on the road ahead. If I do, and I can't protect you, you will be shot as a traitor."

"I am not afraid to die," Ruscart answered proudly, and Lindquist knew the man was sincere.

"I know," Lindquist affirmed. "But the Germans . . . the SS, they may not stop with you. They may seek out your family. I do not want to put them in danger."

Ruscart thought for a moment. He considered his daughters and his grandsons. He wanted so badly to do his part for the war, but knew Lindquist was right.

"You have completed what the U.S. Army has asked of you," Lindquist said, hoping to appease the man's pride. "I thank you as does my crew."

Ruscart nodded solemnly. "I will make sure the Germans make it home," he said lightly. Lindquist liked the reference to home, and shook the man's hand. Ruscart did likewise with Delminico and Smitty, then started back along the road toward Hierheck with the German prisoners.

Lindquist watched until the darkness consumed them all. He then looked at Delminico. "Let's get moving again. It's been start and stop all night."

Delminico moved toward the half-track motioning to Smitty they were moving out. Just before entering the vehicle he looked back to Lindquist. "I don't mind the stops as long as there is another start. I'm not ready yet for the final stop."

"Neither am I," Lindquist replied. "Neither am I!"

45. Ryan, Tiny, Tucker – New Friends

December 25, 00:17 Hours – Ardennes Forest, Luxembourg

The trio of American soldiers traveled with purpose. They knew the Germans occupied Eschdorf in force and felt the enemy would soon stumble upon the barn given the gunfire that had ensued there. They didn't know how far ahead their lines were or what they might encounter along the way, but knew their chances were far better on the move than in the barn. So on this early Christmas morning they traveled, hoping for the holiday miracle of finding their lines.

As they approached the road, they heard vehicles and took cover under some trees nearby. They watched as two armored German half-tracks passed and came to a stop just to their left by an over-turned half-track off the road. The squad unloaded and investigated the incapacitated vehicle. They heard the crackle of a radio, as one of the men announced himself as Unteroffizer Brandt from the Fuehrer Grenadier Brigade. There was more dialog, but nothing Ryan and Tiny could interpret.

"What do we do, boss?" Tiny asked Ryan quietly as the trio peered out from under the tree.

"Sit tight for a minute," Ryan said hoarsely in reply.

Tiny sighed, "Maybe we should return to the barn. Might be safer there and a whole lot warmer."

"You think so?" Ryan said sarcastically. "It's just a matter of time before the Krauts find that barn. Conley is as good as a dead man."

Tiny strained his neck to get a better look without being seem himself. "They're just looking at the truck. Maybe they won't search."

"Yeah let's hope," Ryan replied. "How's Tucker?"

Tiny checked on the injured man. "He's cold as hell," he whispered.

"He's alive, though," Ryan replied. "If those bastards get him he'll be dead for sure. Stay down and quiet, something's happening."

What Ryan heard was the squad as they dispersed with orders to search the area. There were two German soldiers ordered to search in their direction up the path.

"We've got guests coming our way," Tiny said softly, with just a touch of anxiety evident.

"Stay still, damn it. If they see us or track our footprints in the snow, shoot them. But if they don't, just stay still."

As the Germans came up the path, another vehicle was heard nearby, but it did not pass them and its engine died somewhere out of sight before they could guess the type or nationality. Tucker moaned and the men thought their position was compromised for sure. Ryan brought his M1 across, lining it up on the closest German soldier. Tiny readied his gun, figuring he'd take out the one who didn't go down. But Tucker's moan was lost in the engine noise and the enemy continued up the path, passing about ten feet to the side of where the Americans were hidden.

As the Germans continued up the path, the Americans lay freezing, breathing into their coats, praying their breath was not seen. Waiting.

"Oh shit," Tiny uttered under his breath as Tucker started to shake uncontrollably. Tiny quietly repositioned himself so that Tucker was underneath him to suppress the quivering and provide some warmth. Tucker initially moaned feeling Tiny's weight, but stopped trembling under the human blanket the large man provided.

The men waited for the Germans to return from up the path, the frigid night air pricking any exposed areas and infiltrating their clothing, chilling to the bone.

"Where the fuck are they," Ryan mumbled impatiently under his breath.

"I think I hear something now," Tiny whispered.

The men strained to listen and softly at first, then gradually more pronounced, the crunching of boots on snow could be heard as the Germans returned down the path. Ryan expected them to have Conley in tow, but they came back alone.

"They mustn't have gone up far enough to find the barn," Tiny said quietly.

"It's amazing they couldn't smell the smoke," Ryan replied. "I can smell it from here."

"God's with them," Tiny offered.

"God will be looking you right in the face if you don't shut up," Ryan remarked.

At the point the Germans were almost parallel to Ryan and Tiny, one of the soldiers said something to the other. He then turned abruptly and began walking in the direction of the tree they were using for cover. Ryan initially thought their footprints had been seen, but there was no excitement, and only one of the men diverted from the path. The German approached the tree very casually and stopped about 6 feet in front of it.

Ryan gulped hard and hoped his uncontrolled quivering couldn't be heard. Tiny prayed silently, trying to remain perfectly still in hopes he wouldn't disturb Tucker. He wished he was in a position to get a hand over Tucker's mouth to muffle any discomfort the man might vocalize but knew it was not an option. At this distance any movement was likely to be detected so he lay there trying not even to shiver.

The German worked the front of his uniform and let out a long sigh as he emptied his bladder. He seemed to stand there forever but in reality it was only a number of seconds. When he was done he fumbled again with his uniform then turned and seemed to be looking right at the Americans under the tree. Ryan couldn't imagine how they could not be seen, their dark uniforms in contrast to the white snow. His finger twitched on the trigger waiting for the German to show any sign of recognition. After a few moments, the German turned, found the other soldier and continued down to the half-tracks.

Ryan and Tiny breathed a sigh of relief.

"That was close," Tiny whispered.

"Too close," Ryan agreed.

"I can't believe they didn't see footprints on the path," Tiny thought aloud.

"Too dark, I guess," Ryan supposed.

Ryan and Tiny heard a sharp retort in German they interpreted as an order, followed by more shuffling of boots on snow as the patrol assembled back at the half-tracks. After some additional discussion between one of the men on a radio, none of which the Americans could understand, they watched as the Germans loaded back up in the half-tracks, turned, and drove past them back toward Eschdorf.

"Are they gone?" Tiny inquired.

"I think so."

"Want me to check?"

"No, you stay here, and keep Tucker warm. I'll take a quick run to the road and check it out."

Ryan wiggled out from under the tree and stood. His legs felt like jelly from the cold and cramped position he had assumed for the last forty minutes. He carefully made his way down to the road surveying the area for any signs of life. All seemed quiet.

Seeing nothing, he returned to get Tiny and Tucker. Tiny checked Tucker quickly. He was still very weak, but somewhat warmer thanks to Tiny's body warmth. Tucker even managed to give Ryan a passive thumbs up, when asked if he could travel.

The men walked down to the road, Tucker perched on Tiny's back, staying low and alert, surveying the area for the enemy before crossing. As they started to cross, they were rattled to hear "halt" in English coming from some nearby bushes. Their anxiety turned to relief when an American Military Policemen or MP came out walking toward them.

"That must have been the other vehicle we heard," Ryan said softly as the MP approached. "Man are we glad to see you," he whispered loudly as the MP stopped in front of them.

The MP looked at them inquisitively, "Who are you?"

Ryan made quick introductions and looked beyond the GI. "What are you doing here?"

"Road block just behind that brush," the MP replied with a slight tilt of his head.

Ryan strained to see in the direction the MP nodded to.

"You got a medic, we got a wounded man?" Tiny cut in.

"No, but we can get him some help," the MP offered. Then quickly dismissing the injured GI, the MP questioned them about their unit and where they were going. Ryan did all the talking and explained their separation during the firefight and their respite in the barn. He also mentioned Conley, the German prisoner, and that he and the German were helping a woman deliver her baby.

"There is no barn up this road," the MP challenged. "Just a burned out house."

"Beyond the house on the edge of the woods," Ryan explained. The MP looked at him curiously.

Tiny was getting frustrated at all the talking while Tucker lay dying on his back when it suddenly registered in his mind that this was a strange place for a roadblock. After all, the Germans still controlled this area and the town.

"I don't understand why MP's would be posted so close to a German held town?" Tiny questioned, trying to clear his confusion.

The MP stammered a bit before replying. "The Germans pulled out," he finally spit out.

"I don't think so," Ryan replied, picking up on Tiny's point. "Just minutes ago a Kraut patrol came through here sniffing around."

Tiny looked at Ryan, "Yeah, and we would have heard the vehicle traffic if they left."

Ryan quickly pulled up his M1 but before he could get to a firing position, a German machine pistol erupted from the nearby woods and he collapsed to the ground in a heap.

Tiny, who still had Tucker on his back, could do nothing but watch. He wanted to act, to do something, but he knew any reaction on his part would get both him and Tucker killed. The MP quickly put a carbine to his chest, a twitch of a finger and he too would be dead. Tiny stood motionless as the MP relieved him of his weapon. He glanced down at Ryan, laying in a gathering pool of his own blood, an expanding dark stain on the white carpet of ground.

The brush ahead shook, then separated as a SS officer exited with another SS soldier carrying a machine pistol. Tiny guessed it was the man who had mowed down Ryan with the automatic weapon. The officer stopped in front of Tiny staring up at the large man.

"What is the nature of his wound?" he asked in English of Tucker, still perched on Tiny's back.

Tiny studied the man, noticed the black uniform of the German SS. He wondered if a shot from the woods with his name was next and the officer was playing with him. "Thigh wound," Tiny replied. "He's lost a lot of blood and is very weak."

The officer said nothing, but looked towards the woods and motioned forward. The engine noise was immediate and a German jeep-like vehicle, the Kubelwagen, emerged out of some thicket and onto the road. It drove in back of the officer and stopped. Two SS guards exited and stood still behind the officer.

"Take these men back to town," he ordered. "The wounded man requires medical care."

165

The guards snapped to attention and escorted Tiny and Tucker to the vehicle. As soon as the vehicle had left, the officer looked up the road.

"Becker, Hirsch," the officer said to the MP and SS soldier with the machine pistol in that order, "let's pay a visit to this barn they spoke of."

46. Gunn, Reimer – Road Brawl

December 25, 00:25 Hours – Ardennes Forrest Road

The Sherman skidded toward the left, Drabowski working hard to keep the steal toboggan on the glassy road. "Sorry Sarge," he yelled up to Gunn. "Can't see shit out there."

Gunn shook his head. He couldn't see much more than darkness out the viewport either. Moyer said what they all were thinking, "It's just a matter of time before we're off the road and stranded in a snowbank."

"I'm tired of this shit," Farner vented.

Gunn knew Farner was frustrated. Hell, they were all frustrated. This was a crappy mission to draw anytime, never mind that it was Christmas. His crew was like family and Gunn kept military protocol in the tank to a minimum, so he let Farner bitch.

"OK," Gunn said after a long pause. "I'm opening her up"

"You sure?" Farner questioned.

"Yeah, more risk of us going off the road than getting ambushed, especially with this tree lined sky blocking all the fucking moonlight."

Gunn didn't wait for further debate. He worked the lever and opened the hatch. Immediately an icy blanket of wind swept through the turret and he shivered like a baby exiting a warm bath. Gunn pulled some worn gloves from his pockets and dawned them before dragging himself up through the hatch and into the frigid night air.

To Gunn's dismay, the visibility wasn't much better viewing from outside the tank than inside.

"What do ya see Sarge?" Drabowski echoed through his headphones, seconds after Gunn had popped up into the icy darkness.

"Steady as she goes," Gunn shouted back, over the rumble of the tank's four-hundred seventy horse-power engine. "Straight for another thirty feet or so. As far as I can see."

Gunn caught glimmers of ice reflecting back toward him and used that along with the varying shades of dark gray and black to discern the pathway.

"You're going to pull left in ten feet," Gunn radioed. "See it?"

"Not yet," Drabowski called back nervously.

"I don't see it either," Moyer reiterated from the assistant driver's seat.

"Trust me guys, thirty degrees in three, two, one... now do it!"

Drabowski followed Gunn's direction and the Sherman navigated the icy black road like a snail crawling along a snowy tree branch.

*

Reimer and his Mark IV Panzer fared little better. His crew also strained to see the road ahead, slipping and sliding as they made slow progress along the narrow blackened corridor of a road. The only advantage Reimer enjoyed was that the canopy of trees that adorned the roadside was a bit more receded where he was than Gunn's position. That meant a little less filtering of the moon's dim light and few feet of added visibility. Unlike Gunn though, Reimer chose to remain inside the tank, not believing there was anything to be gained by riding topside in the artic-like cold.

*

The Sherman crawled along with Gunn navigating. The chill stung at him like a million little pin pricks, and Gunn fought the impulse to drop back down into the body of the tank where it was comparably warm. Gunn knew slow and steady would keep them moving forward and the extra few feet of visibility he gained from being topside could mean the difference between arriving and getting stuck. He'd just have to tough it out.

The cold triggered thoughts of those poor bastards in the infantry. Sleeping on the ground on frigid nights like this, always numb, bones aching with little chance to thaw. Constantly wet, feet blackened due to trench-foot, no that wasn't for him. Gunn applauded himself that he had made the right choice and picked the tank service. He always loved cars and working on engines so it seemed a good fit. Not that riding in this metal coffin of his was a bargain. He knew too many good men who had their tanks blown out from under and died painful horrid deaths. But in his mind, it still beat the infantry...

A noise found Gunn's ear and at first he thought it was his Sherman's engine misfiring. As he listened more intently he was able to separate the pitch and rev's that left no doubt another vehicle was sharing the road ahead.

"We've got company," Gunn bellowed into his mic.

"Fucking nice," came Drabowski's reply.

"It gets better, I think it's a tank," Gunn said dryly.

"Shit – all we need is to run into a fucking Tiger Tank out here. Our shells can't penetrate its armor and that mother will blow us to fucking hell!" Drabowski added, his voice rising.

"Don't get your panties in a bunch," Gunn replied with a calm he didn't feel. "There's another bend coming up, see it? The road swings left. Pull over to the right side of that bend but leave our back end on the road. I'll position the turret so it faces the bend. Understand?"

"Yeah, so we get a quick shot off as soon as he comes around the corner and then back up out of sight."

"You got it!" Gunn answered. "I don't know what it is so I'm going to take out his threads first. If we immobilize the bastard we can figure out the best way to take him down."

"What are the chances it's friendly?" Drabowski asked.

"Don't worry, I'll get a look before we fire."

"You're the boss," came the reply.

Drabowski pulled the Sherman to the right edge of the bend. Gunn positioned the turret, facing the turn on the left side. As soon as the vehicle came into sight Gunn would make a quick identification and hopefully put a shell into the enemy's tracks, stopping it on the spot. The Sherman would quickly back up out of view and away from the gun sight the German vehicle might have.

Gunn took a deep breath and felt the frigid air fill his lungs. A lot would happen in a furious few seconds and Gunn didn't kid himself that the plan was fool proof. The closer it came and louder it got, the more convinced Gunn became that the vehicle was an enemy tank. The question was – was it a Tiger or something else? The German Mark IV tanks had vulnerabilities and could be destroyed. The Panther Tanks were tougher but at this close range, and a good first shot, Gunn felt he could take it. The German Tiger tanks left him far less confident. The Tiger and King Tiger were the German monster tanks with so much protective steel that shells from a Sherman often bounced off it like tennis balls. To take down a Tiger typically required a rear shot and Gunn knew he'd never get that. If that bastard was a Tiger it was critical to disable the threads. He was certain they'd be as good as dead if the approaching tank was a Tiger and their first shot didn't immobilize it.

Gunn was convinced the tank was not American. From all the reports he heard there was nothing to indicate the area was in American hands. That was part of the frustration his crew felt about the job they had been assigned. No use whining about it now, anyway.

The German tank was getting closer, clamoring away as it clawed along the rugged frozen road. Gunn wondered if its commander was riding atop like him and had detected his tank. If so it would make for an interesting evening, especially if the German tank stopped in wait on the other end of the bend like Gunn's crew did. Given the continuously changing pitch Gunn knew for the moment anyway that wasn't the case.

"We're all loaded and ready to go, right Ellis?" Gunn asked, knowing the reply that would come.

"You bet," came the immediate reply from Ellis. "AP (Armor Piercing) shell loaded with a kiss."

"On my command fire. Remember we want a tread shot."

"Relax Sarge... You say go and I'll nail that Kraut bastard."

The approaching noise was so loud now that Gunn couldn't understand why the German tank hadn't rounded the bend. He even looked behind him to insure himself it hadn't been approaching from behind. The loudness gave him reason to believe a Tiger was approaching. *God save us*, he thought as a number of ugly scenarios filled his head.

*

Reimer looked at his watch. He felt like he'd been on this road all night, yet it had been just over an hour. The trip out had been uneventful thus far. He gauged even the Americans were smart enough not to be joy riding in the middle of the night on such awful roads. Wolf was thorough, he'd give him that much. Still Reimer thought, *all I'm likely to find out here is another mine that was missed, like that poor bastard Mueller found.* The toughest part would be returning to Eschdorf. If the Americans had started their attack his tank might run smack into their advance. *That would shake them up real good*, Reimer concluded. *Forces coming from two directions.* The smile quickly left him however, when the realization struck him that his single tank would be destroyed once the Americans regrouped and countered.

"Sharp left ahead," Reimer instructed his driver.

"I see it," the driver replied.

As the tank navigated into the turn a strange shape began to emerge. Reimer knew without question that the shape was a Sherman.

"Fuck," Reimer swore in German. "Americans... Fire," he yelled to his gunner.

Immediately there was flash.

*

Gunn found himself sweating in the cold as the noise kept getting louder. Finally, the shadow of a barrel protruded out and behind it the outline of a German tank. Gunn had been in battle long enough to recognize the form as a Mark IV Panzer, and he released a short sigh, grateful he was not pitted against a Tiger or even a Panther.

"Into the threads," he yelled into his mic. "Fire!"

There was a slight hesitation as the gunner adjusted the barrel, then the gun exploded.

In the same instant Gunn dropped down the hatch, closing it behind him. "Back her up, fast!" he yelled.

Drabowski had been waiting for the order and the tank lurched backwards almost as fast as the words left Gunn's lips. A second later a high explosive shell from the Panzer struck, erupting the space they had occupied moments before into flames.

"Damn," Gunn yelled. "That was close."

"Reloaded," yelled Ellis.

"Did we hit him?" Drabowski echoed from the driver's seat.

"We hit him, too close to miss," Gunn answered. "Question is where? We should know in a second if he pokes his nose around the corner. Next I need a shot right under his turret. Mark IV's are vulnerable right under the fucking barrel. You got that Ellis?"

"I got it... and don't you worry Sarge, I'll get that fucker!"

*

The impact jerked the Mark IV backwards like it had been slapped by a giant hand. Reimer was slammed against the far wall of the turret, the pain immediate, head engaging a rigid steel support. For a second his world went dark, but he fought through it, cursing loudly, bringing his head to the viewport, struggling to maintain focus. The Mark IV reacted less than a second later as his gunner returned fire. Reimer saw the

171

explosion of his tank's shell but there was nothing where the Sherman had been.

"Missed him, he pulled back," Reimer yelled, adrenaline now fueling him. "Load armor piercing rounds."

Reimer heard groaning from down below. "Who got hit?" he inquired, sneaking a look to the lower compartment.

"Shultz," the assistant driver yelled back up. "I think they took off the lower quarter. Threads aren't gripping."

"How bad is he?"

"Bad... his leg is mangled."

Reimer sighed and looked down at the wounded man. "Shultzy...," he started in a compassionate tone, but the injured soldier cut him off.

"Kill the Americans!" Shultz screamed out in an agonizing tone. "Kill them!"

Reimer said no more. He turned his mind toward the American tank, just around the bend. *That bastard did exactly what he planned to do*, he rationalized. *Took out our threads and pulled back behind the curve where we can't get him. Now he'll play peek-a-boo, jumping around the bend to pump a shell in us before retreating back until we're finished. Not on my time*!

"Watch for the American," he cautioned his gunner. "He will jump around the bend soon to take another quick shot, then retreat. Be ready!"

"The ice may make him think twice," his gunner replied. "But if he tries I'll blow his Sherman to hell."

Reimer allowed himself to pull his eyes from the viewport and gaze to the lower compartment. "Do you think you can move this beast forward at all?" he asked Heydrich, the assistant driver.

"If that shell didn't rip the tracks completely off."

Reimer processed the information. "I need you to get us around that bend."

"I can try," Heydrich replied as he assumed the lead driver role.

"On my command full revolutions forward and around that bend," Reimer ordered.

He looked up and over to Weber, his gunner. "You ready?"

"Ready," Weber replied.

"OK, now!" Reimer screamed and almost immediately the tank lurched forward.

While Reimer was contemplating his next move, Gunn had also been planning the Sherman's.

"Drabowski, we're going to need to motor up quick on that curve, get a shot under that Kraut's turret, then back out again. Can do?

"Sarge, you know on dry ground I can make this old girl dance. But on this skating rink of a road all bets are off."

"Drab-ski, you got a better idea?"

"We could just get the fuck out of here," Farner chimed in.

"Nothing I'd like more, but orders are orders," Gunn replied. "Drabowski, what do ya say?"

"Let's kill this fucker, and get on with the war."

Gunn nodded, turned to Ellis. "What about you? You going to be able to nail that bastard right under the turret? You might only get one shot.

"You get my barrel in sight of that tank and his ass is history."

"OK guys, let's make this happen," Gunn yelled out.

*

The Mark IV leaped forward, then stopped well short of the bend as her broken track spit out from underneath.

"That's it," Heydrich yelled up to Reimer. "Track's gone."

At almost the same time the Sherman spun around the corner, the two tanks separated by no more than thirty feet. Ellis got the look he wanted, made a quick adjustment through his site and fired his armor piercing round, aimed just under the Mark IV's turret.

The German gunner reacted as the Sherman suddenly came into view. He fired almost instantaneously with the American. Despite the firing of the two shells, there was little initial explosion because of the armor piercing type of munition. The shell from the Sherman hit the Mark IV exactly where it needed to. The shell ripped into the turret and penetrated the tank, projecting slivers of white-hot fragments throughout. Reimer, Weber and his loader were all killed instantly, their flesh and blood splattered against the far interior. The smoldering metal fragments were driven into the high explosive shell that Reimer had ordered replaced with the armor piercing one and it ignited, resulting in a huge fireball. The tank become a burning coffin for the crew of five.

The shell from the Panzer IV hit the rear flank of the Sherman, driving it across the road and against the embankment. In the front driver's compartment, Drabowski and Moyer were cut up and shaken but had no life threatening injuries. Up in the turret, the concussion snapped Farner's neck, killing him instantly, while Ellis had his leg nearly ripped off and Gunn broke an arm.

Thick, black, acidic smoke filled the back engine compartment and flames began to dance into the turret area.

"Son of a bitch!" cried Gunn. He looked over to Farner and could see from the contorted expression and awkward position of the man's face relative to his body that he was dead. Ellis moaned, his pant leg a dark mass, a bit of bone protruding out.

Drabowski stuck his head in the turret area as Moyer worked to open his driver's hatch in the forward area.

"Shit," Drabowski said to no one in particular. Then to Gunn, "You OK?"

"I think I broke my arm," Gunn hollered back. "Help me get this hatch open and let's get out of here."

Drabowski needed no encouragement as the crackling flames nudged closer. No one spoke but all noticed the strong smell of gasoline, not to mention the ammunition that was precariously close to the burning. Drabowski pulled himself up into the turret area. In the confined space he stepped over Farner on his way to the hatch. "Poor bastard," he muttered as he worked to free the hatch. They could hear Moyer pounding on the turret hatch from outside, having exited from the driver's exit. He was yelling something but all they heard was muffled shouts. Drabowski unlocked it and pushed it open, only to be met by thick, acidic smoke and a choking Moyer. It was now evident what Moyer was trying to say. The men quickly closed the turret hatch, gagging as they did.

"Ain't going to work," Drabowski said, literally coughing out the words. "Use the driver's hatch."

Gunn tried to drag Ellis with his good arm. Between the darkness tinted by flame and the smoke, visibility was near zero and he tripped over Farner landing on his bad arm with Ellis' dead weight following. "Ugh," Gunn muttered, having the wind knocked out of him. Drabowski lifted Ellis off him and began to drag the wounded man down toward the driver's hatch. Moyer was by the driver's hatch now, waiting to pull them out.

Gunn's own choking brought him out of the daze he was in. It was brighter in the turret which seemed a good thing until Gunn realized it was the fire making an entrance. He forced himself to his knees. "Come on guys," he yelled. "She's going to blow."

Drabowski had Ellis in the driver's compartment now. He tried to grip the wounded tanker, to pull him up toward the hatch, but his hands slipped on the blooded uniform and Ellis fell to the floor. "Come on man," Moyer instructed as he reached down, trying to get his hands in the tank to offer help.

Drabowski finally had Ellis up. Moyer locked him under his arms and began to pull him up and out from the hatch. Gunn felt scorching heat on his back. He turned and looked up from the driver's seat to see the whole turret area a ball of flame. "Hurry!" he yelled, knowing they had but seconds.

Moyer had Ellis out of the tank. Drabowski jumped out the hatch. Both Moyer and Drabowski reach down toward Gunn to help him out. They needed but a few more seconds...

The explosion generated a huge fireball, triggered by the flames igniting gasoline and the high explosive shells. The Sherman tank, which weighed in at thirty tons, left the ground as pieces of twisted, burnt metal were projected for hundreds of feet. The main blast initiated a series of other detonations igniting other shells and rounds of ammunition. The wreckage would burn for many hours.

It was early Christmas morning in Europe, 1944. Back in the states it was still Christmas Eve. For two tank crews it had been just another day of war. For ten men it was their last day of war. For ten families the Christmas of 1944 would forever change a day of celebration into a day of remembrance.

47. Wolf, Becker, Hirsch – The Walk

December 25, 00:40 Hours – Ardennes - Pathway to the Barn

Adolf Wolf was a young officer on the rise. Like his father before him, he served the fatherland well and had been given increasing responsibility as part of a little known SS unit. Thus far, in his short career, he had carried out every order and mission he had been given with blinding efficiency. Having a father who was a General in Berlin only helped his cause, and his exploits quickly found their way up to the ranks of the German High Command. Even the Fuehrer knew of him and his reputation for getting things done. Wolf himself expected to be made captain (Hauptmann in the German army) almost any day, and even thought there might be a possibility of a double jump to major.

"An exceptional night, Untersturmführer Wolf," Hans Becker said casually as the trio of SS men walked the snowy path toward the barn Ryan had told them about.

"And, the night is still young," Wolf commented, confident his streak of luck would continue.

"It was fortunate to locate the supply truck so quickly," Hirsch, the other SS man, chimed in.

Wolf smiled. He knew that Becker and Hirsch were sucking up or what did they call it in America – hitching up to his wagon. They knew he was a rising star and would be a powerful man in the German SS soon. Wolf would let them play the game – hitch up to his wagon… for now. Perhaps he could use them to accelerate his ascent, trumpet mention of his name repeatedly at the highest levels of the Reich.

The men continued up the path speaking in soft, low tones. "It would be nice to know who planted the mine that destroyed that vehicle," Wolf said thoughtfully. "Given what our American friend told us about a German soldier being held captive in this barn, we may find our missing sergeant and the men responsible for laying the mine."

"Did the American also say a civilian woman was giving birth to a baby?" Becker questioned amusingly.

"He did say that," Wolf agreed. "Imagine, a woman giving birth on Christmas Eve in a barn – how novel."

The SS men chuckled.

"Perhaps that makes us the three wise men," Hirsch added to additional snickering.

The trio passed the timbers of the house and their smiles left – a grim reminder of the realities of war.

"The barn must be just ahead," Wolf whispered, suddenly serious. "I feel certain that this birth or whatever they're passing this ruse off as – is part of a local Resistance movement."

Thus far, his investigations regarding civilians in Eschdorf aiding the enemy via the Resistance had not been productive - this might be the break he was looking for. He would get to the bottom of all of it in his methodical, no nonsense fashion.

It seemed to him a nice Christmas present all wrapped up. He had solved the mystery of the missing supply truck, captured American prisoners, and would soon uncover a local Resistance movement. His father would be proud, and surely the Fuehrer would hear!

"Untersturmführer, perhaps we should have kept Hauptmann Decker's men for backup," Hirsch suggested.

"Nonsense," Wolf immediately countered. "I ordered them back to Eschdorf to help defend the town. The Americans will attack soon – perhaps at daylight."

"Does Hauptmann Decker have patrols on the roads leading into town?" Becker asked.

"Some," Wolf commented. "But I have placed patrols along those roads Herr Hauptmann thought not a risk. When Eschdorf is held, Hauptmann Decker will have me to thank."

Wolf thought briefly about the German soldiers straggling in from Hierheck that he encountered earlier in the day and had ordered to hold one such road-block. He would check on them after dealing with the situation in the barn. He thought about sending Decker's men to reinforce them, but dismissed it. *Those men never should have retreated from Hierheck*, he reasoned. *They should have held that town, and I will ensure they hold that road-block if I have to do so upon threat of treason.* Wolf knew the Americans would approach that flank in their attack on Eschdorf and that the men he positioned there would be swallowed up swiftly and decisively before they could muster any type of defense. Wolf felt it was their fate for retreating from Heirheck. He deemed their sacrifice would serve the fatherland by providing notice and direction to Decker's troops when the Americans were attacking.

As they rounded the next turn in the path, the barn came into view, a smoky shadow on a black backdrop. Wolf quickly pushed all these things from his mind as he fashioned a plan to infiltrate. He brought his fingers to his lips, notice for the men to stay quiet as they closed in on the barn and those inside. Instead of talking, he used hand signals to Becker and Hirsch to indicate the plan he wanted to execute. Becker smiled in acknowledgement – he seemed to like his role. Hirsch nodded as well, taking a long look around the perimeter, enacting the guard role he was given.

Wolf looked at Becker and gave the SS man a wave with his gloved hand. *Showtime*, he thought, anxious to see this assortment of characters and to piece together this strange but amusing puzzle.

48. Kohl – The Hunter

December 25, 00:35 Hours –Pathway to Hierheck

Yeager Kohl was a dangerous man. He alone killed hundreds, had a knack for evading detection or capture, and like a lone wolf had instincts for survival that had kept him alive through multiple perilous encounters. Kohl's first name, Yeager, meant "hunter" in German, and in likeness to his namesake, had predatory intuition like few others. His prey seldom escaped his sights and of those who did, few came away unblemished.

Yeager Kohl was a sniper.

He had grown up in a modest house in Ramsau, in the Bavarian Alps, and could shoot almost before he could walk. Hunting provided the means to eat and Yeager learned at an early age that to shoot and miss meant to go hungry. It was a lesson his father ingrained in the young boy when they headed to the mountainous areas in search of pheasant, rabbit or elk. When Yeager's aim was off target and the family dinner ran or flew off, the boy would be denied dinner that evening. Even when his father's aim was true, he would sit and watch the family dine, punishment for what his dad called a job undone.

Kohl honed his skills with a rifle quickly given the incentive his dad provided. When drafted in the German army in 1941, he so impressed his superiors with his marksmanship that they recommended him for special training as part of the Fallschirmjaeger or paratroopers. While training he was approached by a General from the Waffen SS and enticed to join the Gebirgsjäger or the Waffen SS Infantry Mountain Unit. The invitation struck a loud chord with Kohl who loved the Alps and little persuasion was needed to get him on board.

He quickly made a reputation for himself with his gun, but he was more than just a sure-shot. Kohl possessed a sharp mind, was at home in the mountainous regions and was driven to succeed. He was also strongly built, the product of years of hard labor and very agile for his brawn, having climbed in the hills to hunt almost his entire life before being recruited in the German Army. Kohl was also an excellent skier, which only added to his impressive resume.

The German army quickly found out the limited longevity of a sniper. Just as rapidly however, they discovered how effective a sniper can be, one or two holding up platoons of men, inflicting both physical and emotional damage. After two years in the Waffen SS, fighting as part of a Mountain unit in Karelia, between Finland and Russia, Kohl was reassigned to an SS Unit in Southern France. Now assigned a sniper's role, Kohl leveraged his diverse skillset and began his reign of terror on Allied troops. The German offensive the following December found him in the Ardennes picking off American troops almost at will. Kohl carried some of the latest German weapon technology including an upgraded Walther G-43 semi-automatic rifle with a night-vision 5x scope, warm camouflaged clothing and a mentality that made him nearly unstoppable. To Kohl, sniping was like hunting, he felt an adrenaline surge when his prey came into range and a rush with each kill. He became proficient at killing from farther and farther away and this made him even more dangerous and difficult to find.

Earlier that day, he was positioned just outside of Hierheck and initially had disrupted the American advance into the town. When it became clear that the town would fall, he relocated to the outskirts where he picked off numerous enemy allowing Wehrmacht troops to escape. An American artillery attack caught him unaware, a tree burst sending pencil sized slivers in his upper leg.

With his snow camouflage now blood-red across his entire upper right leg, he hobbled his way toward Eschdorf. Kohl was closing on the town when he heard noise on the path in front of him. It sounded like a patrol. Like a cat he silently climbed a tree, grunting only once in protest to the throbbing in his leg. Probing with his night scope he saw German soldiers, but something was wrong. They were not heading to Eschdorf, they were heading toward the American lines. Seeing no weapons Kohl thought the German soldiers were captives, but he viewed no guards. Blood pooled in his stomach, eyes became like slits, his trigger finger flexing. He had risked his life for these men, had killed and came close to being killed to give these soldiers another chance to fight, to honor the German army, their homeland. The thought that they would turn that opportunity and the blood he and so many others spilled into surrender burned more than the wound in his leg. Kohl looked for a target, the one in charge. This treason would end and he would see to it – one by one, eventually all.

49. Conley – Unable to Leave

December 25, 00:44 Hours – Ardennes Forest, Barn

As soon as Conley was out of the barn door he heard voices down the path in front of the burned out farmhouse. He quickly worked his way around the back side of the barn and hid behind an empty feed barrel. He loaded his last clip into the Thompson and watched as a trio of men approached. He saw what appeared in the limited light a curious group; an American MP, a German SS officer and a German SS soldier carrying a machine pistol. He studied the figures to be sure, the uniforms, cartridge belts, boots and helmets. Initially he thought the MP was the German's prisoner, but as they got closer he noticed the MP carrying a weapon and could hear the men all softly speaking German.

Conley's Sergeant had told his squad about Germans being parachuted in, wearing American uniforms, but he thought that most had been captured. He looked at his hands on the Thompson and found them shaking. He thought of all he'd been through this night. Conley considered opening up with the Thompson. Clearly he could mow the trio down before they could react, but he assumed more troops must be nearby. He quickly pieced together that Ryan and company must have stumbled onto the Germans, at least the MP, and likely told them about the barn before they were captured. He remembered hearing the sound of a German machine pistol when he was in the barn and wondered if what Ryan had said about the Germans not taking prisoners was true.

Conley decided he would monitor the situation and act only if he needed to. Mueller was a German soldier, and should have nothing to fear from his own troops. At least he hoped so. However, if Elise was left alone, or if she and the baby were in any way put in danger, Conley would do what was necessary to protect them. He had promised Andre, and after seeing that innocent little life being born in the midst of the chaos of war, he vowed that he'd give his life to do so.

As the Germans passed the edge of the barn, Conley retraced his steps and relocated to the other side of the barn, providing himself a better vantage point to listen. He would also be closer to the door if he needed to gain access. He quietly made his way down the side wall of the barn until just around the corner from the SS men, outside the barn door. Apparently, two of the men remained outside while one of the men – Conley guessed the MP – entered. Conley rationalized the MP, masquerading as an American, tricked Ryan into revealing the circumstances in the barn. By sending in the disguised MP, it would be easier to see access the situation and disarm the American.

But the American was not in the barn. He stood aside it cold, alone and contemplating many things. And for William Conley, what kept dominating his thoughts was how close he was to death.

50. Kohl – The Hunted

December 25, 00:38 Hours –Pathway to Hierheck

Wheaton sent out a partial squad to meet Ruscart and the prisoners as they returned from Lindquist. He wasn't concerned about the Germans changing their minds about surrendering, Wheaton was more concerned about the self-appointed prisoners exiting the woods prematurely and walking into the withering machine gun fire that had relentlessly tormented his men most of the night.

Sergeant Kline led the five man team, almost half of a squad, more than enough to retrieve the group of beaten-down, hapless, and unarmed Wehrmacht soldiers. Kline, a New Jersey kid, whose family roots marked him as a German-Jew, spoke fluid German and would hopefully be able to keep the prisoners calm, returning them to camp quickly so as not to interfere with the Eschdorf attack, now forming up.

The Americans moved along the path swiftly but cautiously, closing the distance between them and German prisoners. The air hung thick and frozen, so crisp Kline felt he could cut it with his trench knife. *Bang…* the unmistakable sound of a gunshot not too far ahead, Kline dropping, his squad doing the same. *Bang…* another shot and with it a harsh scream. German voices, in great distress, Kline picking up verbiage about them being easy targets, no cover on the road.

"Krauts?" Basehart, one of his men, questioned in a grunted whisper. "Krauts shooting Krauts?" he asked, confused.

"Sniper, I think," Kline answered. "You take Mills and circle around through those woods. Boggsy, Thomas, on me!"

Without question the group was up each man following the order given. *Bang! Bang…* more screams. *Damn*, Kline thought as he ran, *it's a fucking turkey shoot*!

Kline rounded a turn, saw shadows of men lying on the path, heard them yelling in anguish, terrified. Now they heard his men coming at them, fearful they too were out to kill them. He spun off the path, his men doing the same, breaths coming hard now, sweat dripping. *Bang…* a

184

shot ripped through bark, inches away. He heard rustling on the path, some of the Germans trying to move, to get to cover, afraid now of both him and woods beyond.

"Stay down!" he yelled in German. "Friends!" With that he raised his Thompson and sprayed the woods where the sniper might be. *Bang...* the shot rang out defiantly, stinging a branch close, too close. *Bang...* this time another one of the Germans along the path shuddered, then went limp.

"Boggsy, set up that BAR behind a rock and keep firing into the trees. Thomas, find good cover, then look for a flash, smoke, anything that might tell us where this bastard's hiding."

*

Kohl couldn't feel his legs, knew he had lost a lot of blood. Through the scope things seemed to be getting fuzzy, his marksmanship slipping away with each droplet of blood he shed. But he still had targets, shadows in fetal positions on the ground as seen through his night vision scope. How sad it was that a man could walk proud in victory one moment, only to quiver and grovel like an infant when hope seemed lost. Such cowards, Kohl thought, as a shadow moved and he instinctively positioned his weapon, took a slow breath as he always did before a kill, and leisurely and evenly compressed the trigger. *Bang...* thud... another victim. Kohl wasn't done yet – still breathed life that harbored death.

Bullets flew in his direction, but they were below him, so he paid them no mind. Kohl noticed movement to his left, positioned the scope to see two Americans trying to flank him. *Bang...* both Americans dropped, but one much more awkwardly. He knew the man was hit. More bullets coming in at him, higher in the trees, closer now. Kohl turned back toward the path, searched with his scope for the automatic rifle peppering at him. He picked it up just to his left. Kohl could see the man was well covered, just the muzzle of the BAR visible. He lined the scope just above the muzzle of the American gun, but the area kept moving, knew the loss of blood was affecting him. Kohl took a breath and squeezed the trigger, not sure of his success. For the moment though, the firing stopped.

*

Kline moved off in the opposite direction, hoping to flank the sniper on the other side. He knew the man must have night eyes to shoot so accurately in the nearly pitch black forest. He also knew that the German killing machine could put a bullet in his head should he turn his scope in his direction, so Kline tried to move silently and stay behind cover. He heard the sniper's gun bark twice more and stopped in search of the German's location. But there was nothing visible and the sound was lost in the night. Kline guessed the German had some kind of device that muffled the sound or redirected it. Time was also the enemy. The assault on Eschdorf would begin in minutes and he was expected back to lead his squad. *This needs to end now*, he thought, *I need a break*.

As if in reply, he saw it, a shimmer – a slight reflection of steel off the dim moonlight. It wasn't much and Kline had no way of knowing if it really was his sniper. He navigated a little closer, needed to, to improve the angle, knowing he was exposing himself. Kline had focused on a section of tree and although it was now dark, he locked in, moving slowly but defiantly to secure an unobstructed shot. He heard the snow beneath him, crunching like popcorn, seemingly amplified but continued unabated. One more tree to clear…

*

Kohl saw the movement, both left and right. He knew the Americans were trying to flank him on both sides. His head spun, dizzy, struggled to process what should be two quick easy kills. The scope revealed a clean shot to his left and he adjusted, took a breath and squeezed the trigger. To his amazement he missed, the man dropping but clearly not hit, for a head shot would have rotated his target around, at least knocked him back. Kohl gulped hard knowing he was dying, the loss of blood affecting his ability to execute kills. He refocused through the scope, could still see the enemy, hidden but still partially exposed. He'd settle for a body shot. *Bang…* Kohl watched the body jerk, sprawl out like a snake suddenly uncoiling itself, then nothing – dead.

Kohl looked to his right, knew he had lost time requiring two shots to down one man, not his usual. The target moved, closer, was now out in the open, almost too easy. Kohl thought the man a fool, couldn't imagine why the American would expose himself from cover… unless…,

There was a flash and plume of smoke as Kline's Thompson erupted, forty-five caliber bullets tearing into Kohl's torso. Initially, Kline had no way of knowing whether he hit the sniper and he hurled himself behind a tree, half expecting a bullet as the answer to his question. A second later, he heard branches split and yield, the shadow of a gun dropping, followed by a blob of what appeared to be dirty snow. The thud at the base of the tree put an eerie finality to it. The cost had been high, three of his men and seven Germans killed. Ruscart had survived the attack, but Schmidt was not among those more fortunate.

51. Becker, Wolf, Mueller, Elise - Confrontation

December 25, 00:55 Hours – Ardennes Forest, Barn

Hans Becker, dressed in a U.S. Military Police uniform, pushed the door open and cautiously walked into the barn, his carbine leading the way. He looked into the dim light and was first surprised with how warm it was within.

Mueller heard the door but continued in his conversation with Elise. He felt his best chance, regardless of who found them, was to depict himself an unarmed soldier helping a civilian who had just given birth.

Becker, his carbine out front, walked quietly to the back of the barn and spun around the fireplace. Elise was startled momentarily, even though she could see the man's shadow approaching. Mueller turned his head and was surprised to see an American MP. After hearing a German weapon only minutes before, Mueller was not expecting an American. He was confused and somewhat suspicious that this man might not be who he portrayed.

The two men stared at each other for a long second. Becker saw that Mueller held no weapon and turned a malevolent glance toward Elise, holding her baby. Elise shivered at the accusing eyes but held his glare with one of her own. After a number of awkward moments, Becker turned back to Mueller.

"Who are you?" Becker questioned, in perfect English that made Mueller question his suspicion.

"Unterfeldwebel Eric Mueller."

"Your outfit?"

"Fuehrer Grenadier Brigade."

"You are away from your outfit, Unterfeldwebel. Why is that?"

"This woman needed my help. She delivered her baby tonight, less than an hour ago."

Becker was unimpressed. "And who is she?"

"She is…," Mueller started.

"Can the woman not speak for herself?" Becker interrupted.

Mueller's doubt about the MP returned. Based on the man's indignant tone the MP sounded like he was Gestapo.

"You have poor manners for a Military Policeman," Mueller said rather callously.

Becker ignored Mueller although he kept his carbine pointed at him. He shifted a menacing glance toward Elise. "You are?"

"The owner of this barn," she replied hesitantly.

Becker was clearly unsatisfied by what he heard. "There were some Americans up the road who said an American GI was here. Where is he?"

"He left," Mueller said flatly.

Becker didn't seem convinced. He spied the flashlight sitting on the mantel and grabbed it, keeping his weapon trained on Mueller. He motioned Mueller to the side and walked past him, flashing the light into the stalls. He quickly came across the bodies of Vogel and the American they had found in the barn when they arrived.

"What is this?" Becker asked.

Mueller had had enough. He didn't like this cat and mouse game. He felt pretty sure the MP was not American and decided he'd play his hunch.

"I know who you are and what you are doing." Mueller blurted out. "Does the German army have nothing better to do than dress up its men in American uniforms and harass its own soldiers? Are they so insensitive to a new mother, who has no family because of the fortunes of war?"

Becker was unmoved. "Unterfeldwebel, your imagination runs wild. How do I know that you are not the American I was told about and that the body in the stall is not that of the real Unterfeldwebel Mueller?"

"What?" Mueller uttered in disbelief at the preposterous scenario.

Wolf, who was listening at the door, entered with the other guard. Hearing the door open Becker broke off conversation and stood silently as the German lieutenant made his way in and around the fireplace, the guard trailing a few steps behind.

Wolf was a man who didn't tolerate fools, and he didn't like that Mueller was beginning to make a fool of his agent.

"You are a perceptive man, Unterfeldwebel," Wolf said when he finally spoke.

Mueller said nothing. He looked at Wolf trying to size the SS man up. The man looked every part the Nazi he was, long black coat, brimmed hat and fur-lined leather gloves, which he began to take off. Mueller thought he had seen Wolf as a character in a movie, but quickly realized that this was not a movie; it was the worst scenario he could imagine for him and Elise. He hoped that Conley had gotten away so at least one life would be spared. Discerning about that made him recall how close he came to killing the American himself. *Crazy war*, he thought.

Wolf continued, now in German. "You do know Unterfeldwebel, there is a town, perhaps a mile from here, where you could have gotten this woman proper medical care and reported to your unit?"

"Yes, Hauptmann, but as I tried to explain to…," he hesitated, not sure what to call the man masquerading as an MP, "… this gentleman, I was held by an American for some time. This woman came to us, needing our help. There wasn't time to go back to town."

"Unterfeldwebel Mueller is it?"

Mueller nodded.

"I find your story amusing. Am I to believe that a strong man, an Unterfeldwebel, with many years of military service, could not overpower a single American soldier? This while you were caring for a woman in childbirth? Did the American hold his gun on you the entire time?"

Mueller started to reply, but Wolf cut him off.

"And you, young lady. Why would you leave the town to come out here to a farm to have your child? There is a civilian body out in the snow. Were you meeting one of your contacts from the Underground?"

"No!" Elise shouted so quickly that she startled the baby, who began to cry. "The town was not safe for civilians. There were soldiers there…,"

An explosion close by suddenly rocked the barn. The town was being shelled and misses were landing in the nearby woods behind the barn. Elise was glad for the interruption, because with a second to think, she realized she couldn't say anything about the SS, which Wolf was obviously a part of. He never let her continue.

"This all sounds like a ploy to me." He looked at Mueller and then at Elise. "Someone tell me what is going on," he said in a raised voice.

The barn became quite tense. Mueller looked over to the MP who seemed to be enjoying the exchange. *You bastard*, he thought. He glanced beyond Wolf to the other guard who was expressionless. Finally, he turned back to Elise. She held her baby tightly, trying to comfort the whimpering infant, but her eyes stared into Wolf's almost in defiance.

"We have told you the truth," Mueller said after the long silence.

"And I have told you I am not satisfied with your answers," Wolf snarled back. "Perhaps you will remember more if I hold the baby."

Wolf took a step toward Elise. She pulled the baby close, her eyes wide with fear. Wolf stopped when another series of explosions nearby shook the ground under them.

"The American artillery is engaging in Christmas festivities," he said, as if it were a good thing. "Soon they will initiate a full attack. We must leave now, all of us."

His eyes found Mueller, "Unterfeldwebel Mueller, get this woman and her child ready to travel. We will continue this discussion later."

Wolf then turned to the guard behind him, "Check the area around the barn. If the Americans are attacking there could be American soldiers nearby." He looked at Elise, "Perhaps even your American friend."

The soldier clicked his heels and left.

52. Lambert – Escape

December 25, 00:57 Hours – Ardennes Forest, Outside of Eschdorf

René Lambert was a wanted man. He fled the Germans from a work location a few weeks before, after an Allied bombing gave him an opportunity to escape. The aerial bombardment came from a dozen P38 Lightning's and to René was a masterpiece of luck. The attacking planes zeroed in on a German railroad, which he and a group of forced laborers had been pressed into service to repair. In addition to destroying the rails thereby delaying movement of German supplies to the front, the bombing also served to create a diversion to spring the determined laborer. With bombs exploding, propelling fragments of hot twisted medal in all directions, René made for the woods versus the railcars as was his instruction from the guards. In the chaos his initial absence was never noticed and he was able to put substantial distance between himself and the railroad before the guards realized he was gone. Given the name and general location of a Resistance fighter's home from a friend at the labor camp, he started his quest back from the grave, a place where few of his fellow countrymen returned. This despite being told he and fellow neighbors were laborers and not prisoners. René could only shudder at what being a prisoner meant. He knew if he was caught he'd find out firsthand.

René was one of the lucky ones. He had a name and location in which refuge could be found. Still he escaped without proper clothing for the frigid winter air and his shoes afforded him no insulation or dryness from the snow and ice that quickly saturated them. Within an hour René was navigating the woods on frozen stumps of legs, exhausted and wondering if he would ever know warmth again.

"Bonjour," a voice softly called out.

René stopped, looked about him.

"Who are you looking for?" the voice uttered.

René turned toward the voice, found a small man holding a German machine pistol. "Marcel, I am looking for Marcel," he said through chattering teeth.

"I am Marcel… and you are René?"

"Yes, you know of me?"

Marcel nodded slightly "I know all I need to know - you are wanted by the SS. Come, I can help you."

René had no way of knowing if this man was who he said he was. The stranger knew his name but that meant nothing - the Germans in search of him certainly knew who they were looking for. For all René knew this was a French partisan, sympathetic to the Germans, who would march him back to custody. Despite any concerns he had, René knew he had little choice but to follow the man, hinge his frozen hopes on any help Marcel could offer.

The men walked a short distance in silence, a small house suddenly materializing, sitting inappropriately in the middle of the woods. What struck René about the structure was that it had no yard, or boundary markings, it simply stood, out of place, among the trees. René collapsed on the floor upon entering, the cold, stress and tiredness finally overwhelmed him. He awoke a short time later, feeling comforting warmth surrounding him and a small rotund woman massaging his feet. She only smiled when he looked at her and called for Marcel in French.

"You have returned to the living and met my mother," Marcel said from a nearby table.

René nodded first at the woman and then at Marcel. "How is it you live here? That the Germans don't find you?" he asked, incredulous to what he saw.

"So many questions for a man so weak he passed out on my kitchen floor. Let us just say we have an arrangement with the Boche. We provide them preserves and watch for Resistance activity and they leave us alone."

"But you are…," René started to say.

"A nice French family trying to survive the war," Marcel finished. "Now what is *your* story?"

"I need, no I must get home," René began. "My wife, Elise, is due to deliver our first child in a week or two."

"Where is home?"

"Eschdorf."

"Hm… that will be tricky. Eschdorf may soon to be occupied by the Boche."

René was not deterred. "I know the town. If I can get in I'm sure I can find my Elise."

"We will do what we can to get you on your way," Marcel said confidently. "But it is a risky journey and you must do as I instruct – is that clear?"

René looked at the man, sized him up, knew he would be putting his life and with it his wife and child's life in this man's hands. "Yes," he answered simply.

A week had passed since then. René's journey had been a tedious and dangerous one. After two days of decent food and healing to regain some lost strength, René was outfitted with warm clothing – mostly layers of shirts and pants, wool socks and a pair of boots, not new but better than the decrepit shoes he escaped in. He was also given a fresh set of papers, forged with a new identify should he be stopped. His old papers would reveal him as a wanted man. René was leery of trying to pass himself off with false papers, but Marcel assured him they would do the job.

He bid farewell and hiked through the rugged forest to a nearby farm Marcel had given him directions to. René then hit the road in the back of a potato truck with a Belgian farmer named Milo, a friend of Marcel's, who had gained the trust of the Germans by providing weekly drops of spuds. Trust aside, the plan was not foolproof. If the Germans had ever searched the truck, both driver and discovered passenger would have found themselves on the end of a rope. Their luck held. The guards at the checkpoint knew Milo from prior visits and let him pass unmolested. To avoid suspicion by not deterring from his normal route, Milo had to drop off René some distance away from Eschdorf. René then hiked an additional five miles before reaching the home of a man needed for the next leg of the journey. After thawing, a hot meal and good night's sleep, his guide took him on another trek through deep woods until René recognized his surroundings at the outskirts of Eschdorf.

René now squatted in brush looking over the road, just outside Eschdorf, not far from where Andre and Elise had escaped hours before. He studied the area, trying to discern if the Germans were indeed hidden in posts along the roadside where a crude map he was given indicated they would be. He finally conceded to himself there was really no way to know without literally walking into these places - they were just too well camouflaged. Knowing he'd have to chance the correctness of the map, René picked a spot in between two mapped guard posts and carefully made his way to the edge of the road. After surveying the area he stepped out of the brush and had but a foot on the road, when he heard "Halt", loudly in German coming from a concealed location in the brush, just feet away.

René froze in place, his mind awash of many things. He endured so much, come so far, minutes away from Elise. Clearly the map was wrong and he picked the best place to enter – to be caught. He was thankful he had no weapon, to be caught with one would mean an awful death, especially if it was of German design. He felt vomit rise to his throat when he saw the black uniform of an SS guard rising out of the bush about ten feet away from him. The guard looked to be a Sergeant and held a Lugar toward his chest. René searched the darkness for other guards but saw none, the post well cloaked.

"Who are you?" the guard queried.

"Paul Jorion," René stuttered, hoping he had correctly remembered his alibi. He expected the guard to request his papers, but instead the guard took a different approach.

"Give me one good reason why I shouldn't shoot you here and now?" the SS guard barked.

René had a story concocted about visiting family for the holidays. With a gun at his chest, it suddenly seemed contrived; however, nothing else came to mind. Fortunately at that moment the shrieking sound of a shell filled the void of silence ending with a thunderous clap, shaking the ground and lighting the town. René flinched and watched the guard do the same even though the explosion was some distance away. Another shell followed, this one closer and again he spied as the guard's eyes diverted, focusing on the fireball erupting across the road, part of a building in the town crumbling to the ground. A third shell landed even nearer, in the field opposite the road, shrapnel stinging nearby trees. René's mind raced. He used an aerial bombing to escape once, he would use this shelling to aid in another quick exit. Another explosion, the guard marking it with a concerned glance. René spun and darted towards the woods. The guard recovered a moment later, his Lugar coming to life, spraying lead at the black form awkwardly fleeing. The first two shots missed, but the third shot appeared to hit its mark, René's arms suddenly flailing before he crumbled to the ground.

It was not what René had planned that night.

53. Conley - Deadly Encounter

December 25, 01:04 Hours – Outside Ardennes Forest Barn

It had all come down to this that dark, early Christmas morning. Conley collected his thoughts as he stood aside the barn, sobered by the shell fragments decimating the woods in back and the SS guard who was just around the corner – so close he could smell the tobacco the man reeked of.

His gut churned as he considered how he could dispose of the German quietly, not letting those in the barn know he was there. He thought of his trench knife but that would be of better use if he could get behind his victim. Another explosion ripped the night in the shallow woods and he shivered, both cold and fear shaking him. Conley decided he would smash the butt of the Thompson in the German's face. He then moved right to the edge of the barn and crouched down in wait.

The SS guard paused after exiting the barn to survey the immediate area. He saw Andre's dead body to his front, then looked out farther ahead of the barn, where two trees stood. A nearby explosion halted his next step and he deliberated whether it was too dangerous to search the woods behind the barn. He reasoned if the American was still around he would be close by, so he decided to at least walk the perimeter of the barn. Another explosion nearby gave him additional reason to be cautious, but he knew he had to make at least one pass around the barn to appease Lieutenant Wolf. He started forward in the direction of Conley.

Conley was ready, although he had never done anything like this in combat. He had practiced it numerous times, but with numbness infiltrating his body he wondered if he could generate the speed and power needed to take the German down quickly and quietly.

The SS guard was no fool and was careful in his approach. As the German neared the edge of the barn, he realized he could be blindsided by cutting the corner too close and made a wide arc to the outside. Another explosion lit up the sky for a moment and the German glimpsed something to his right out in front of him. He gazed for a moment curiously at what appeared to be a dog, lifeless in the snow, then stopped and peered around him, everything now dark again. He altered his course slightly and instead of turning toward the side of the barn headed toward the dead animal.

The light around the barn was very dim and Conley could see only faint shadows. He could hear the German's footsteps, echoing like the crushing of broken glass and could sense his nearness, but not as close as he thought for him to engage in close up combat. As the guard's dark form became visible, two explosions occurred in the pasture in front of them and cast light that exposed both soldiers for a brief second. Conley saw that the German was some fifteen feet away, and the German saw that there was something crouched against the side of the barn.

Conley had the advantage in knowing the German was there, and it saved his life. He was a fraction of a second quicker getting his burst off than the German and his bullets spun the man around, the SS guard's machine pistol firing harmlessly into the snow.

The silence following the gunfire lasted only a few ticks of the clock before a swishing noise and three more explosions ripped the field behind the dead German, sending burning shrapnel whizzing in all directions. Conley dropped and hugged the ground as metal fragments tore into the barn above and in back of him.

He realized the area around him, including the barn, could be a kill zone at any moment as the shells began to fall more indiscriminately near. More importantly, Conley knew the SS men inside the barn had heard the gunfire and knew that he was out there.

54. René – New Life

December 25, 01:07 Hours – Outside Eschdorf

The SS Sergeant barked an order into the nearby brush as he studied the dark, inert figure, clumped in the woods ahead of him. Explosions lit up the night around him, one hitting the road, rocketing burning shrapnel into the trees and bushes nearby. A young SS Private appeared, machine pistol at his hip.

"Yes, Sergeant," the soldier said in German, his eyes blinking at the flashes of light, seemingly rattled by the deadly barrage.

"Get control of yourself," the sergeant snapped. "The civilian I just shot, make sure he is dead, retrieve his papers."

"Jawohl," the SS Private replied, giving a hesitant stare into the woods where the body lay.

"Raus!" the sergeant impatiently growled. *Not long ago the SS was an elite fighting force*, his mind wandered. *Now it has been reduced to boys playing soldier*. He quickly pushed the thought from his mind, turned and harshly issued orders to the remaining men manning the machine gun post in the hidden brush. Almost immediately there was rustling as the men needed little incentive to relocate further down the road and away from the immediate shelling.

The young SS Private stepped cautiously towards the dark shape in the snow. His Sergeant had spoken as if the man in front of him was dead, but how could he be sure? He held his machine pistol at the ready as he came up on the body. With his boot he rolled the lifeless form over on its back, gave a long stare, contemplating who the civilian might be. He could understand a man wanting to exit the town, escape the carnage from the shelling, but this civilian was trying to get in. *Probably why his Sergeant wanted the man's papers*, he thought. More explosions ripped the road and shrapnel was heard stinging the nearby woods. He gave the *corpse* a last gaze before taking a knee, sliding a hand into the coat in search of papers. The body felt warmer than expected. He started to back off, instincts kicking in, when something struck like a cobra, pierced him deeply in the chest, driving him backward to the ground.

*

Minutes before, René thought he might make it when he felt the burn, the bullet grazing his ribs. He knew then the game was up... the next shot would end it all. Instinctively he flailed, leaving no doubt he had been hit, falling awkwardly trying to sell the ploy. René played a hunch, hoping that if the guard thought he was dead, the SS man would save his own skin and retreat to a safer location. The SS Sergeant played it both ways however, calling on one of the lowly privates to check him while looking out for himself.

René heard the dialog, knew the SS Private was young, inexperienced, not a typical SS Nazi hardliner like those he remembered from his captivity in the labor camp. René felt he could take the untried private unless the soldier shot him from a distance out of fear to ensure he was dead. As the man moved closer, René let the penknife Marcel gave him and kept up his right sleeve slide forward until it was along his wrist. He wasn't sure how to attack the enemy soldier but when the German rolled René from chest to back, using his boot, the plan quickly formulated. As the SS guard began to crouch by him, René maneuvered the penknife from his sleeve to his hand under his body and out of sight. When he felt the SS Soldier reach into his coat for papers, he thrust the knife towards the man's chest, with as much force as he could muster. The sharp blade tore through the guard's coat plunging deep in his heart.

The SS man's eyes bulged, his mouth opening as if forming a scream but it never came – he was dead. The soldier's eyes remained open, protruding widely in a shocked, disbelieving, hypnotic stare.

René eyed the man's machine pistol in the snow but knew he couldn't take it. To be seen with a weapon would mean getting shot, no questions asked. The Americans were laying waste to the town; he questioned his own sanity for attempting to enter it. He thought about camping out at the farmhouse until the fighting was over. Wondered if perhaps Andre and Elise had ventured there. *No, he rationalized, the Boche would never have let them stay at the farm. They would have relocated them to town.*

The shelling seemed to abate. Now the sound that dominated the background was that of heavy machine gun fire. He pulled to his feet, made his way to the roads edge, where he had first been held up by the

SS Sergeant. Knowing the post there had moved, René felt this was now the safest place to cross. He stole glances up and down the empty road. Machine guns clattered and much yelling could be heard further down where René guessed the Americans were making their advance. He watched his breath rise, small white clouds in the crisp, clear, frigid air. He then inhaled deeply and bolted across the open roadway as he exhaled. René counted his steps as he ran, waiting for a hail of bullets to mark his entrance into town and the German welcoming. He had cheated death once already this night. René doubted he could do it again.

55. Wolf – Ultimatum

December 25, 01:10 Hours – Ardennes Forest Barn

Adolf Wolf waited impatiently as Mueller prepared Elise to travel. Mueller hoped he could pull Elise and her baby in the cart they had used as her makeshift bed. He tucked in the blankets as best he could to ensure she and her baby were snug and warm.

Explosions landing closer to the barn made Wolf more animated and hearing shrapnel hit the back of the barn drove him to announce immediate departure. Mueller staggered as he brought the cart around to the front of the barn. His ribs were screaming and he wondered how he could possibly maneuver the cart in the snow. He hoped that Wolf would have the MP help him pull the cart, but he knew if the shelling became too tense, Wolf would either abandon them or kill them. He felt certain Wolf would choose the latter.

Ignoring the burning in his chest, Mueller coerced the cart to the front of the large double door, the only means of exit for the awkward wagon. He was about to remove one of the cross-boards that held the double door in place when two distinct eruptions of gunfire were heard. As a soldier, he recognized the first as an American Thompson and the second as a German machine pistol. He also knew that all things being equal, usually the first to fire won a gunfight.

Mueller immediately concluded that the gun was Conley's and his initial reaction was relief that the man was still in the area and might be of help. Then Wolf spoke and his optimism vanished like a light bulb shattered in the night. Apparently, Wolf had assessed the situation and came to the same realization as Mueller – but had other plans.

"Leave that beam in place!" Wolf ordered Mueller. "And move away," he pointed with his Lugar to the back of the cart.

"You," Wolf said under duress and looking at Becker, "cover the entry door should the American burst through."

Becker hurried to a position on the near side of the barn that gave him a clean shot at the entrance should it open. In the seconds that followed everyone in the barn just stared at the door. There were additional explosions and muffled gunfire heard erupting from the town, but in the barn all eyes remained fixed - waiting.

After a number of seconds ticked off, Wolf moved to the side of the entrance. He stopped a few feet away and yelled through it. "American, put down your weapon and come in the barn with your hands on your head! Otherwise I will be forced to take the life of this civilian and her baby!" he added.

Mueller's stomach soured as he heard the absurdity of Wolf's words. "You take her life and you're a murderer!" he cried out.

He was about to say more but Wolf silenced him, pointing the Lugar directly at his chest. "You shall remain silent, that is an order! If you do not, I will shoot you now!"

Mueller suddenly realized that if Wolf killed the civilians, he'd kill him too, to ensure anonymity if nothing else. Mueller swallowed what he was thinking in a sigh. More time passed in silence only interrupted by the rumble of explosions and gunfire in the distance and an occasional stray boom in the nearby woods and pasture.

Wolf's impatience finally reached a crescendo - he screamed out to Conley in a menacing, high-pitched shriek, "I will not speak again! You have ten seconds to decide."

Mueller looked at the MP. The SS man in the American uniform looked calm and returned his gaze. Mueller had few doubts that he would carry out Wolf's orders to kill them all if directed to do so.

56. Lindquist – New Orders

December 25, 01:11 Hours – Ardennes Forest Road, Luxembourg

Just as Lindquist was about to resume his patrol, his radio buzzed. It was command giving him a change of orders. Miller's tank had been freed from the culvert. Miller's Sherman, now accompanied by another half-track, were on their way to meet him. Lindquist's orders were to wait for Miller and company to arrive, then proceed to the road junction he was close to intersecting. Once at the road junction, he was to take up defensive positions so that nothing would get up or down the road. Additionally, a Sherman was being sent from Heiderschied to check for Wheaton's lost patrol and any enemy presence along the main road. It would meet up with Lindquist at the road junction and add to the blockade. Between this Sherman, Lindquist's and Miller's, plus the two armored half-tracks, a formidable post should be established.

Lindquist strolled over to the half-track and informed Delminico and Smitty of the new orders. As they waited for Miller, night seemed to turn into day as the American artillery began shelling Eschdorf in advance of the 1:00 AM attack. Through it all, a German machine gun could be heard rattling off in defiance of the bombardment and Lindquist wondered if it was the same MG-42 that Wheaton mentioned had been raking the ground near his position.

"Nice Christmas present for the Krauts," Deliminco stated quietly as he watched the pyrotechnics less than a mile away.

"Yeah, the shit's starting to fly," Lindquist commented.

"The Germans will still put up a hell of a fight, even with all that shelling," Smitty added.

Lindquist and Delminico nodded their agreement.

As they watched the barrage batter the town, the men heard a vehicle making its way up the road behind them. Delminico looked at Lindquist with uncertainty, but Lindquist seemed to recognize the engine sound. Delminico relaxed a bit. "That Miller?" he asked, speaking over the engine noise.

"Definitely a Sherman," Lindquist replied.

Soon Miller's tank, followed by a half-track, came up on Lindquist's position. Lindquist and Delminico left the half-track and hurried over. The two men climbed on the tank as Miller opened the turret hatch and popped out.

"Didn't think I'd see you so soon," Lindquist remarked at Miller, who looked cold but was wearing a smile for the first time that night.

"Neither did I. Turns out at the end of the ravine it becomes less steep." Miller shifted toward the half-track immediately behind him. "With a little help from Joe Jackson and his half-track back there, it wasn't that difficult getting out."

Lindquist stared back at the half-track but couldn't make out much in the darkness. He nodded in Jackson's direction.

Just then a large explosion hit the woods rather close to their left. The men flinched, their eyes blinking at the bright flash.

"Close miss," Miller commented. "Be ironic getting killed by our own artillery."

"Sadly, we wouldn't be the first," Delminico replied seriously.

"We have new orders," Lindquist hollered, above the noise. Now the sound of heavy gunfire coming from town filled the air.

"I heard about those orders," said Miller. "Hold the road junction."

"Yes, and we should get on it," Lindquist added. "I'll cross and take the far side of the road; you and Jackson hold this side."

"Roger that," said Miller.

"Let's go," Lindquist ordered, as he and Delminico slid off the tank and fled to their vehicles.

Miller dropped below, buttoned up the tank, then buzzed Jackson on the radio to relay the plan. Once Lindquist pulled out, he barked orders to his crew below to join the procession.

57. Tiny, Tucker, Delminico – Crossroad

December 25, 01:14 Hours – Ardennes Forest Road

For the two SS soldiers and their American prisoners, the drive toward Eschdorf had been more than eventful. After being placed rather harshly in the back of the Kubelwagen, Tucker began coughing up blood and convulsing. His thrashing in the back of the Kubelwagen became so severe, the SS men pulled the vehicle over. Tiny wasn't sure if the stop was to allow him to attend to the critically wounded man, or to shoot him.

Tiny knelt over the dying man to administer one of the morphine shots that Conley had given him. One of the SS guards nudged him with his machine pistol. "Rasch machen," he uttered menacingly. As if hearing the order to hurry up and complying, Tucker stiffened then went limp. He was dead - the morphine had been too little too late.

There was no doubt that Tucker's passing had been slow and painful. The man had literally bled to death. Tiny took a deep breath, felt a wave of emotion riding over him. He had known his friend was dying, knew he would succumb given the harsh conditions and lack of medical help. Yet death still hurt like a kick in ribs, the finality of it, the friend he had literally carried for miles, another casualty of a senseless war. Tiny was still leaning over his dead companion, eyes glassy, mind awash, when he felt the icy steel of the SS soldier's gun muzzle dig into his neck, this time harder - it was time to go.

Tiny rose slowly on shaky legs, still staring down at his dead friend. He wanted to gather Tucker up, bring the man to town for a proper burial, but he knew that wouldn't happen. Tucker, like Ryan, would become another frozen corpse, to be retrieved by the graves registration units once the area was secured. The SS guard shoved him hard, clearly miffed at his sluggish response to the order. Tiny stumbled his way to the Kubelwagen, hitting the side of the vehicle with a thud. He was escorted in via a hard push into the back seat.

As the vehicle proceeded down the road, it was obvious to Tiny that they were heading toward a town under siege. Explosions lit up the sky and the sound of gunfire was rampant. He wondered if the SS men had an alternate destination in mind, maybe someplace north of Eschdorf, where the Germans still held ground.

The vehicle rounded a curve and headed down a straight section of road where the tree line broke, exposing a narrow secondary road. It was hardly visible in the dark from either side. As the Kubelwagen began to cross, a shadow appeared that materialized into a large heavy vehicle, vying for the same piece of road. The SS driver applied the brakes but it was too late. The Kubelwagen skidded directly into the other vehicle's path. As metal hit metal, the Kubelwagen was deflected by the much larger vehicle, rolling it on its side where it slid to a stop across the road.

*

With little light to guide him, Delminico had little time to see that the road ahead was ending and intersecting with the main road. He was driving by instinct and as the road quickly came upon him, he reacted, turning onto it. As he spun the wheel he heard a screech and then the sound of metal being deformed under the front end of the half-track. He initially thought he had hit a road marker, but quickly realized he collided with a vehicle, a much smaller one he had literally rolled and pushed across the road.

"What was that?" Smitty called to him from his gun perch above the cab.

"I hit something," Delminico called up. "A car I think – be ready on that Fifty."

Lindquist's tank skidded to a stop in back of the half-track, not sure what happened. Lindquist buzzed the half-track's radio.

Delminico picked it up and spoke before waiting for his Sarge to ask. "Just hit a vehicle. Knocked it over and across the road. Not sure if it's a friendly or not."

Lindquist had his Sherman nose around the edge of the half-track. He couldn't go past the half-track – the road was too narrow – but he was able to angle the Sherman just enough to directly face the disabled vehicle. He lowered his turret, ready to disintegrate the vehicle with the tanks 76mm gun. Between the tanks weapons and the half-track's fifty caliber machine gun the vehicle was well covered.

Lindquist couldn't make out the vehicle. "What's the deal?" he yelled into his mic.

"Can't tell! I need to get out and check," Delminico replied. "Cover me!"

"Don't be a hero," Lindquist countered.

"You never have to worry about that," Delminico quipped in reply.

Delminico grabbed the carbine in the seat next to him and gave the Kubelwagen a long stare. He could see nothing but the dark form of a vehicle. There seemed to be no movement or life coming from within. Delminico carefully exited the half-track, keeping his carbine pointed at the vehicle as he did. He glanced across to Smitty who had the large fifty caliber machine gun zeroed in on the damaged car. If there was as much as a hiccup from the vehicle Smitty was ready to plug it full of large holes.

*

The driver in the Kubelwagen was rendered unconscious by the collision with the half-track. The other guard and Tiny were also badly shaken by the impact. Both men's heads had hit the frozen ground through the side windows as the vehicle flipped on its side. Their helmets deflected some of the blow but both blacked out for a few seconds after the crash.

Tiny opened his eyes and found himself looking upward into darkness. All around him there was silence, and he wondered whether the two SS men were alive. He thought about making a move to exit the vehicle but wasn't sure how to move his contorted body.

*

Delminico approached the vehicle, circling from the back. The vehicle started taking shape and he recognized it as German in the pale moonlight. He was tempted to back away and just have Lindquist fire his cannon, but thought Command might not appreciate that. This looked like an officer's car and given they were attacking the town, taking an officer or two prisoner might be of high value.

He deliberated briefly on how best to close in on the vehicle. Being on its side, the driver's door was facing up and opening it would be difficult without making himself an easy target. Delminico decided he'd peek through the front window, which was at ground level, and see who or

208

what was inside before trying the door. He carefully made his way toward the front of the Kubelwagen.

*

Tiny sensed motion outside the Kubelwagen, but figured it German, given the proximity to town. He wondered why there was so much caution, thought it concerning that the vehicle might explode, although he smelt no smoke or saw any flames.

He looked up over the seat in front of him. Both SS men seemed to be unconscious, no movement evident. The driver had slid across the seat upon collision and now lay on top of the other SS guard in a heap.

Suddenly the little light provided by the quarter moon faded as a shadow appeared in front of the glass. Tiny strained to see what appeared to be the outline of an American GI. He was about to call out, but caught movement in the front seat. The SS man under the driver had regained consciousness and had also seen the shadow. He was working the muzzle of his machine pistol up to a firing position.

Tiny found it hard to move in the restricted turned space but twisted and snaked his way, managing to lodge his large body between the two seats. With a grunt he came down on the SS soldier bearing considerable weight. While the driver on top of the guard buffeted the blow, Tiny's weight locked the SS man in. His right hand found the SS guard's throat. While he couldn't engage his left arm due to the confined area, the pressure on the German's throat was enough to force the man to release the grip on his weapon.

Unable to turn the gun toward Tiny, the SS guard opted for a new plan. He felt for his trench knife at his waist, finding it barely within reach. The SS soldier, fighting for his life, struggled to get the grip he needed to retract it from its sheath. The guard knew it would be a race to see if he could remove the knife and use it before the big man choked him to death.

Tiny knew nothing of the knife. His immediate concern was not getting shot by the man outside the vehicle. "I'm an American GI!" he screamed.

Meanwhile, the SS man found the grip he needed on the knife. He slid it out of its sheath.

*

Delminico heard the American shout out. "Hold fire!" he yelled toward Smitty and Lindquist. He spun around and climbed up the vehicle reaching for the door.

*

The knife was out. All the guard needed to do was swing it. Tiny was still oblivious to the weapon, trying to keep the pressure on the man's throat from a difficult angle. The SS man tried to will the strength to swing the blade, but things were going dark. He wanted to give in to the darkness that was surrounding him. He fought it.

*

Delminico was on the door pulling to open it.

The guard swung the knife.

The door opened.

The knife blade winged by Tiny's shoulder embedding itself in the seat. For a moment, Tiny didn't know if he should release his grip to deal with the knife or continue applying pressure.

"Move!" Delminico screamed.

Tiny released his grip from the man's throat and collapsed in the back seat.

Delminico looked at the SS man who was gasping, struggling to breathe. The German's eyes slowly focused on him standing over the open door of the vehicle. The guard defiantly moved his right hand back toward his machine pistol in an attempt to free it. Delminico had seen enough and the carbine erupted.

58. Conley – Decision Time

December 25, 01:15 Hours – Outside Ardennes Forest Barn

Conley had no illusions – he realized the exchange of gunfire between him and the guard had been heard in the barn. He also knew the sound would travel for some distance across the woods and expected German troops to arrive from the road below, but in the seconds that followed there was nothing but silence.

Finally Conley stood up, not seeing any movement from the shadow he had shot. His body felt stiff all over and the nervous perspiration that covered him from the brush with death moments before now stung like a horde of needle pricks as the chill enveloped him like an icy blanket.

Conley heard a voice, muffled through the closed door but clear enough that he understood the demand. It was the German officer ordering him into the barn. Then came the *"forced to take the life of the civilian and her baby."* A different kind of chill suddenly cloaked his body. Ryan's words about the Germans not taking prisoners came to mind. Given that he'd just killed one of his men, Conley doubted whether the German Lieutenant would let him live. Still, if it meant life for Elise and her baby, Conley would do whatever he had to - he was a man of his word.

But… how could he be sure the officer wouldn't kill him and then kill Elise and Anna? Mueller wouldn't let that happen. But how could Mueller stop it? Conley thought about yelling back for an assurance that Elise and Anna would be safe, but realized that would gain nothing. He held none of the cards! Conley was playing this hand of poker with only the joker – and in that moment, the joker was him. His mind raced for an answer, thoughts careening like a pinball bouncing from bumper to bumper.

Wolf screamed from the barn again, giving him just seconds to decide. For a moment panic consumed him and running away felt the right thing to do. But Conley stood firm, knowing time had run out and with it his options. It was now up to Mueller to protect Elise and Anna. Perhaps

Mueller couldn't save them, but he believed that, like him, Mueller would do whatever he could to try. Conley laid down the Thompson, and approached the door.

He gulped hard. "I've dropped my weapon. I'm coming in!"

Conley paused for a second, looked upward and said a quick silent prayer. Then he slowly opened the door and entered. In the dim light of Andre's lantern, he saw the German Lieutenant standing to his left. The man was looking at him but for some reason his Lugar was pointed at Mueller who stood by the cart with Elise holding her baby. Looking right, he saw a man dressed in an American MP uniform with a carbine pointed at him.

The German Lieutenant smiled, or at least it appeared to Conley that the corners of his mouth rose.

The Lieutenant looked over at the MP then back at him. "Shoot him," he said casually.

59. René – Empty Search

Without realizing it René had traced the same route in reverse that Andre and Elise had used to escape the forsaken town. Now he stood in the cobbler shop basement, breathing heavy, trying to imagine where they might be. He remembered that before the Germans came, the townspeople gathered together in the basement of the school house for air-raid drills. It made sense that during the American shelling, the locals would gather together for support. It was also Christmas Eve or it had just been... perhaps the townsfolk wanted to spend some time in fellowship and prayer.

Making his way as quietly as possible, he navigated his way around the block to a vantage across from the school house. René studied the area around the school for several minutes, searching for any signs of German troops. He spied a half-dozen Grenadiers in a half-track in direct sight of the entrance of the school, but otherwise the street seemed vacant. He hoped it meant that most of the soldiers were positioned elsewhere, defending the perimeter of the town. René knew a way to the school basement through an adjacent building, figured it would be safer that way, avoiding sneaking by the Grenadiers. He could still hear the dueling machine guns spitting out hot lead, where the main road entered the town, hoped he could use the American attack as a diversion to buy him the time he needed to find Elise.

René sprung on soft heels, retraced some steps to pull out of sight of the Germans at the half-track, quickly crossed the street, then closed the short distance, slipping into the building next to the school. René searched frantically for the stairway he knew would take him down to the basement, but the front of the building had been hit by a shell during the bombing. Where he expected stairs he found instead a small mountain of wood, twisted metal and cement. René groped in the dark to the building's far side finding a stairway there. He felt his way down, step by step until they gave way to a cold, dirt floor. René wondered if the shell

213

that hit the building had penetrated down that far and if his passage was obstructed by rubble. René navigated across the basement floor in slow motion, unable to see more than a foot in front or behind him. He crawled at a snail's pace, his hands reaching out ahead, feelers. René was a blind man in a mine field, not knowing where he was or when he might run into something. He was making progress, at least he thought so, but René really didn't know if he was even moving in the right direction.

Panic ran up his spine like the rats he knew shared the underground space. He fought back, felt his life wasn't worth anything if not with Elise and their child to be. He had beat worst odds to get to the town, he could overcome the darkness to find her… he had to.

René continued, unsure but determined. As he looked up a dim light appeared a short distance away. He stopped, tried to focus. Thought there might be voices too. If he could just hear over his thumping heart. René took a long, slow breath, then another. He felt better. There *was* thin light filtering through – flickering, perhaps a candle. He crawled another ten feet or so, until he found it, the small corridor that linked the two buildings. On the other side, he heard them, voices now resonating clearly. René stopped again, listening intently, needed to know who owned the voices before making an appearance. What he heard was not the dialog of German soldiers, it was townspeople. René had found the school cellar. He gave thanks, his mind anticipating Elise being there, in his arms soon.

Sadly for René, she was not there and worse, while Elise was not far away, at that moment she was in grave danger.

60. Conley, Wolf – A Time to Die

December 25, 01:21 Hours – Ardennes Forest Barn

Wolf gave the order and with that there was an immediate crack. Elise screamed and Anna wailed. Conley braced and closed his eyes momentarily, expecting to be driven back by the bullet's impact, but upon opening them, instead saw the MP jerk and crumble to the floor. Conley turned quickly back toward Wolf, to glimpse Mueller behind him with a Lugar in his hand moving away from Elise and positioning the weapon toward the German Lieutenant for a second shot.

Mueller had executed his hastily conceived plan. He correctly guessed that Wolf would shoot Conley when the American entered the barn and kept his Lugar concealed but ready. What he hadn't considered until he pulled the trigger was that Elise and Anna were immediately behind him and in the line of fire should Wolf shoot at him and miss. Mueller believed he could get a second shot off at the Nazi Lieutenant before the SS man could react, but even if hit, Wolf could return fire. Not willing to take a chance on Elise or Anna's lives, Mueller jumped quickly away from the cart and in the direction of the fireplace.

Hearing the crack of the gun, Wolf also expected the American to fall, but instead watched Becker collapse. He immediately pieced together the situation and cursed himself for not searching Mueller. Wolf spun his head quickly, spied Mueller retreating away from the cart, hastily repositioned his aim and fired. For a moment Conley found himself lost in the action, like he was watching a Saturday matinee. But when Wolf turned his gun on Mueller, Conley sprung, leaping on Wolf's back in a punishing tackle, a second after the Nazi triggered the shot. As he was being savagely driven to the floor, in desperation Wolf fired twice more. One bullet went wide hitting the edge of the fireplace, the second chewed up the dirt floor. Conley knew if he missed the chance to put the German away it could cost all of them their lives. He couldn't reach the gun in Wolf's extended hand. Instead, when he hit the floor with Wolf, he slammed the German's head into the ground.

Elise screamed out some words that Conley could not understand as the baby continued to wail. He stole a quick glance at Mueller, saw him down and not moving. *Was Mueller dead he wondered? After all that happened this night, to be shot by one of his own countrymen.* Conley felt the rage surging, like a volcano beginning to erupt, the need to kill Wolf now consuming him. He reached down his leg for his trench knife.

After his head hit the floor, everything went fuzzy for Wolf, but the Nazi was able to quickly shake it off. When Conley shifted his attention to Elise and Mueller, Wolf felt the American's hold on him relax slightly and saw an opportunity to strike. He spun swiftly and swung his Lugar in a sweeping motion that would connect with Conley's jaw.

Elise shrieked a warning to Conley but was a little late. Conley felt his face go numb as the back of the Lugar connected with his cheek. Fortunately for Conley, Wolf couldn't generate the power he needed from the ground to administer the blow with real force. Somewhat dazed, Conley grabbed the German's arm and twisted the gun away. In doing so, he realized he was inadvertently positioning the weapon at Elise. Wolf recognized this as well. He blurted out an unintelligible snicker and applied force to the trigger. His finger slid over it, however, as he had lost the grip he needed when he hit Conley's jaw. Wolf frantically clawed to reposition his finger to get the pressure needed to fire. Conley used that precious time to force Wolf's gun hand down. At the same time he drove his trench knife into Wolf's ribs with his other hand. Wolf's throat gurgled as he turned his attention back to the American. It was too late though as Conley, now in a frenzy, incensed that Wolf would shoot a young mother and baby, punched the blade, slamming it deep into the Nazi's chest four more times in rapid succession. Blood spurted and air hissed as the knife ripped through flesh and punctured lung. Wolf gasped with each thrust, his eyes bulging before his body went limp on the floor.

Conley suddenly felt exhaustion consume him and his body buckled over the dead Nazi. Through the baby's cries, he heard Elise calling for Mueller. When he looked up, Conley saw her struggling to get off the cart with Anna in her arms in an attempt to get to Mueller. With considerable effort, Conley pulled himself up. His head pulsed like waves pounding a shoreline and with his first few steps he swayed like a drunken sailor on shore leave.

"Stay in the cart," he fumbled words to Elise, who was herself weak and still working to get off her makeshift bed, baby held tightly in her arms.

She stared at him in resignation, too tired and too feeble to argue. "Please help him," she muttered, tears streaming down her face.

The throbbing in Conley's head eased slightly after he had been standing a few seconds and the swirling room seemed to slow down. He managed a nod to Elise and stumbled his way to Mueller, almost falling over as he bent down to examine him.

The German stirred as Conley touched him. "Come on, don't die on me now," he said, searching for Mueller's wound.

"Is he alive?" Elise called out, straining to see from the cart, heavy emotion in her voice.

"Looks like a wound in the upper chest area," Conley replied. "I'm hoping it's a shoulder wound, but I can't tell, there's a large blood stain and little light to see."

Conley rummaged in his uniform pockets and retrieved the last bandage he had. With much effort he also salvaged a wet towel and the flashlight by the fireplace. With the added light and towel, Conley was able to find the wound.

"Did you find it? His wound – did you find it?" Elise asked in an anxious tone. She was now sitting up on the cart, overseeing Conley's triage.

"Yes... in the shoulder."

"So he will survive?"

"I believe so."

Mueller regained consciousness as Conley cleaned and treated his wound.

"You alright?" Conley asked, taking Mueller's good hand and having him hold the gauze in place against the wound.

"Take's more than a single bullet to kill me," Mueller grunted in obvious pain.

"Good to know," Conley replied, smiling.

"The shelling has stopped," Mueller pointed out, something they had all missed in the frenzy of the last few minutes.

"That is good – correct?" Elise asked from the cart.

"Well," said Mueller. "When the shelling stops, it usually means the infantry moves in... that the fighting will begin."

The words were sobering and for seconds there was nothing, the group contemplating their meaning. To each they held something different, but the common thread was evident. War indelibly changed lives and the words uttered by Mueller moments ago played as a private movie, flashing vivid images of war to each. Mueller was transposed to Eschdorf, saw his men fighting bravely but being chewed up by the big American machine one by one. Too many men, too many weapons, such a waste of life. Conley thought also of the besieged town, knew he should have been part of the attack, felt guilty that he wasn't. Still, Conley struggled to get beyond being the sole survivor of that firefight the night before. Was he special or just buying time for another bullet on another day? For Elise, the movie played out across two scenes – thoughts of René, dead or barely alive in an SS work camp, and the Gestapo again swarming the barn, taking Anna from her. Elise pledged she would die before she'd let that happen. Interestingly, a third scene found her mind's eye and she let it in, welcoming the hint of optimism it brought, offsetting those dark scenes that cloaked her in panic and despair. With a sigh she considered how this displaced trio had worked together despite their varying allegiance's to preserve life. Such an idiosyncrasy on this fateful night.

With Conley's help, Mueller moved closer to the fire. Conley also navigated the cart back to its prior location, by the fireplace, so that Elise and Anna could also enjoy the fire's warmth. It had waned since Wolf's terrifying visit, but with a little hay and some logs, it quickly regained new life. Conley considered whether stoking the fire was wise or if it would announce their location. Given all they had been through that night, the last thing they needed was more attention.

61. René – Coming Up Empty

December 25, 03:27 Hours – Town of Eschdorf

The shooting had stopped. The town was a hive of activity again as German troops regrouped. The wounded were evacuated to the town hospital, fatal casualties removed, troops repositioned, defenses strengthened, ammunition redistributed. The American attack had been repulsed, but at a cost... there was always a cost. And, the only sure bet to be made was that the Americans would be back.

The question in René's mind was when? With the town buzzing in the aftermath of earlier fighting and in anticipation of another attack, he was unable to resume his search for Elise. Every exit he attempted to use was blocked with soldiers from the Fuehrer Grenadier Brigade or worse, the SS. René knew that once daylight came, it would be nearly impossible to remain unseen, traversing building to building. With the passing of night he would lose his cloak of invisibility, his freedom to blend into the shadows. He had beat great odds to be so close, but until Elise was in his arms, a mile or five-hundred made little difference... they were still apart.

The townspeople in the schoolhouse basement welcomed him, seemed incredulous that he was able to escape the labor camp, for few had. They told him about the frightful incident, when the SS had carted people away for interrogation. While all agreed that Elise and Andre were not among those removed that day, no had seen them since. Given that the mother-to-be and her uncle weren't found in the cobbler shop, many feared and speculated the SS took them away, perhaps as retribution for René's escape.

René was not willing to admit defeat – couldn't accept that his escape might mean torture and death for Elise and Andre. It wasn't that he didn't believe the SS would use such tactics, it was more a gut feeling that his wife and her uncle could avoid such a scenario. René began to build his own theory as to their whereabouts.

"They must have left Eschdorf, retreated to the farmhouse," René tried to expound his case, to convince others of what he was trying to convince himself.

The few people around him looked at each other tellingly. While none came out and said so, consensus among them favored a notion of Gestapo involvement, the incident with the SS still too fresh in their minds.

"There is something else you haven't considered," a man named Rolf, a good friend of Andre's offered up.

"What is that?" René asked, pushing the last piece of bread, graciously shared by those in the basement, in his mouth.

"When I last saw Elise, she was very pregnant. Perhaps she was brought to the hospital to deliver the baby."

The words hit René hard. "Of course!" he blurted out loudly, rising to his feet, swallowing. "It makes perfect sense! Why hadn't I considered that?"

A new plan quickly formed in René's head. It would be difficult getting inside the hospital undetected. In his desperation, he considered killing a guard and using the uniform or perhaps playing the role of a medic, or an orderly. First however, he needed to make his way to the hospital from the schoolhouse without detection. With the streets now teeming with German troops – it seemed an impossible task.

René shared his plan with Rolf and those around him. They were aghast and let him know in no uncertain terms that killing a German soldier would lead to severe reprisals. "We can make it look like the result of the American attack," René said, a meek attempt to defend his idea.

"The Americans have not penetrated this far into town," Rolf argued. "There is a better way."

"Yes?" René asked anxiously.

"Axel Janssen, the town doctor, has been pressed into service by the Germans. If we can locate him, he would know if Elise is there and if she's delivered the baby."

"Finding him will be difficult and take time," René countered.

"I will go with you. I know where his office is." Rolf said.

"But how do we get to the hospital amongst the soldiers on the street?" René questioned.

"We don't use the street," Rolf replied as a coy smile found the corners of his mouth.

Shortly after, they headed out, using René's detour through the adjacent building. This time it was a little easier, aided by a candle. But they did not exit via the stairway René had used to get to the basement from the street. Instead, Rolf led René deeper into the building until they were amongst the sewer chambers. The network of pipes that serviced the city were a maze that René had never seen, nor could have negotiated without Rolf's help. The elderly Luxembourg civilian seemed comfortable guiding him along. The odor was not the most pleasant, but nor was it as pungent as René would have expected. He guessed the cold helped in that regard. After a lengthy, damp stroll guided by Rolf and a number of rats, they exited a short block from the hospital, behind it and in view of a rear door.

"Where are we?" René questioned.

"In back of the hospital," Rolf whispered. "Someone is coming. This way…,"

Rolf quietly led René around a corner and down an alley, away from the threat. They stopped behind some rubble, the rear entrance only a feet way. To reach Janssen's office, they would need to enter the hospital and navigate down a stairway. It wasn't far, but to do so undetected would be a challenge, for even at the rear entrance there was activity. They needed to wait until all was clear before proceeding. As they crouched, hiding, they could hear voices, soldiers nearby. Cigarette smoke stung their lungs as they waited, rigid and cold. Without warning, a soldier rounded the corner of the rubble, almost careened into René. "What is this?" the German snapped, startled at the sudden appearance of the two men in the dark.

René let the penknife drop down his sleeve, had it at the ready. He was about to strike at the German when Rolf intervened. "Dr. Janssen summoned us from the basement of the schoolhouse. He asked us to help him with stretcher duty. Unfortunately, we can't find him."

The German looked at them with doubt, then shoved them forward with is rifle. "Raus!"

René struggled to stay on his feet after the push. He knew his opportunity to kill the German was lost. Even worse, once the Boche checked his papers they would likely figure out who he really was. He and Rolf needed another plan... fast!

62. Conley, Elise, Mueller – Aftermath

December 25, 03:45 Hours – Ardennes Forest Barn

It took some time for Elise to settle Anna, but once done, one by one, the exhausted group succumbed to their tiredness. Only Conley remained awake, monitoring the sporadic gunfire coming from town. An undistinguishable clunk outside the barn, led him to patrol around its perimeter, concern burning within him that the SS might be probing the area in search of their missing lieutenant and his men. After two such trips, Conley nodded off into a fitful sleep, trying to stay alert to exterior sounds.

The baby's cries woke them up.

Conley noticed that the fire had waned and wondered if the baby awoke because of the chill settling in. He retrieved some hay and cut logs from the back of the barn and in little time had it rekindled and propelling heat. Elise bundled Anna in her arms, soothing the infant with a gentle sway. Elise's tenderness and Conley's fire soothed the baby and quickly Anna returned to sleep. Mueller seemed unaffected by Anna's waking. If he awoke he never let on.

In the quiet of the barn and glow of the fire, Conley and Elise exchanged glances. Despite his tiredness, Conley's eyes radiated at the sight of Anna snuggled up against her mother in makeshift swaddling and he smiled.

"What is it?" Elise asked him, a soft grin in return.

"This is new to me," Conley said humbly. "I've never seen a newborn interact with her mother."

"This is new to me too," Elise replied honestly.

"She definitely seems to know you're her mother," Conley said, sounding still in awe of what he was seeing.

"Why shouldn't she," Elise commented. "We've been together for nine months."

Mueller grunted and Conley came closer to the cart so as not to wake him with their talk. The truth be known, he was more concerned about stirring Anna. As he closed on the cart he could see the outline of Elise's face in the faint firelight. Her high cheekbones were accented and her eyes glowed softly. Conley suddenly felt like a youngster with a crush on teacher. He thought again about Elise's husband but couldn't bring himself to broach the subject. His mind wandered to her age. She couldn't be much older than he. It was another question Conley wanted to ask but wasn't comfortable doing so. In the end, it was Elise who asked, catching him off guard with her timing.

"How old are you, Private?" Elise queried. "You saved me and my baby and yet I know so little about you."

"Nineteen, ma'am," Conley answered, suddenly flushed, not sure if it was the fire or the discussion that fed the warmth he felt.

"You are so young to be so far from home."

"The war has displaced a lot of people," Conley replied, trying to sound worldly. As the words came off his lips though, he thought they sounded corny.

Elise responded with a bemused "Yes...," making Conley wonder if she was thinking of her husband, parents, Andre or even... him. His mind began to drift to a romantic place – he and Elise. After all, Conley rationalized, his bravery and bravado had saved them. Why wouldn't she fall for him, the hero...?

Helen flashed into his thoughts. When she heard of his heroism, Helen too would want to be his girl. His mind played out the fantasy - first he had no one, now two attractive woman sought his company. Conley looked at Elise and smiled, her eyes tired but as striking as ever. She smiled back and began to speak, "You and I...,"

Conley waited. His heart pulsed in circles feeling like a spinning top, but for the first time that night, not out of fear. *Here it comes*, he thought.

"...Have been through so much this night," she continued. "First, Uncle Andre and I had to run for our lives to escape from Eschdorf. We trudged through snow and bumped into dead Germans on our way, only to find our home reduced to tinder. Then, all that's happened in this barn. Losing Andre...,"

Elise signed deeply, her eyes becoming moist, welling up. A long second elapsed before she went on. "My precious Anna!" She paused again, trying to maintain composure. "And that horrible man, Wolf."

Conley nodded. "I know, hardly a typical Christmas Eve."

224

"I only hope…," Elise said, her voice cracking, "…that my René could have been here. I pray he is alive and will see his beautiful daughter soon."

Feeling like a child whose balloon abruptly deflated, Conley suddenly became uncomfortable. A quick glance cast to Mueller, revealed the man sleeping as though he had no cares. When Conley's eyes made their way back to Elise, he found her drifting off, either succumbing to exhaustion or lost in thought with René. Conley sighed, slowly made his way to an adjacent stall, and settled down once again.

As Conley lay on the hay, his mind ran in many different directions. He could hear renewed gunfire in the distance. Conley assumed it was coming from the town and hoped it was the American army driving the Germans out of Eschdorf in retreat. His mind conjured images of vicious house to house fighting and the thought of all the killing happening on such a holy night made him shudder. Conley paused and repeated what had been a ritual that night, uttering some words in prayer. Though a good Catholic boy, Conley had never prayed so much as he had since spending time in Europe.

Conley's attention shifted to Elise, disappointed how their conversation played out. He felt like an adolescent schoolboy for thinking that a married woman, with a newborn infant, would ever consider a young, inexperienced, grubby, GI-Joe like him. Conley replayed their dialog over and over, each time thinking how much better his words could have been phrased, feeling embarrassed that he came off sounding so immature.

What was it about her anyway? Or perhaps it was him, always playing the white knight to a damsel in distress. Helen found him again and with her, images of that day at Harvard, punching out that bully. A subtle realization washed over him like a mild rain on a summer day. Elise was a lot like Helen. Both women were strong and independent, yet feminine and attractive.

Conley drifted into a dreamy slumber, finding himself back home. It was the last time he saw Helen, saying goodbye as Conley, in army dress uniform, stood on her porch. A sea of emotions surrounded him and much like his discussion with Elise moments ago, finding the right words was like fishing on a slow day in the harbor.

Since the incident at Harvard, Conley and Helen had nurtured an unusual but close friendship. Helen was attractive and popular, and by senior year almost the whole school knew of her. She was runner up as prom queen and one of the school's best students. Conley in contrast, was little known, even amongst his own class, and with much effort, managed a low "B" average.

Although sought after by many boys in high school, Helen dated but did not have a steady boyfriend. Conley wasn't sure if it was Helen's choice or had something to do with her dad, who everyone knew as coach and respected to the point of fear. It was one of those topics Conley always wanted to ask Helen about, but knew he would never do.

As he stood on her porch facing her, the words she spoke reverberated over and over. "I'm so proud of you, Bill."

She leaned in and kissed him on the cheek, his face suddenly becoming flush in response. Standing there, like a bronze statue, Conley didn't know what to do. His dream played out like it had in real life, Conley doing nothing until Helen motioned him to sit down.

In that moment, Conley wasn't thinking of getting killed and not coming back. He was locked on how to keep Helen in his life, while he was overseas. As Conley sat on the porch bench, he uttered some words that should have come much easier, given he was talking to his best female friend. "Will you write?"

"Of course I will," came the response.

"I'll write every day," Conley blurted out, immediately knowing he gave away much too much of his feelings.

Helen smiled that captivating smile. "I would like that," she offered in return.

Conley received mail from Helen at least once a week for the first few months, but since he had been in combat, letters from her were less frequent. Conley wondered if the mail was just not finding him or if she had found other activities, or people to occupy her time. Letters from his parents still found him regularly after all.

In fitful sleep, Conley rationalized that girls like Helen and Elise were just not in his league, and he'd be best not to carry high hopes. Besides, his priority now was just to stay alive.

Conley drifted back to Helen's porch for a moment, but as he stared into her eyes the sound of a motor droned. He turned from Helen, looked up and down the street but could see nothing, yet the noise was still there... getting louder and closer. Wait, it's not a car, it's much bigger. Rousing from the broken dream, Conley instinctively reached for his Thompson. He rolled to the far side of the fireplace to give him line-of-sight to the door and focused on what might be out there. As he listened, Conley recognized the sound was a rumble, slowly increasing in pitch and volume. He determined vehicles were coming off the road and moving toward the barn. One sounded like a tank.

Conley rose, grabbed his helmet, and ambled to the door. He carefully opened it a crack and peered out, trying to be stealth. Seeing nothing and hearing only the droning engines, Conley swiveled it enough to step through, crouched low and entered into the dark, frigid abyss once again.

The icy air singed Conley's throat with each breath and the warmth gained from the barn was quickly drained from his body. Once outside, he could better discern the sound. Conley couldn't see in the dark, but was certain now the noise was a tank and at least one other vehicle. The question was – was it friend or foe? Conley found the feed barrel used to spy Wolf earlier that night and stared into darkness as the vehicles doggedly trudged a trail up the narrow road. He guessed the vehicles were passing the burned remains of the house and would come into view in less than a minute.

Conley caught a faint flash of light to his side, spilling from the barn door. He cursed silently, knowing the glow would be seen by the approaching vehicles as soon as they rounded the bend. Wondering if something was wrong, Conley left his position and retreated hastily to the barn. He found Mueller standing uneasily against the doorway, needing its frame for support. Mueller had also heard the rumbling engines and had wanted to investigate.

"You OK?" Conley asked.

"What's coming?" Mueller ignored his question.

"Don't know. I was waiting to find out."

"If they are American, I will surrender," Mueller said.

Conley thought about Mueller's statement. In Conley's mind the German had already surrendered to him, but he didn't question.

"You must save yourself," Mueller whispered hoarsely. "I will take care of Elise. No one will question... I am wounded."

"Could be more SS men," Conley cautioned.

"Go… I will fashion a story," Mueller continued, genuinely concerned for Conley's life.

The rumble was getting louder, the ground beneath them now quivering in response. Elise called out asking what was happening, and Conley knew he needed to get out of sight quickly.

He gave Mueller the briefest of nods, then retreated around the back of the barn, returning to the barrel. But Mueller wasn't fooled. He knew Conley wasn't ready to leave until he knew what or who was paying them a visit. They would both find out soon enough.

63. René – Hospital Visit

December 25, 03:47 Hours – Town of Eschdorf

The German who found them brought them to a room inside the hospital that acted as a holding area. There were other soldiers there, some sick, most waiting for treatment of minor wounds. The German soldier gave René and Rolf's papers a quick check, then left them in the care of the other men in the room, while he ventured off to find an officer to deal with them. Most of the other soldiers in the area paid them little mind, each nursing his own ills, but one of the Germans, a Corporal Hamm, seemed to make the men his personal responsibility.

"Why isn't an able bodied man like yourself fighting for the good of the Fatherland?" he inquired sarcastically of René.

René said nothing but Hamm wouldn't let it go. "What is it with you? Are you ignoring me?" he badgered.

"Ah... no," René finally responded, trying at all means to avoid trouble. "I didn't realize you were speaking to me."

The German rose, impressing René with his size. Hamm limped over to him, stood over René who was sitting on a bench. "I think you are arrogant!" the Corporal said, his finger poking René's chest.

"Come now," Rolf cut in. "We mean you no harm. My friend here has served, he was sent back because a shell has impacted his hearing," he lied.

Hamm was not impressed, seemed to see through the charade immediately. He fixed a glare on Rolf, clenched his fists and opened his mouth to say something but was interrupted from behind.

"Gentleman," the voice said. It was doctor Janssen.

"Hello Axel!" Rolf sputtered, turning quickly away from the big German. "I'm so happy to see you!"

Doctor Janssen shot Rolf a curious look. When his eyes fell upon René he gasped slightly, as though he had seen a ghost.

"Hello...," he said again, his voice nervously rising.

Rolf jumped in as René was beginning to understand he did often. "We are here per your request for stretcher help."

The men exchanged long glances. "Yes... I see," Janssen said unevenly after an extended pause. The doctor guided the large German back to a seat. "Please come... Someone will be with you shortly," he offered before returning his attention to the two townspeople.

"Perhaps we could discuss our duties in your office?" Rolf inquired, leading slightly with nodded head.

"Ah... yes...," Janssen replied. "This way...,"

"Halt!" Hamm, the big German shouted turning a number of heads in the room. "Those men were told not to leave this room. We," he looked around at other soldiers in the area, "were asked to ensure it."

Janssen walked over to the German Corporal, standing before him but talking to the room. "I am Doctor Janssen. I requested these men to help me with stretcher duty during the pending American attack. If there are questions, my office is down the hall and clearly marked with my name." He exited stiffly, escorting René and Rolf as he did. Janssen thought he might be challenged, but was not, despite a number of glares. René and Rolf followed him to his office, a small, overstuffed room, smelling of sterilizing alcohol. He shut the door behind them, found his desk and sat heavily, placing shaking hands on its paper-strewn top.

"Are you trying to get me shot?" he gagged out.

"I'm sorry Axel," Rolf began. "It was the only way."

"Only way for what?" Janssen looked over at René. "And you... did they release you?"

"I left," René said, careful of his words.

"What! You mean escaped!" Janssen blurted out forcefully.

René ignored him. "Elise... is she here? Has she had the baby?"

It started to make sense to Janssen. He took a long breath. "No, I have not seen Elise in three or four days now. She was well when I last examined her. It won't be long now – any day I'd say."

Janssen looked at the two men before him, saw their concerned looks. It was then he realized, "Is she no longer in town?"

"We don't know," Rolf replied. "René has been to the cobbler shop and the school, has not been able to find her or Andre."

"They must have left for the farmhouse," René said through a trance-like stare.

Janssen nodded. "That sounds like something Andre would do. Perhaps with an American attack coming, he felt it better to leave."

"I must get there," René spit out, turning for the door.

"Hold on my friend," Janssen called out nervously. "Those Germans will be back, looking for you. As it is I will catch hell for requesting, what did you call it, stretcher help, without getting authorization. If the Germans suspect that I am in any way helping the enemy, my family..." he stopped, looked down. "You know...,"

Just then there was an explosion nearby, flickering the lights. There were shouts in the hallway. *Boom*...another one, the Americans were shelling again.

"That was close," Janssen said, rising. "There will be injured, they will be looking for me."

"This may be the diversion we need," Rolf cried, stopping Janssen as he came around the desk.

Janssen looked at Rolf, then René. He turned back to his desk and opened the side drawer, pulling out a pair of scrubs. "René, put these on. If anyone asks you're an orderly looking for wounded. The back entrance is to the right. Good luck." He turned to Rolf. "You, stay with me."

Rolf smiled at René, grabbed his hand and shook it. "God be with you," he said. He then followed Janssen out the door. René knew he was on his own again.

64. Conley – New Visitors

December 25, 03:55 Hours – Ardennes Forest Barn

The vehicles came into view and Conley could now make out the outline of the tank and half-track. He recognized the silhouette of a Sherman and breathed a sigh of relief. A thought crossed his mind regarding the German posing as an American MP, and Conley wondered if the Germans might have stolen American vehicles at their disposal as well. He knew he'd have to take that chance.

Conley realized he couldn't just step out when the vehicles drove by or they'd shoot him dead long before they recognized him as a fellow GI. He rested his Thompson across the barrel then walked out into the open, well ahead of the vehicles, making himself visible from a distance to hopefully be identified as a friendly. Conley placed his hands up to present as benign an image as he possibly could. Even then, given the black of night, he'd be just a shadow on a white carpet. Conley had little choice but to accept the risk he wouldn't be at the end of a large caliber machine gun bullet. This was still German held ground as far as the Americans were concerned. *Damn, perhaps there was a smarter way to approach this than stepping out in front of a half-track and tank*, he considered. *Too late now. Try to run and I'm a bullet ridden piñata.*

*

Delminico saw the shadow step out and slowed the half-track trying to discern the situation. Tiny had given him and Lindquist a full accounting of what had happened in the barn, including a warning regarding the SS and an American MP imposter. He would proceed with caution and take no chances.

Delminico grabbed his microphone. "Sarge, there's someone out on the path. Appears to be unarmed, hands are up."

"American?" Lindquist asked.

"Think so, really can't tell. After hearing about Krauts dressed as MP's... does it matter?"

Lindquist considered his options. "Have Smitty keep him sighted in his fifty. If he so much as sneezes wrong, yell *Gesundheit,* then plug that bastard full of lead."

"Will do, Sarge," Delminico answered.

After a pause Delminico's voice-box squawked again with Lindquist's voice, "Where it opens up just ahead, let me pass you. Then motor over to the barn and cover anything or anyone that might try to exit."

"Copy," Delminico acknowledged.

Lindquist looked around, saw nothing but darkness through his viewport, then spoke into the intercom for the men in the tank to hear, "Stay alert, eyes open for anything out of place. We'll shoot first, worry about the resulting shit later. Our lives trump anyone else's about now." Within the tank there were a number of silent nods as the men stood vigilant.

*

Conley stood shivering in the frigid air, arms up, exposed and in the open. He counted each frozen second as the vehicles slowly approached. Conley eyed a dark figure in the half-track covering him with the fifty caliber machine gun as it slowed, letting the tank pass. The huge Sherman closed in and Conley felt the ground shaking under his feet. With a sudden jerk the steel monster came to an abrupt stop beside him. For seconds it sat idling, as if sizing him up. Conley pictured the commander inside the tank, looking all around, deciding if it was safe to open the hatch, making himself and the crew vulnerable to ambush. *Hell, do something,* Conley thought, but as he put himself in the tank commander's spot, he understood the hesitation.

Conley held the stone-like pose, rigid and unmoving. He wanted, needed, to drop his hands and wrap them around his shuddering body, but to make any unwarranted move would not end well for him. He remained silent and statuette while the tank commander determined his fate.

Finally the turret hatch opened and the head and partial shoulders of the tank commander's dark form surfaced. For a moment the commander ignored the shivering Conley, still surveying the area prudently, eyeing the barn and the space around it before letting his gaze fall upon him.

"Who are you, soldier?"

"Bill Conley, Private, 328th, G Company, Squad three. On patrol last night... my platoon got ambushed. I'm all that's left."

Conley hoped his words were convincing. They were the truth.

Lindquist, nodded. "328th you say. G Company... That was Sergeant...,"

Lindquist paused and Conley guessed he was waiting for him to fill in the blank.

"Bo Morgan," sir,

"Yeah, Bo Morgan. Good man."

"The best," Conley quickly added.

Lindquist kept a steady fix on Conley as though still trying to size him up. After a few seconds he asked, "Who is your lieutenant, private?"

"That'd be Roger Wheaton sir," Conley spit out. Conley wondered if baseball questions would follow. He heard of GI's using this line of questioning to flush out German's in American uniforms.

Lindquist's demeanor relaxed a bit, hearing Conley's answers, but his questions continued.

"Who's in the barn?"

"A wounded German Sergeant, a mother and her newborn," Conley said flatly.

"That all?" Lindquist questioned.

"Yes sir," Conley answered.

"We heard there were some Krauts... SS, in this area," Lindquist said.

"Yes sir. They're dead."

"You killed them?" Lindquist inquired.

"Yes sir, with help."

Lindquist saw Conley's body shaking, his voice quivering in answering the questions. He knew the man was cold and scared. He had heard enough.

"OK, let's check out this barn of yours and you can tell me about how you killed those Krauts."

Conley nodded, grateful at the thought of thawing in the barn.

Lindquist yelled down the hatch to his driver and the tank lurched forward. He maneuvered the Sherman between the two trees that stood in front of the barn then positioned the turret so it pointed down the path. The half-track had pulled just forward of the barn, at the foot of the pasture, facing the woods behind the barn. This gave the vehicles fields of fire to cover the most likely approaches of the enemy in the event they were needed.

Conley was left standing alone when the tank drove off. He dropped his arms and tried to jog over to where the vehicles were assembling. It was like running in slow motion for Conley, his legs felt like timbers, struggling to accommodate the commands issued from his brain.

Conley arrived to hear Lindquist grunt a command to the men in the tank to keep the engine running and to take turns on watch. With that Lindquist pulled himself out of the turret and jumped down to the ground. "Sergeant Roger Lindquist, 735th Tank Battalion," he said by way of formal introduction.

Conley started a nod and was about to give the Sergeant his name and rank, but realized he had already done so. He drew back awkwardly and said nothing.

Lindquist smiled as one of the men from the half-track came up. "This is Delminico" he said, pointing.

"Private Bill Conley," Conley said, finally getting his introduction in.

Delminico nodded broadly. "So you're the patrol we were supposed to find."

Conley looked at him, confused, and was about to question him. He never got the chance.

Lindquist shivered and said, "Too cold to talk out here."

With that, Lindquist started walking toward the barn. Delminico quickly followed, leaving Conley again to catch up.

65. René – Dark Woods

December 25, 04:21 – Ardennes Forest, Outside Eschdorf

René embraced the woods as though welcoming an old friend. He had doubts when he fled the hospital that he'd ever make it this far and see these woods again. In truth, though, it had been much easier getting out than entering the ill-fated town. The Americans resumed their attack and the Germans in response were loud and visible, officers barking out orders and men moving to defensive positions. As a result René was able to map out and execute a clean get away.

As he crouched in the woods, René now faced a dilemma of a different kind. The woods were alive, the Germans manning perimeter defenses and the Americans sending probing attacks in an attempt to flank their way in. Initially he had the advantage coming up from behind the German troops lying in wait of the Americans. René found himself almost in the midst of a German machine gun position before glimpsing the white ground in motion, snow camouflaged soldiers searching the woods ahead for targets. He spun on his heels, slid away and circled in a wide arc away from the ambush in waiting. Shortly after, he encountered another German nest, but was more alert, saw it well in advance and was able to thread his way through undetected.

Although it was frigid, the cold did not bother René this night. Too much had happened, was happening now, to allow his mind to focus on the icy air. Instead he pondered the quickest means to get to the farmhouse. He knew the shortest route would be too dangerous, he'd continue to circle rather than travel as the crow flied. René traversed the woods putting distance between himself and the German perimeter defenses. He thought of how much time over the years he spent in these woods, as a child and as an adult. This part of the Ardennes had been like a friend to him, a place to hike, hunt and now take refuge. René hated that the forest, his forest, was now a place of death where men hunted other men. He recalled playing army as a child with his friends and having such fun. René wasn't having fun now.

He continued on a circuitous route finding the going sluggish in the deeper snow, as had Andre and Elise before him. When René was satisfied he was clear of the German defensive positions he turned toward the farmhouse. Now he needed to concern himself with the Americans. They would likely think him a German scout, probing their defenses and would likely shoot anything moving from the direction he came.

He improvised a plan, whereby he'd study the area immediately out front, looking and listening, hoping his instincts and knowledge of the Ardennes would help him discern any danger. Then he'd travel from tree to tree as quickly as possible, trudging through the snow until he felt the need to check again. On this night the forest was teeming with peril. Gunfire seemed to come from a number of directions, but was most prevalent toward the town as expected. Still, not far away, a machine gun hammered, spitting lead at shadows vying for entry into the town.

René rested, crouched behind a tree, catching his breath. He had completed four intervals of this makeshift plan and was beginning to feel comfortable that it afforded him some measure of secure travel. René pulled himself up, had taken but two steps forward when a sudden crack broke the silence around him, a bullet whizzing by his head and smacking the tree he used for cover. René spun, stunned by the loud pop, lost his footing on the slippery snow and tumbled forward. The slight pitch rolled him over and René skidded to a stop on his backside by some brush. Somewhat shaken, but still aware of the danger around him, René pulled himself into nearby brush, anything to provide cover. As he turned, hoping to get his bearings, René found himself staring at the barrel of a Thompson machine gun.

All things considered, René was a lucky man. Had he landed next to a less experienced soldier, his life might have ended at that moment. Fortunately for René, the GI at the other end of the Thompson was Sergeant Guy Calloway. Calloway was a seasoned soldier, having made the June landings on hellish Omaha beach and fighting his way through Belgium to Luxembourg from France one grim town at a time. Calloway noticed the civilian garb, held his finger on the trigger. "Freeze!" he ordered, his voice low and direct.

René did as instructed, eyed the GI cautiously. He hadn't gotten this far to be gunned down by those he considered allies. "I am a civilian," he said, in slow low tones.

Calloway seemed unmoved, the gun didn't waiver. "At least you're dressed as one."

"I have escaped Eschdorf and am searching for my wife, Elise, at our farm. She is due to have our baby any day."

The words struck Calloway like a two by four. Prior to leaving Hierheck he had heard radio intercepts from a tank commander named Lindquist, saying he was heading to a barn to pick up one of Bo Morgan's men and a local woman who had delivered a baby that night.

Calloway studied the man. If what he said was true, he could be very helpful. "You say you just came from Eschdorf?"

René nodded, "Yes."

"See many Krauts on your way out?"

"Yes, there are a number of Boche hiding in these woods."

"What if I told you I could get you to your wife before daylight in exchange for you guiding me through those Kraut positions?"

René fell back, reeling as if he'd been gut punched. "You can do that? You know where my Elise is? She is safe?"

Calloway hesitated at the word *safe*, because he also heard about SS in the barn's vicinity. "I heard some radio transmissions. No guarantees but a pretty good hunch." He looked at the civilian. Even in the dark the man looked desperate. "You in?"

René nodded, "This way…,"

66. Conley, Mueller, Elise, René – Departure/Capture

December 25, 06:02 – Ardennes Forest Barn

The sun came up late that time of year in Luxembourg. At 6:00 AM it was still dark as night with a smoky haze that hung in the frigid air like a frozen wreath. For the remainder of the night the barn had been quiet, although only a short distance away in the surrounding woods and town, a violent battle raged. Gunfire could be heard consistently, as well as the detonation of grenades, a grim reminder that war knows no holiday. Despite the town under siege the exhausted occupants in the barn slept undeterred, turning the sounds of battle into a curious kind of background lullaby.

The noise was subtle but discernable, low voices talking outside the barn. Conley turned, his hands on the Thompson before his eyes were open, a reflex action now. The tenseness in his chest yielded a bit, when it occurred to him that he was among friendly forces. After all, there was a guard outside; the voices he heard likely posed no threat.

Lindquist stirred as well and picking up on the muffled garb he opened one eye then the other. When he pulled up to his elbows he saw Conley on his feet, shuffling toward the door. The door opened just as Conley approached it and he found himself eye to eye with a young GI.

"Sorry to bother you sir," the soldier said. "I'm looking for Sergeant Lindquist."

"I'm Lindquist," the Sergeant said, coming up behind Conley. He waved the man inside, Conley quickly shutting the door to minimize the chill.

"Orders sir to escort a Private Conley and German POW back to command."

Conley and Lindquist exchanged glances, "It appears the US Army is most efficient at the most inopportune times," Lindquist said quietly.

Conley signed, "It was only a matter of time, Sir."

Lindquist nodded in agreement. "Give us a minute to gather up," he said to the GI. "What about the young mother, do you know about arrangements for her?"

"Yes sir, they're freeing up an ambulance from the fighting in town, should be here shortly."

Lindquist acknowledged the GI with another tip of his head, looked at Conley, "OK, let's get Mueller."

*

Calloway looked through brush at the roads edge. Thanks to his Luxembourg guide he had been able to slip the German defenses then surprise them from behind. By his count he had lost 7 men out of the three squads (thirty six) he led, but he had killed three times as many of the enemy. He was certain beyond a doubt, that without the guide, his losses would have been horrific.

René came up next to him. "What else can I do for you Sergeant?" he asked sincerely. Calloway looked at the map René had crudely fashioned of the town, shot the man a grateful look. "We're good here. You certainly kept your part of the bargain."

"I'm glad you feel that way."

"I'd like to offer one of my men to ensure you get back OK, but I'll need them. I scribbled you a note, in case you get stopped. Have them bring you to Sergeant Lindquist."

René smiled, taking the note. "Thank you Sergeant… And don't worry about me, I know my way back."

"I was told your wife is in a barn, on a farm you would have run into had you not found me. Do you know the place?"

"I know it well, Sergeant. It is my wife's property. I am surprised though she is at the barn and not at the farmhouse."

"The house is gone," Calloway said flatly.

The words caught René unaware and he jerked slightly, a bit of a gasp. "The war," he said in response, after a pause. Then he added, "As long as I have my Elise, all is good."

Calloway hoped that was the case, but held back any thoughts he had. "Thank you, my friend," he said instead.

René squeezed his shoulder, nodded to the other men, the few shadows he saw around him, then dashed into the woods. He hoped this time he would make it.

*

The goodbyes were difficult, usually are. Elise thanked them profusely, wished the two men well through a number of tears and called them her shepherds once again. After the somber farewell with Elise and Anna, Conley helped Mueller to the front seat of a waiting jeep, then hopped in back, before it drove off down the path and onto the main road. The men rode in silence, lost in their thoughts of the night and wondered what the new day would bring.

The sky took on a different look, Christmas day slowly evolving, clear and very cold. The sun would still not show for some time, but its nearness turned the black to a tepid gray and inky shadows now took on more form and shape. Conley and Mueller eyed one such shape – that of a German Kubelwagen on its side. The sight left both to wonder what carnage happened there, but neither imagined the vehicle as playing a role in the events of their night. Ahead of them the battle loomed as a murky canvas of smoke and gunfire. Both men were grateful when the jeep veered off, turning in the direction of Hierheck and away from the nightmare that Eschdorf now seemed to be.

*

René moved quickly, too quickly he cautioned himself. The woods were still alive and dangerous. He had come too far, endured too much, was so close to seeing his wife to throw it away by being careless. René resumed the plan he used before, of surveying an area ahead of him prior to covering it, although he was less enthusiastic given his not so successful attempt before. The start and stop approach slowed him down and René had to fight his impatience to continue with it. He was getting closer now, nearing where the woods ended by the pasture, when he saw them. René crouched low, the snowy brush providing cover, keeping out of sight, rifle sight.

It looked to him an American patrol, or perhaps just a guard post. Either way they could assist him or kill him. René considered re-entering the woods and circling the GI's but knew he was likely to encounter more. He swallowed hard, "Hello," he said in the best English he could form.

There was no reply, just a scurry as men repositioned their weapons.

"I am a civilian," he called out. "I am unarmed and would like to approach. I was a guide for Sergeant Calloway and have a note from him."

"Never heard of him," came a nervous reply.

René swallowed hard. This was not good. He tried another tack. "My wife Elise is in a barn, just ahead. I am trying to reach her."

Again there was silence.

"If you'd let me bring you this note from Sergeant Calloway," René called out, desperation seeping in his voice.

"I told you I never heard of him," came the harsh reply again.

René could hear movement to his side, knew he was being flanked. Would they shoot first he wondered? He knew he'd soon find out.

67. Conley, Mueller – Where the Road Ends

December 25, 07:45 Hours – Hierheck

The jeep entered Hierheck, drove up to a house used as an aid station for prisoners and skidded to a stop. The driver looked back, threw Conley a curious glance then uttered, "This is the end of the road for your Kraut friend."

Conley started to react but caught himself. He initially wanted to belt the driver, a young private, but after he thought about the situation, he understood the soldier's mindset. Until last night, he had never met a German soldier, had felt the same way this private did. Even now, he wondered how well he really knew Mueller other than their mutual respect for and willingness to help a pregnant woman.

Conley said nothing, jumped out of the jeep, then helped Mueller exit. When he turned toward the house he found a guard had come over. The GI looked them both over, then spoke to Conley in a slow southern drawl, "I can take it from here."

"He needs medical care," Conley noted.

"Inside the house," the guard grunted, as though Conley had stated the obvious.

"Can I go with him?" Conley asked.

"Why?" the guard snapped, suddenly defensive.

"Because he's weak, lost a lot of blood. He needs help to walk."

The guard gave Conley a pensive look. After a few seconds he uttered, "Suit yourself, but all weapons must remain in the jeep."

Conley braced Mueller against the front of the jeep, dropped his Thompson on the seat, then shed his belt and trench knife. When he was clean of weapons, Conley took Mueller under his good arm and the men slowly strode towards the house, the guard curiously pacing behind them.

*

The plan was executed perfectly. Almost as soon as René perceived movement on one side of him, a soldier burst through the other leveling an M1 with a bayonet at his chest. A nice piece of deception he thought.

He was patted down then pushed ahead to the remaining squad, where the GI he initially spoke to was waiting. René thought it interesting that when patting him down, they missed frisking his lower arm and did not detect his penknife. He also found the man in charge, a corporal named Ferguson, very young and very hard to convince that he was a friend.

"… I've told you I don't know how many fucking times, I don't know a Calloway," Ferguson said in a harsh whisper, turning away.

René signed, wanted to run, knew he'd be shot. Then the other name came to him. "Lindquist!" he blurted out. "Do you know a Sergeant named Lindquist?"

Ferguson turned back towards him, "How do you know Lindquist?"

"That's who this message is for."

"You realize, I have no idea where Lindquist is. For all I know he's in Eschdorf killing Krauts," Ferguson moaned.

"He is at the barn," René countered. "I can take you there."

"Slow down Frenchie," Ferguson uttered sarcastically. "I have orders to secure this flank and work my way toward town. I don't have time to play nursemaid to a civilian."

René sighed, this corporal was unyielding. His penknife brushed against his arm, the cold steel stirring a quick plot to strike and escape. Shove one into the other, he thought… outrun them to the barn... René felt panic rising and with it his level of desperation.

"Let me see that note," Ferguson ordered, giving pause to René's extreme planning. The corporal read the note, staring at it for a number of seconds. René thought he was trying to discern if it was genuine. "Stewart!" Ferguson suddenly called down the line in a whispered scream.

A short but stocky young GI made his way over, "Sir?"

"Stew… Josh Miller, one of Lindquist's men, is commanding a Sherman back on the road. Take this… civilian with you, ask him to verify that Lindquist is at a barn nearby and not in Eschdorf. If Lindquist is at that barn, bring this man to him and give him this note."

René's heart leaped. Finally! "Thank you," he said offering out his hand.

Ferguson stared at it for a second, didn't reach out. "Go Stew!"

*

Conley got Mueller to the door, knew it was time for goodbye. He put out his hand and Mueller pumped it.

"Good luck to you," Conley said.

"Good luck to *you*," Mueller stressed. "For me the war is over but for you…,"

Conley and Mueller's eyes locked, a knowing exchange, before Mueller turned and walked slowly but deliberately into the house where another guard waited. Conley stared at the door for a number of seconds, genuinely wishing the man well. He then pondered Mueller's last words, considered what his wartime future held. He looked up to the brightening sky, another day dawning, sighed, and started back to the jeep in the same slow, deliberate fashion as Mueller had moments before.

68. Elise, Lindquist, Delminico – The Breaking Dawn

December 25, 08:11 Hours – Ardennes Forest Barn

There would be no ambulance available to transport Elise and Anna away from the barn, that Christmas morning, while wounded and dying lay in the streets, houses and yards of Eschdorf. Additionally, now that the area around the barn was deemed secure, Command wanted Lindquist's Sherman and Delminco's half-track engaged in the fighting to provide much needed infantry support. Lindquist's orders were to see mother and daughter off safely, then join up with Josh Miller's tank, leading both Shermans to the battered town to face the Germans. Delminico was instructed to escort Elise and Anna in his half-track to Hierheck for medical care, then also proceed to Eschdorf as quickly as possible to provide fire support.

The barn was a flurry of activity as Lindquist and Delminico assumed the caregiver roles of Conley and Mueller. The men bundled Elise and Anna in preparation to wheel the cart out the barn's central double doors to the waiting half-track. Delminico had Smitty park the vehicle just outside the barn entrance to minimize time in the frosty air. Though the half-track wasn't heated the new mother and her child would be snug under the blankets and out of the elements.

The men had pulled the cart around the fireplace to the front of the barn and were almost ready to open the large double doors, when Smitty's voice echoed from outside. "Hey Sarge, need you out here."

Lindquist finished tucking in a corner of the blanket which worked itself loose at the edge of the cart during the move. He took a second to admire his work, stole a look behind him towards the door, then turned his attention to Elise, "Be right back ma'am," he said.

As he stepped outside, Lindquist noticed the new day was dawning, the sky much lighter now. It looked like it would be a bright day, sunny, although another cold one. He also noted two men, standing with Smitty... a young GI and a civilian. His mind raced at seeing the local man, wondering if the Resistance knew of German troops nearby.

"What's up?" he asked, approaching the men.

"Sarge," Smitty said, "You're not going to believe this."

"Try me," Lindquist challenged.

"Read this," Smitty said, handing him a note.

Lindquist read the short note and a huge smile spread across his face, the concern he had moments before fading away. "I'll be damned!" he said loudly. He looked at the civilian standing impatiently next to Smitty and motioned a hand toward the barn. "Merry Christmas, my friend. Merry Christmas!"

Lindquist watched the man bolt to the barn, heard Elise scream with joy seconds later. He smiled at Smitty and the other GI, snuck another look toward the barn, "… And to all a good night!"

*

A few miles away, eating a K-ration before rejoining his outfit, Bill Conley sat discerning all that ensued since his patrol set out the evening before. Conley felt a different man for the humbling experience, knowing he had played a role in bringing life into the world at a time when killing prevailed. He hoped his presence and all the blood shed by those who fought this *good* fight could create a better world for Elise to raise Anna and for both to lead fulfilling lives. Conley also thought of Mueller, had trouble now perceiving the man as an enemy. Perhaps Mueller was fighting because, as a German soldier, he had no other option. Given what he had learned about him, Conley found it difficult envisioning Mueller as embracing Hitler's Germany as a way of life. Mueller had taken a bullet for him, obviously he did not align with the Nazi cause as had the fanatical SS Lieutenant Wolf. Conley found he had only good thoughts for Mueller, wishing he survived the war and enjoyed a decent life. Conley warned himself that he couldn't let his empathy for Mueller make him indecisive on the trigger once back in combat, or his own life might come to a sudden, violent end.

As he took a swig of ice water from a nearly frozen canteen, that Christmas day in 1944, his restless mind shifted once again. Conley recalled Elise referring to him and Mueller as her shepherds. He had never considered himself one, Mueller either for that matter. But looking back he realized that perhaps there was truth in her words… and more. Not only had he and Mueller watched, guided and sheltered that memorable night, both had bonded together and fought savagely to

protect Elise and Anna as well. They had been shepherds indeed...
shepherds who roared.

Epilogue

Despite this being a story of fiction, I thought the reader none-the-less might be interested in the post-war lives of the main characters involved. What follows is a short summary of each character and the aftermath of that memorable Christmas in Eschdorf.

William Conley – While the war had turned sharply in the Allies favor following the Battle of the Bulge, there was still much bloody fighting to endure. Bill Conley, supported by a strong faith, close squad and letters from Helen Kinkaid, fought gallantly as part of the Allied Campaign to defeat Germany until the war's end in May of 1945. Upon returning home to Boston, he resumed work for his father's By-Products Company, eventually taking ownership. Bill married Helen and fathered two children, who in later years blessed him with three grandchildren and eight great-grandchildren. It took years for Conley to return to Europe, the loss of so many fellow soldiers affecting him deeply. He finally returned for the 60th reunion of the Battle of the Bulge in 2004 and was able to reunite with Elise and Anna. Conley died in 2006 at age 81 of natural causes with Helen and his family at his side.

Eric Mueller – Mueller spent the remainder of the war in a US prison camp. He returned home and lived his remaining years in Darmstadt, the town he grew up in. Mueller never married, instead preferring the carefree life of a bachelor. He returned to Eschdorf a number of times to visit Elise and Anna, endearing himself to be called "uncle" by the latter. Mueller became a successful business man, working as a manager for a German high-end car manufacturer. He was killed at age 59 in a car accident driving at high speed on the Autobahn.

Elise Lambert – After the war ended, Elise and René rebuilt the farmhouse on their property where they resided over their remaining years. Elise never had additional children and perhaps as a result she and Anna built an especially close mother – daughter relationship. In her later years Elise developed Alzheimer's, her memory intermittently fading so severely she had trouble placing even Anna at times. While not initially remembering Bill Conley when he visited, Elise was able to enjoy a reunion with him, her memory returning for a short while, surprisingly after Bill used the word "shepherd" in reference to that night. Elise died peacefully at age 83, only a few months after seeing Conley. Elise always believed he would return and Anna was certain her mom waited until his visit before passing.

Anna Lambert – Anna grew up on the farm with Elise and René as loving parents and enjoyed a wonderful childhood following the war. She married her high-school sweetheart, who became an attorney, moved to nearby Wiltz and worked in Real Estate. Anna and her husband, both retired, are the proud parents of three children, seven grandchildren and eleven great-grandchildren (and still counting).

René Lambert – Fortunately for René, the Battle of the Bulge turned the tide in the war with Germany and with it any concern regarding reprisal for his escaping the labor camp. Once reunited with Elise and Anna, he would never leave their side again, enjoying many memorable years in the farmhouse he rebuilt. A loving father, he was a devoted husband and caregiver to Elise, patiently standing by her through her Alzheimer's until her passing in 2005. His own health deteriorated shortly after and he died two years to the day of Elise's passing at age 85. Anna believed it was her father's way of honoring her late mother.

Helen Kinkaid (Conley) – There is an expression "the pen is mightier than the sword" and nowhere was this truer than with Helen and Bill. During the war, written correspondence allowed expression of an inner self Bill Conley couldn't easily communicate otherwise. As a result, Helen watched her friend mature into a man one letter at a time. While many of his letters were censured and Conley never shared of war's horror, Helen saw the progression. Though she dated other guys while Conley was at war, no one found the place he had touched with his weekly notes. Their relationship rekindled upon his return from the war, Bill and Helen married two years later. It was a relationship that stood the test of time, producing three children and spanning sixty years until Bill's passing. Helen was to pass three years later at age 83.

Nathan Lindquist – The Sergeant tank Commander never saw the end of Christmas day. One of the last casualties of the battle for Eschdorf, his tank was hit by a panzer-thrust rocket as the Germans retreated the town. His driver was the only member of his five-man crew to survive the blast.

Sal Delminico – The half-track driver survived Eschdorf but was wounded when his vehicle hit a mine during the Allied push into Germany. The "million-dollar wound" gave Delminico an early discharge and returned him home to New Jersey, where he ran a gas station on a busy corner in Trenton until he retired. He lived out his years at home in the same city, passing at the age of 87.

Josh Miller – Corporal Miller rode his tank all the way to Germany and was a witness to the fall of the Third Reich. Following the war he returned home to Denver, received an Engineering degree and worked for Boeing for thirty-two years until his retirement. He married a girl he met in college, had four children and lived happily until he passed at age 77. Even in civilian life the phrase most tied to him was "Son of a bitch"!

Tiny Anderson – Tiny was reunited with his unit later that day and fought until the wars end. Upon returning home, he finished high school, attended college, got married and took a job as a school teacher. His wife died of cancer only five years into their marriage and Tiny never remarried, instead putting his time and energy into his work. His nurturing ways and competence saw him rise to school principal, a role he maintained until retirement in his hometown of Austin, Texas. He died of natural causes at the age of 79.

Philippe Ruscart – No one was happier for the American's presence in Hierheck and Eschdorf that Christmas than the aging civilian from Hierheck. After providing invaluable help, guiding Lindquist and Delminico and surviving death via the sniping attack during the return to Hierheck, Philippe returned to a more docile lifestyle with his wife and two daughters. He lived out his remaining years on his modest farm in the Luxembourg country-side living until the ripe old age of 94.

Guy Calloway – The seasoned Sergeant that René guided to the edge of Eschdorf was killed later that day in town towards the end of the fighting. At the other end of the bullet that ended the Sergeant's life was a 13 year old "Hitler Youth". In a strange twist, the fanatic young German was riddled with bullets from the gun of a young Corporal named Ferguson.

Historical Note

When writing any fictional story tied to history, there is always the question of where to deviate from the factual and how to do so without minimizing or detracting from what actually took place. This includes date and location, the people involved and most importantly the specific events that occurred.

The Battle of the Bulge was a significant event in World War Two. The Christmas of 1944 and the town of Eschdorf also played important roles as part of that history.

Eschdorf was the scene of a hellacious ordeal between American and German forces and a number of unfortunate civilians caught in the middle that Christmas day. While historians have done their best to document this battle, some questions still remain regarding the exact units involved and who did what and when. It is not the intent of this narrative to provide a different perspective or to verify any historical viewpoint.

When Night Awakens is a work of fiction. Like many fictional narratives it blurs the truth of what actually happened with the author's storyline to provide a hopefully entertaining and thought provoking read.

This narrative hopes to engage the reader via its characters, plot, action and subplots. In doing so it also attempts to inform the reader of the stark agony of war that knows no holiday and makes no exception for combatant, civilian or even innocent child.

The fight for Eschdorf was a very real event. The order of battle as supported by a number of historians began as an American attack on the town at 1:00 AM local time early Christmas morning. The initial attempt by American forces to take the town was repelled by the defending German armies. A second assault with supporting armor recommenced at 4:00 AM local time. It was to continue throughout Christmas day as brutal house to house warfare before American forces eventually drove the Germans out of Eschdorf early the morning of December 26th.

The author tries to maintain this historic truth throughout the narrative's storyline. Any errors, omissions or inaccuracies as it pertains to this historical fact lie solely with the author.

Beyond this much poetic license has been taken to weave the plot and storyline of this story:

The author depicts the U.S. 26th Division, the U.S. 735th Tank Battalion and the German Fuehrer Grenadier Brigade as the main combatants in the battle for Eschdorf. There were certainly other units involved on both sides that were not recognized in attempts to keep the storyline from becoming over complicated. The author means no disrespect for the contributions made by the many units not named and for any suffering endured as part of this conflict.

Nazi security – the SS and Gestapo - certainly played a role in the Battle of the Bulge. It is also fact that Nazi security forces were near Eschdorf during that time. However, the author has not been able to confirm specific actions by these groups in Eschdorf during the period of this novel. Therefore, any mention of the SS or Gestapo in Eschdorf as part of this story is without factual basis and from the author's imagination. For an informative if not chilling read of the civilian toll, including that inflicted by the Nazi SS, during the Battle of the Bulge, the author recommends "*The Unknown Dead – Civilians in the Battle of the Bulge*", by Peter Schrijvers.

All characters in this storyline are fictional with the exception of Lieutenant Colonel Paul Hamilton. His Task Force, consisting of infantry, tank destroyers, tanks, and engineers, had orders to secure ground to the north of the bulge and make a crossing at the Sure River.

However, the strong German presence in the towns of Eschdorf and Arsdorf thwarted this action and Hamilton had to commit an additional Battalion to secure these German held towns. Lieutenant Hamilton's presence in Heirheck that Christmas Eve is part of the author's narrative as is all attributed dialog. In fact, the storyline has Hamilton in a warm command post on Christmas Eve, whereas a number of historical accounts have him on the frontlines directing preparations for the attack on Eshdorf.

Other liberties taken by the author to develop the plot are focused in three areas: 1.) Geography of the land around the town, 2.) The layout of buildings and structures within the town and 3.) Positioning of troops on both sides that Christmas Eve.

The town of Eschdorf sits on high-ground above a number of rolling ridges. It resides in relatively open space versus the close tree line the author proposed to aid Elise and Andre's escape from the town.

The surrounding woods in the narrative do not lie exactly as depicted. They were adapted to support the storyline. Likewise, there is no farm or barn where portrayed in the story. Additionally, the back roads and geography that is described and ravines that are defined along those back roads behind Eschdorf and Heirheck were all created to support the storyline.

The town of Eschdorf is depicted to support the storyline, not as it was. Even the buildings depicted are not all factual, and of those that are, interior layouts were depicted to suit the plot. The Eschdorf sewer system layout was all fabricated as well.

Historically, the Germans held more ground surrounding the town of Eschdorf than the novel gives them credit. The narrative depicts the German army largely concentrated in the town with minimal peripheral support. In truth, much of the area where Lindquist's tank patrol and Conley's adventure took place was likely held by German forces on that night.

To all those who partook in any role in the Battle of the Bulge, be it soldier or civilian, I salute you for your courage and perseverance during that almost unimaginable time. May this narrative depict a small piece of your struggle with sincere hope this time in history never be forgotten.

Glossary

BAR – Short for Browning Automatic Rifle. This was a .30 caliber auto-firing weapon that held a 20 cartridge clip. It could be fired multiple ways; from the shoulder, hip or mounted bi-pod.

Blitzkrieg – means "Lightning War". First executed by the German Army during World War Two, this tactic employed speed, surprise and a strong military presence to overwhelm an opposing army. This tactic was used with devastating effect during the early years of the war. Hitler also employed this means during the Battle of the Bulge and initially saw great gains until the Allies were able to regroup.

Carbine – a .30 caliber, lightweight, semi-automatic rifle, which along with the *M1* rifle became a stand-issue firearm for US troops in WW2.

Company – Two or more platoons typically commanded by a Captain (see platoon below).

Flank – The side of a military unit. To "flank" the enemy means to approach for attack from the side, thereby gaining advantage by surprise and reducing the enemy's ability to defend themselves.

Grenadier – a Private in the German Army.

Hauptmann – a Captain in the German Army.

Herr – sir, mister in German

Jawohl – yes; yes sir in German

Kubelwagen – a light duty military vehicle, manufactured by Volkswagen during the Second World War. It was a highly reliable vehicle that served the German Army in much the same fashion as the Jeep served the Allies.

Luftwaffe – the German Air Force.

Machine Pistol – A hand gun style weapon capable of firing in automatic or single shot mode. Its name was derived from the pistol-like grip and a number of variations were used by German soldiers in World War Two.

M1 – A U.S. Military rifle, the M1, its formal name the M1 Garand (John Garand was the rifle's designer) was a .30 caliber, semi-automatic weapon. It was standard issue among U.S. infantry. The semi-automatic feature allowed a soldier to fire an 8 shot clip as fast as he could pull the trigger. This was a distinct advantage over their German counterparts who had to draw back their rifle's bolt to put a bullet into the chamber for each shot.

Panzer – Typically associated with German tanks. "Panzer means armor-plate. A Panzer Unit was usually an armored group consisting of tanks and other armored vehicles.

Potato Masher – A German grenade which had a distinctive appearance leading to its being called a stick grenade or potato masher. It consisted of a long handle with a cylindrical charge at the end. A pull cord ran down the hollow handle from the detonator within the explosive head. To use the grenade, an end cap was unscrewed, permitting a cord to fall out. Pulling the cord moved a steel rod through an igniter starting a five second timer. This allowed the grenade to be hung as a trap, the slightest disturbance causing it to fall and set the fuse.

Raus – scram, quickly in German.

Replacements – Soldiers sent to war to "replace" combatants pulled from the ranks due to death, wounds or other means of attrition. This became significant for a number of reasons. Two of the many reasons were 1.) Squads and platoons became a "band of brothers" enduring serious hardships and difficulties together. Adding new men to ranks did not always sit well with men who saw their comrade's die, and the replacements needed to earn their acceptance into battle-hardened units. 2.) As attrition took its toll, replacement soldiers were not trained as thoroughly as the original troops and often paid the ultimate price during their first combat engagements.

Sd.Kfz. 7 - a military vehicle – specifically a half-track, used by various German military groups during the Second World War. Sd.Kfz. is actually an abbreviation of the German word Sonderkraftfahrzeug, which translates to "special purpose vehicle". The Sd.Kfz 7 was indeed a multi-purpose vehicle whose utilization spanned from hauling troops (up to 12 soldiers, equipment and ammunition) to a gun platform for a number of anti-aircraft weapons. It was also used to tow artillery.

Sherman – A medium sized tank that played a pivotal role in Allied operations in North Africa, Europe and the Pacific.

Squad - The number of soldiers in a squad could vary from four to sixteen but the typical number of men in a U.S. squad was twelve. A German squad in World War Two consisted normally of ten men although later in the war when manpower shortages mounted, this was reduced to nine.

SS/Gestapo – The group of police and security organizations consolidated under Heinrick Himmler and responsible for many crimes against humanity during World War Two. As such, the SS and Gestapo were greatly feared by both Allied soldiers and civilians. During the Battle of the Bulge, a number of SS Units were deployed to monitor civilian activities primarily looking for those engaged in spying or sabotage.

Third Reich – Another name for the Nazi government in Germany. The word *Reich* in German means "empire." Adolf Hitler called his government the *Third Reich* with the belief he was orchestrating the third in a line of German empires; the first being the Holy Roman Empire and the second the Empire created by Hitler's idol Chancellor Otto von Bismarck, who unified Germany in the nineteenth century.

Thompson ("Tommy Gun") – The Thompson machine gun was an American used fully automatic .45 caliber field weapon that held a thirty round magazine.

Unit – A general term used to describe a military grouping of personnel or subdivision of a larger military organization. A Squad, Platoon, Company or any part there-of could be referred to as a "unit".

Unteroffizier – a Corporal in the German Army.

Untersturmführer – a second Lieutenant in the German SS.

Acknowledgements

There is an expression – "It takes a village" – and while not initially quoted in the context of publishing a manuscript, it certainly does apply. Without question, this book would not have been possible without the help and input of a number of people, and I would be remiss if I did not give them the credit they so rightly deserve.

First, thank you to Justin Thrift, my initial contact to the publishing world, who graciously read my early drafts and provided many useful edits and advice, imploring me again and again to visually tell my story. Justin was also a great mentor, providing tremendous insight to the writing and editing process.

Additional thanks go to my good friend Smita Bhat, who enthusiastically offered to read my manuscript and utilizing her honed skills as a quality engineer, provided a number of language and spelling corrections after I thought the book was good to go.

Another reviewer I'd like to acknowledge is Patricia Camaioni, who provided great input regarding finalization of each characters story at the end of the novel.

Many thanks also to Todd Jewett, who offered his expertise in all things legal. Todd's input and responsiveness to my many legal questions was greatly appreciated and I couldn't have finalized the contractual pieces without his help.

Thanks as well to Jack Butler and James Faktor from Endeavor Press for all their help in engaging in the publishing process.

Finally, to my wife, Kimberly, whose support and encouragement never wavered throughout the two years that it took to finalize this manuscript. Over that time, she read and reread each revision, always providing quality edits and suggestions to enhance the storyline, personalize the characters and stabilize the plot. For this book and the past twenty-five years in all I have done, she has been my main champion and cheerleader. Without her input, reassurance and undying patience, this book would have never come to fruition.

64776294R00156

Made in the USA
Middletown, DE
17 February 2018